ADVANCE PRAISE F
DEAD EXTRA

"Dark, seamy, and complex, *Dead Extra* is, at first glance, an excellent, faithful foray into old school LA noir. Jack Chesley is a hard-drinking former cop and World War II vet, pushed into investigating his wife's suspicious death. But Sean Carswell is a writer who understands this genre well enough to subvert it left and right, particularly when it comes to the dead woman, whose gutsy misadventures occupy almost half of the book. Come for your hardboiled comforts—the violence, the corruption, and the mood are all there, as are the sharp prose and snappy dialogue. Stay for Carswell's fresh, intelligent point of view."

— **Steph Cha,** author of
Dead Soon Enough and *Follow Her Home*

"Sean Carswell has written a moody, atmospheric page-turner that kept me up all night and left me hungover with longing for glamorous, gritty 1940s Los Angeles. Carswell's shell-shocked, world-weary vet is a realistic protagonist, but it's the dames who really steal this show."

— **Denise Hamilton,** *Los Angeles Noir* editor and
author of *Damage Control* and the Eve Diamond mysteries

"Like a deadly cross between *The Day of the Locust* and *LA Confidential, Dead Extra* is a stunning exploration of Hollywood's postwar history: dark, dream-like, and very dangerous. I loved it."

— **Phoef Sutton,** *New York Times*–bestselling author
(with Janet Evanovich) of *Wicked Charms* and
Curious Minds and author of *Heart Attack and Vine*

"Sean Carswell's *Dead Extra* is a refreshing take on classic hardboiled '40s noir. There's a world-weary hero who can take a knock and give plenty back, a dead woman with a scandalous past, corrupt cops, and Hollywood skeletons, but what's really striking is the extent to which the story is largely driven by women—not your typical femme fatales, but smart, flawed, determined women with their own dreams, traumas, and stories. Carswell's women live in a time that limits their ambitions and routinely victimizes them, but they push back in spite of the consequences, finding both tragedies and triumphs."

— **Lisa Brackmann,** *New York Times*–bestselling author of *Rock Paper Tiger* and *Black Swan Rising*

"Dirty cops, unscrupulous mental health workers, and shady Hollywood actors—Sean Carswell spins a noirish tale with razor-edged prose and memorable characters who confront sexism, corruption, and the exploitation of the powerless. *Dead Extra* is a compelling story from the way back when that feels uncomfortably contemporary."

— **Patricia Smiley,** author of the Pacific Homicide crime novels

DEAD EXTRA

SEAN CARSWELL

PROSPECT
· PARK ·
BOOKS

Published by Prospect Park Books
2359 Lincoln Avenue
Altadena, CA 91001
www.prospectparkbooks.com

Distributed by Consortium Book Sales & Distribution
www.cbsd.com

Library of Congress Cataloging in Publication Data
Names: Carswell, Sean, 1970- author.
Title: Dead extra / Sean Carswell.
Description: Altadena, CA : Prospect Park Books, [2019] | Description based on print version record and CIP data provided by publisher; resource not viewed.
Identifiers: LCCN 2018045540 (print) | LCCN 2018048072 (ebook) | ISBN 9781945551482 (Ebook) | ISBN 9781945551475 (pbk.)
Subjects: LCSH: Murder--Investigation--Fiction. | GSAFD: Mystery fiction.
Classification: LCC PS3603.A7764 (ebook) | LCC PS3603.A7764 D43 2019 (print) | DDC 813/.6--dc23
LC record available at https://lccn.loc.gov/2018045540

Cover design by David Ter-Avanesyan
Book layout and design by Amy Inouye, Future Studio

JACK, 1946

JACK LAY ABOVE his own empty grave. Brown grass poked into the back of his neck. He kept his eyes closed and his breathing slow, but he tried to stay awake. The springtime sun soaked into his darkest suit: a navy blue that could pass for black if not for the clear skies above.

His name was etched in the grave marker closest to him. "John Walter Chesley, Jr.," it read. "Born March 31, 1920. Died February 8, 1943. Lost over the skies of Germany." Most days, he felt like crawling into that empty coffin six feet down, but the fact remained. He wasn't dead yet.

The stone next to it laid out the particulars for the woman Jack had widowed, who then widowed him. Wilma Greene Chesley. Born April 12, 1918. Died July 14, 1944. Wife. Sister. Author.

Jack hadn't read the book yet.

Footsteps crunched in the grass nearby. A sharp heel dug into the dirt. The flat of the shoe hit the grass. The steady rhythm grew slower as it approached Jack. A shadow covered his face. The woman knelt down. She was so close that Jack could smell the soap she washed with. Cashmere Bouquet. The same brand Wilma used to use.

Quick as cats, Jack rolled away from her and popped up. He stood on the balls of his feet, ready to run or wrestle. Instinctively, his hand went inside of his coat. His fingers grazed the cool grip of his Springfield 1911. He looked across the gravesite.

The woman who had knelt at his side was standing now, flowers at her feet, hand over her chest. Her red hair was parted cleanly down the middle, the curls spun into submission and twisted into a hair comb on the back of her head. The afternoon sun pulled the freckles out from beneath her foundation. Her blue eyes burned underneath a furrowed brow. Christ, she looked identical to Wilma. If not for her broad-shouldered business suit, Jack could've convinced himself that he was standing over two empty graves.

It's peacetime, Jack told himself. Hold it together. He pulled his hand out of his coat, smiled, and said, "Gertie."

"Jackie?" Gertie glanced down at Jack's tombstone and the imprint his body had left in the brown grass. "You're alive, or you're a ghost?" she asked.

"A little of both, I guess."

Gertie put a hand to Jack's face. "You feel alive."

"That's what I tell myself every morning. It gets me out of bed."

"And you're back?"

"Standing in front of you."

Gertie pointed to the full vase atop Wilma's grave. "Those are your flowers?"

"They're Wilma's now."

Gertie looked at Jack. Jack looked at Gertie. The air hung still over Evergreen Cemetery.

Jack squatted down, picked up the bouquet Gertie had dropped, and handed it to her. She sniffed a pink lily. Her brow loosened but her eyes still burned. "So you're alive and you're back, Jackie. What now?"

Jack cast a glance over toward the potter's field. "I don't know."

Gertie tossed the flowers on Wilma's grave. She crossed herself and turned back to Jack. "Let's get a bite and bump gums."

Jack had taken the red interurban to Evergreen Cemetery. Gertie had driven. She drove them both to a sandwich joint off Alameda, not far from Union Station. The place was packed. They found a small table jammed between bigger tables. Gertie dug into her sandwich. She'd spent a long day on the lot, putting a shooting script back in order, running from one department to another to make sure everyone had the current changes, juggling a drunk screenwriter, a disengaged director, and the egos of a half dozen actors. This French Dip was the first food she'd touched since before sunrise.

Jack sipped his beer and watched her eat. His years in Germany made him wary of meat in general and suspicious of meats with sauce on them. He still smelled all his food before eating it. In a packed, smoky joint like this, where he couldn't trust his nose, he let his sandwich sit.

Gertie polished off her plate, pickle and everything. She took in the immediate surroundings. To her left sat a few men in corduroy suits. They talked about fabric prices and young seamstresses. Another man, deeply engrossed in a newspaper, sat to her right. Gertie leaned in and caught Jack's eye.

"I hear you've been at Wilma's grave every day for the lasts few weeks."

Well, that explained why Gertie wasn't very surprised to see him. "Who told you that?" he asked.

"The guy who cuts the graveyard grass," Gertie said.

"He told me you come every afternoon at the same time and lie there in your suit. Said you turn on the waterworks when you think no one's looking. Said you bring fresh flowers every day, and two times you polished her stone with car wax. That true, Jackie?"

"More or less." Jack rubbed the side of his cheek to make sure it was dry. "Only I don't wait until I think no one's looking to turn on the waterworks. I just let loose when I have to." Which might be any minute, what with Wilma's spitting image staring him in the eye.

Gertie scooted even closer. "What do you know about Wilma's death?" she asked.

Jack shrugged. "Just what they told me at debriefing."

"Which was what?"

"She fell in a tub."

"That's it?"

"Is there more?"

"I think so." Gertie leaned back in her chair. She took a pre-rolled cigarette, tapped it on her tin case, and placed it between her lips. Jack dug a lighter from his inside coat pocket and offered Gertie a light. She inhaled and blew the smoke out of the side of her mouth. A red fingernail dug a strand of tobacco off her tongue. Her eyes never drifted. She held Jack's glance. "I think there's more."

Of course there was. Jack figured as much from the minute he'd heard the story of Wilma. It didn't make sense. Wilma was too tall to land nose-first on the edge of a tub. If she slipped, she would've fallen out or dropped to her knees or cracked her hip on the edge. The physics of landing nose-first were implausible. Jack was no genius, but he'd always been smart enough to know bullshit when he heard it. So, when the doctor at debriefing told him about his wife's death, Jack fought back the urge to kill.

Germany had taught Jack something about survival, something about tucking away his rage until he needed it, something about staying in the moment when he needed to be there. He prodded Gertie. "Like what?"

"I identified her body. Mom was off drunk somewhere. You were dead. A cop dragged me out of Musso and Frank's to have a peek. And that's all they gave me. A quick peek. It was enough to see bruises around Wilma's throat."

Something homicidal rumbled deep inside Jack, threatened to tear him apart. Simple routines helped him keep himself together. He took a pouch of tobacco from his jacket pocket and started to roll a cigarette of his own. "Sometimes blood pools in strange places."

Gertie tightened her lips into a white line. Her nostrils flared as she took a slow, deep breath. She let the air out. "So I went by Wilma's bungalow that night. No cops were there. I had a key but it didn't matter. The lock had been busted. I turned on the lights and stepped into the empty little house and found all kinds of suspicious things. The needle was still down on her Victrola, at the end of a record. There was a little puddle of water in front of it. And right by the front door, speckles of blood. Like someone cut her foot and was running around anyway."

"She could've gotten out of the tub to play the record, then went back in." Jack dug a fingernail into the worn wooden table in front of him. "The blood could've been from any time."

Gertie reached across the table. She put her hand under Jack's chin and lifted his glance to meet hers. "Her bathrobe had blood and snot all over the front lapels. If you die naked in a tub, you don't bleed on your bathrobe."

Jack's eyes followed a stream of cigarette smoke snaking its way up to the dark rafters.

"Plus," Gertie said, "I talked to the neighbors."

"And?"

Gertie reached into her purse. She pulled out a few sheets of paper. They'd been folded in half and in half again. She passed them to Jack. "This is what I think happened, based on everything I could find and what everyone who would talk to me told me."

The paper was worn soft. It felt almost like a handkerchief. The typed letters looked to be pressed down by carbon, not ink. A copy. Gertie probably kept the original back at her place. Some of the letters along the folds had been worn away. Jack lit his hand-rolled cigarette. He took a deep drag, made a slow exhale. He angled the paper into a pool of light and read Gertie's story.

It was too much. Too sudden. Jack could read some of the words, even make meaning out of some of them. Mostly, they were just squiggles on the page. More than he could take right now. He pretended to read and thought of the bruises Gertie had seen, imagined some tony bastard choking the life out of his Wilma. It's peacetime, he told himself again. Hold it together.

"Nice story," he said. He folded the pages and stuffed them into the inside pocket of his jacket. "You write like Dashiell Hammett. You should be a novelist."

"This isn't about my writing."

Jack nodded. "So you think she was murdered."

"Of course she was murdered, Jackie."

Jack felt the weight of the Springfield on one side of his coat and the weight of Gertie's story on the other.

"And who was the man?"

Gertie pushed her empty plate aside and leaned her elbows on the table. She looked over Jack's right shoulder as if she were hoping to find someone there who was entirely smarter and more reasonable than her former brother-in-law. "If I knew that, I'd do something about it."

Jack pulled his uneaten sandwich closer. He wrapped it back up in its wax paper and stuck the whole thing in his outside jacket pocket. She must've tried to do something, Jack figured. Nearly two years had passed. Gertie must have followed trails until she was scared or bullied off. Jack would try to get that part of the story later.

He said, "Let's say she was murdered. Just for the sake of argument, let's say that." He rubbed the back of his neck, felt the tension in his taut muscles. "Then what?"

Gertie burned into Jack with her blue eyes. "Then you find out who did it."

"*I* find out who did it? Me?"

"Why not you? You were a cop."

"I was a shitty cop. I never investigated anything."

"You know the right people. You can get into the right places, find some answers."

"I knew people. I don't know them anymore."

"Of course you still know them."

"It's been too long. Everyone thinks I'm dead." He thought, but didn't add, *I'm mostly inclined to believe them.*

"Excuses, Jack. You're just giving me excuses."

Jack shook his head. "I'm not sure what you want from me. I don't know what you think I can do."

Gertie stubbed out her cigarette and tapped her bun

to make sure every hair was in place. "You can find the bastard who killed your wife, Jack."

He took stock on the red car home. For two of the past three years, he'd been in a POW camp in Germany. There were also the months he spent alone behind the lines in Germany, and the months he spent after the camp, trying to make it home. The Army paid him a lump sum for those years. It wasn't a fortune, but it was enough money to give him time to think. He didn't want to go back to the force. He was no cop and he knew it.

He could've taken over his father's PI business, but he was even less of a dick than a cop. And his father never really investigated anything. The old man had spent a life as a hired thug. Not much more.

The PI license was still around the house on Meridian Street. Same name as Jack's, only missing the junior. Jack Senior wouldn't be using it anymore. Like almost everyone else, he'd died while Jack was in Germany.

A baby in the back of the interurban screamed out. Her mother cooed and held the child close. Jack looked at the little boy swaddled in a blanket, snot dripping from his nose, spit gathering around his mouth as he screamed. Jack looked at the mother, with loose strands of hair falling onto her face and dried mucus smeared on her shoulder. A thought flashed across his mind before he could tuck it away: I dropped a bomb on that baby. That baby and his mom. He glanced around the car, saw men in factory blues, mechanics with motor oil wedged in the cracks of their skin, seamstresses with that sewing squint, maids and men in business suits, and women with bags of groceries. I killed the German equivalent of every one of them, Jack thought. I killed them all and slept through the night.

The next thought Jack didn't want to think but couldn't keep from bubbling up was this: wartime and Germany and Nazi soldiers weren't the only things that drove him to kill. The war had taught him that most people can't kill another person. Even when soldiers are getting shot at, even when their lives are on the line, most can't shoot back. Or, really, they can shoot back, but they subconsciously shoot high or low or wide. Most men can't shoot to kill. Most humans can't kill other humans. But some can. For whatever reason. And Jack was one of those people who could. So it wasn't that he didn't want to find out what happened to Wilma. It wasn't that he didn't want her killer to pay. He just feared the horror show once he did find out. He wanted the killing to stop. For the rest of his life.

Jack pulled out his packet of tobacco and started to roll a cigarette. Small routines helped.

He'd have to find ways to keep his thoughts in check if he was going to look for the man who murdered Wilma.

WILMA, 1943

WILMA HADN'T INTENDED to throw such a party. Gertie stopped by with one of her pals from the studio, a wardrobe girl named Ethel. Ethel had a bottle of red. Wilma poured three glasses. They sat on the dusty chintz loveseat and matching chintz chairs that came with Wilma's new bungalow on 243½ Newland Street. Conversation drifted everywhere it could as long as it avoided the war. Less than a month earlier, two Air Force officers—one a chaplain—had showed up on the doorstep of Wilma's then-apartment in Los Feliz to deliver the bad news that Jack's plane had been shot down over Germany. "There were no survivors," the chaplain told Wilma. As if she couldn't take the next logical step from that one, the chaplain made it perfectly clear. "Your husband, Sergeant John Chesley, was killed in action."

Wilma didn't want to talk about it anymore. All she'd done for the past month and a half was talk about it. She asked Ethel, "Any new talent over there at Republic?"

"Oh, honey, is there!" Ethel said. "We have this new dreamboat on contract. Tom Gutierrez. He's a Mex but you wouldn't know it to see him. All you'd know about is those deep, dark eyes. A woman could get lost in those."

"He is a handsome fellow," Gertie said.

"Honey, handsome ain't the word. That lug walks on the lot and my panties try to walk off me."

"When did you start wearing underwear?" Wilma asked.

"Touché." Ethel sipped her wine. She repositioned herself on the loveseat, legs tucked under her, floral skirt spread over her knees and calves, only ankles and bare feet visible. "Anyway, he's not going by that Mex name. They're calling him Tom Fillmore, for some reason."

"Because he's from Fillmore," Gertie said.

"What's Fillmore?" Ethel asked.

"A little farm town north of the San Fernando Valley."

"What's it near?" Wilma asked.

"Nothing," Gertie said.

"So Tomas Gutierrez, a little Mex farm boy from next to nowhere, is about to take over Hollywood and slide inside Ethel's skirt. Am I getting this right?" Wilma asked.

"Hitting the nail on the head," Gertie said.

"Oh, honey, let me tell you about this boy. We had him playing a G-man in a tight blue gabardine suit. It was all I could do to put that suit on him. I had to measure his chest and inseam a half-dozen times before I got it right. He just stood there and let me run my fingers across him." Ethel adjusted her bun. "My goodness, I'm getting flushed just thinking about it."

"Call him up," Wilma suggested.

"Really?" Ethel asked.

"Sure, why not?" It was Saturday night. They were adults and could do as they pleased. What could be the harm?

Gertie plucked that question right from Wilma's brain and offered the answer, "Haven't you been drinking a bit too much since, well...for this past month?"

Wilma waved her hand like a matador would. "We're young. We deserve to have some fun."

Gertie gave in to Wilma's twelve extra minutes of

wisdom once again. "Okay, Ethel, call your dreamy To-mas. Tell him to bring some friends."

"And more booze," Wilma added.

"And some records for the Victrola," Gertie said.

An hour later, Tom and his friends and his booze and his records filled Wilma's little bungalow. Rather than risk the enmity of her new landlords, Wilma invited the Van Meters to join the party. They brought more booze. Mr. Van Meter spun Benny Goodman's "Sing Sing Sing." Gene Krupa's opening drumbeats got Wilma up and dancing. Tom's friends pushed the furniture against the wall and cleared the floor. Pretty soon, everyone was hopping.

As the music and hum of the little party spread to the houses on either side of Wilma's, more folks dropped by, more folks were called, more records spun, more booze drunk. Party favors just seemed to appear: a bowl of peanuts, chicken on the grill in the front driveway, a tub filled with ice and bottled beers, marihuana cigarettes for the group milling around by the Van Meter rose bushes, a little mound of cocaine on the bar of the kitchenette, a bag of leftover biscuits from the hash house where Wilma worked, musical instruments. Someone put a uku-lele in Wilma's hand between records. She launched into a rendition of "Five Foot Two"—just because everyone knew it, and would sing along—then tore into her favorite Benny Bell number, "Everybody Loves My Fanny." The artist from down the block produced a pair of bongos and joined in. Folks made instruments out of spoons from Wilma's kitchen drawers and pill bottles and hair combs. One thoughtful pal of Tom's had brought a kazoo with him. The makeshift orchestra ripped through a handful of numbers, loud and boisterous, if not necessarily skilled.

The booze kept flowing after the orchestra took a break. Mr. Van Meter stayed on top of the Victrola. Mostly, he kept things swinging, spinning sides by Cab Calloway, Duke Ellington, Fletcher Henderson, and the like. When he played Harry James's hit, "I Had the Craziest Dream Last Night," Ethel nuzzled up to Tom. You might call it dancing. It looked like something else. The wardrobe girl made a suit of herself and Tom wore it.

If any eyebrows were to be raised, they'd have to wait until the morning. This party was inertia unto itself. Sure, you could hear the water gushing in the toilet every time someone used the tiny bathroom in the middle of the bungalow, but as Wilma pointed out early, "This ain't a shindig for gentlemen and ladies. It's for guys and dolls like us."

The little bungalow swelled and sweated with party guests. The lawn around it was trampled by revelers. Various guests used Wilma's bedroom for one of the things bedrooms are used for. Her sheets were left in no condition to be slept upon. A fight broke out. Maybe a few of them. Who could tell among all the madness? It stretched until the first light of dawn colored the eastern sky.

The problem with Wilma was she could never keep her drinking to just one night. Her party had been a hit. She should've slept it off that Sunday afternoon and been back to herself by evening. She just couldn't.

She found a little bit of orange juice and a lot of vodka when she woke up that Sunday. Screwdrivers carried her through the cleanup. Leftover gin hid in her flask during her lunch shift on Monday. She may have accidentally-on-purpose dumped a tray of dishes in the lap of a regular who grabbed her ass that one too many times. Otherwise, it was a good shift. Tom Fillmore, who'd blown his chance with Ethel late that past Saturday, kept Wilma company through Monday evening. On Tuesday after her shift, he took her on a tour of Hollywood nightspots. They drank whiskey neat with showbiz types at Players on the top of Sunset. They grabbed a quick bite and a slow martini at the Formosa Café. He took her to see Lena Horne at the Little Troc. She washed down the songs with her own set list of gin gimlets. They finished the night off at his house on Fountain.

Tom had ideas and Wilma played along.

She woke up in Tom's bed around 6:30 Wednesday morning. She had until 4:00 to get to work. She could've slept a while longer there and, surely, Tom would've have driven her home, but that seemed like the worst plan of all. She didn't want to talk to Tom, didn't want to look into those dark, empty eyes, didn't want to think about the night before, about how rough and rude Tom had been at the end. She climbed out of bed as gently as she could, stuffed her bra and panties into her purse, pulled on her black party dress, and tiptoed out of the house. On the front porch, she considered walking the two blocks to the red car stop on Sunset in her bare feet but decided that her high heels would be slightly less painful.

She dozed on the red car down Sunset and on the next one up Figueroa, trying not to think what she looked like, wild red hair styled by a pillow, breasts loose under the black rayon of her dress, only the dregs of yesterday's makeup clinging to her face, crust around her eyes. She could tell her story to the morning commuters without opening her mouth.

It'll be all right, she told herself. I don't know any of these people. I'll never see them again. She listed off the things that would heal her from this brannigan. A little sleep. A lot of water and coffee. A long bath. A hamburger and fries. Feeling human again was only seven or eight stops up Figueroa.

The red car braked around Avenue 52. Wilma idly glanced at the passengers boarding the trolley. One of them looked a lot like Jack only older, alcoholic, mean, and sporting a nose that had been broken at least a dozen times. She was too slow about turning away. He saw Wilma and steered a course in her direction. Wilma put her purse on the empty seat next to her. He picked up the purse, tossed it in her lap, and sat down.

Christ, the last thing she needed on a morning like this was a visit from John Chesley, Sr. She looked out the window to her right and tried to pretend she couldn't feel his shoulder pressed against hers.

The red car started rolling again. John said, "You look like you've had one hell of a night."

Wilma kept facing the window. "I don't see how that's any of your business."

"When my daughter-in-law is whoring around town, it's my business."

Wilma faced him, caught his brown eyes with her baby blues. "I ain't your daughter-in-law anymore, palooka."

"You're still carrying my last name, aren't you?"

Actually, Wilma had gone back to calling herself Greene instead of Chesley. Nothing against Jack. She'd just always been a Greene. Wearing his last name felt like wearing his underwear. It never really fit. She didn't want to explain this to the old man. She didn't owe him a damn thing. An old thug like him had no right looking down his busted-up nose at her. She said, "Find another seat before I start screaming rape, old man."

"You little fucking trollop." The old man grabbed his briefcase and stood from his seat. "You dirty fucking whore. I hope you know that the State of California takes alcoholism very seriously. I hope you know that."

Wilma jerked her thumb toward the back of the car. "Tell your story walking."

Two hours later, after a little sleep but before the coffee, bath, or hamburger, Wilma got a knock on her bungalow door. It was the boys in white coats from Camarillo. No doubt as to who called and where she'd be going.

JACK, 1946

JACK SAT on a low wall in front of a rooming house on Newland Street. Wilma's second-to-last moments were spent on the street in front of him. He unfolded Gertie's account of Wilma's death and let his eyes graze over the words again.

A cowbell echoed through the bungalow. Someone had sprung the front door lock and forced himself inside. Wilma grabbed the edges of the tub. Panic poured in. What do I do? Hide or run? Hide or run? What do I do?

For the past year, she'd been telling herself to move into a place with a back door. She hadn't done it. The only way to walk out of this bungalow was through the front. She looked up at the bathroom window. It was too small for a full-grown human to crawl out. There was nothing in here to hide behind or under.

Heavy heels clomped across the hardwood floor. One man. Letting himself in. Letting himself be known.

The door to the bathroom led into the living room, in full view of whoever thumped his brogues on the floorboards. She could walk out and face him or stay in the tub and wait for him. She stood. Water rolled off her bare skin. The cool evening air pushed aside the residual warmth. Soap bubbles clung to goose bumps. She stepped out of the tub, letting the dripping water puddle underneath. She wrapped her wet hair into a towel and slid on a terry-cloth robe and scanned the bathroom again. Nothing to use as a weapon but a hairbrush. It was hardly worth wielding that.

In a gamble, she left the robe untied.

The heels clomped closer. Wilma turned off the bathroom light, gave her eyes a few seconds to adjust to the darkness, and stepped through the doorway.

He stopped walking when he saw her and stood next to the loveseat. His hands were buried deep in his jacket pockets; his Homburg brim dipped low like it was shielding his eyes from a sun that had set an hour ago. With two quick steps and a dive, he could tackle her. Too close. Inside the bungalow was too close for him to be. But this ten-foot gap: way too close.

Wilma slapped a half-smile on her face and twirled the loose, dripping end of a curly red lock. "Well," with nothing else coming to her mind, she said, "this is a surprise."

He said nothing. His eyes presumably stayed locked on her. She couldn't see them to say for sure. A little bit of the whites glistened in the moonlight that crept into the bungalow, but that was it. And, truth be told, Wilma wasn't surprised. This wasn't a surprise. It was inevitable he'd show up, sooner or later.

Wasn't it?

It was.

Wilma took a couple of slow steps away from the bathroom. This put the loveseat between her and the man. She needed time, an excuse, something to stall him until she could make a run for it. The only thing in front of her, the only thing she could be walking toward if she were acting casual, was the Victrola. She patted her towel turban and glanced over at the man. "I'll play some music," she said. The low brim of his Homburg swiveled to follow her steps. Something about this made her even more aware of the open front of her robe, of the white skin that caught glimmers of moonlight.

As luck would have it, Wilma had been listening to her Chester Ellis record that morning. She didn't want to bend down with her back to the man and seek out another side, so she stuck with the one she had. A risky move, playing Chester Ellis in a scene like this, but Wilma took it. She cranked the arm of the little Victrola, dropped the needle on the record, clicked off the latch, and let it play. Chester's piano filled the room. The man didn't flinch.

He was screwing up his courage to kill her. She knew it. She could taste it like a stink drifting off him. It was too dark to tell if he had a gun in those jacket pockets or a sap or was just wearing a pair of gloves to keep from doing it with his bare hands. But it was there: the murderous vibe tangling with the notes of the Chester Ellis record.

Wilma looped around a dusty chintz armchair, walking this time toward the man. He'd left the front door open. Wilma was slightly closer to it than he was. She eyed the kitchen behind the man. "You must want a drink. I have a new bottle of Vat 69 behind you there. I haven't even cracked the seal." She pointed at a cabinet directly behind the man. He turned to look. This felt like Wilma's only chance. She raced out the front door.

He took off after her.

Her bare feet hit the gravel drive in front of her bungalow. Small rocks dug into her soft soles. With one hand, she gathered the lapels of her bathrobe and pulled them tight. Her other arm flopped as she ran. The towel on her head unraveled and fell at the end of the drive. Wilma turned

right onto Newland Street and crossed maybe half
the block before realizing that she had no idea
where she was running to and nowhere to go.

The man turned right at the end of the drive,
also. He picked up the towel and twisted it into a
rope.

The wet night collapsed on the pair. Thick fog
blurred the moon into a vague glow above them.
A red interurban car rumbled past the nearby intersection of York and Figueroa.

Wilma assessed her options again. This night
just wasn't getting any better. She needed a car or
a friend or a gun or something. She needed shoes
because her feet were already torn up and bloody.
She needed clothes. She needed help. She needed
Jack but he'd gone and got himself shot down in
Germany a year ago. That was where the trouble
started. If he just hadn't gone to war. If he just
hadn't died there. If he had just come back like
he was supposed to and lent her a hand now and
then. Goddamn it.

With no better ideas, she started screaming,
"Jack," again and again, ripping apart her vocal
chords doing it. The screams bounced down the
street and vibrated off stucco walls and got ab-
sorbed into nearby porches and potted plants. A
small dog joined in, yapping as hard and loud as
Wilma. This stopped the man. He and Wilma faced
each other on the street, no more than twenty
feet apart, Wilma screaming, "Help," now instead
of "Jack," the man's eyes darting from door to
door, waiting for someone to intervene.

The neighbors stayed inside, letting it all
wash underneath the sounds of the Gas Company
Evening Concert or the new episode of Boston
Blackie. No one came outside to check.

The man walked toward Wilma, twirling her

towel. Water dripped from her hair onto her bathrobe. She gave the screams a rest and waited.
When he got an arm's length away, she feinted
left. He lunged. She danced around him and
sprinted another fifty yards down the street. The
soles of her feet left small red drops with every
step.

When her breath would allow it, she screamed
again. One neighbor slammed his window shut.
Another screamed, "Pipe down out there." The
dog kept yapping.

The man picked himself off the tar and turned
back for Wilma. He made his dash. She made her
fake. He fell and she sprinted. They paused for
breath. He pounced again. She fled again. Maybe it all looked like something from a burlesque
stage, Wilma the flaming-haired Gypsy Rose Lee,
the man one of her rotating casts of comedians,
only instead of witty repartee with each pause,
Wilma screamed. Instead of an audience at the
Old Opera, the neighborhood tuned out.

On one sprint, the man threw down the towel. Wilma tripped on it. She flung her hands out
too late. Her nose hit the street, broken for sure.
She squirmed up before he could drop on top of
her. She ran with blood and snot racing down her
chin and soaking into the wet collar of her white
bathrobe. When she hit the drive this time, she
decided to try her bungalow again. Maybe the
lock would hold. Maybe the man would give up
and leave. Maybe she could telephone somebody.
Maybe Gertie.

Her feet ripped across the gravel driveway.
She launched into the bungalow and swung to
slam the door shut behind her. The man's brogue
wedged in the frame. Wilma pushed. The man
pushed harder. He forced his way in and shut

the door behind him. The screams stopped right about then.

Jack had read this story enough times to get through it without crying. Enough times to have it memorized and almost enough times to believe it. He folded it once again and stuffed it back in his jacket.

He climbed the concrete steps of 243 Newland Street and paused on the porch. A poinsettia plant in a glazed black pot bloomed its flaming red flowers. Two rockers sat next to the front door. One was painted yellow, the other blue. The sun had paled them both. The yellow rocker's seat had been worn down to the original wood. Jack knelt to inspect the knitting bag between the rockers. He found a handful of cream-colored doilies. The name on the mailbox read "Van Meter." He had to start somewhere, so he started here, by knocking on the door.

It took some shuffling and mumbling, but eventually a woman opened the door. She was too young to be called old, but too old to stick with that platinum dye job. Jack said, "I'm sorry to bother you. I'm looking for either a Mr. or Mrs. Philip Van Meter. Would I be right in assuming you're Mrs. Van Meter?"

The woman jutted her hip to the left and planted a hand on it. "What are you selling, honey?"

Jack pulled his father's badge and license from his back hip pocket. He showed it to her. "Mrs. Van Meter, I'm an investigator." He flipped his wallet closed and replaced it. "I'd like to ask you a few questions about an incident that occurred in your backyard about two years ago."

"You're either talking about the orange tree I planted

there or the whore who took a face plant in my bathtub."

A wave of heat raced through Jack's veins. The nerve endings on his face tingled. He tucked it away under a polite tone of voice. "I'm speaking of Mrs. Chesley. Wilma."

"Her name was Wilma all right, but you got the wrong last name. She was no Missus."

"She was widowed. Maybe she used her maiden name with you. Greene."

"Sounds right." Mrs. Van Meter blew a wayward bang off her eyebrow. The bang fell right back where it had strayed to begin with. "Anyway, there's not much to tell. She got drunk, fell in the tub. What's to investigate?"

Jack pointed at the rockers. "Perhaps we could sit and chat for just a couple of minutes."

Mrs. Van Meter nodded. She walked around Jack and took up residence in the yellow rocker. Jack settled into the blue one. Mrs. Van Meter said, "Tell me your story before I tell you mine. What are you after?"

"Mrs. Van Meter, I do freelance work for an insurance company. I've been asked to determine just how accidental Miss Greene's death was."

"What for?"

"They don't tell me, exactly. My guess is someone took out a life insurance policy on her and now he wants to get paid."

"Who would insure that tramp?"

Jack dug out a bag of tobacco and set to rolling a cigarette. "Like I said, they don't tell me."

Mrs. Van Meter snapped her fingers. "I bet it was her husband. I bet she wasn't a widow like she said. I bet she was a grass widow. Now that husband wants to collect. But, hell, maybe he did it."

Jack offered Mrs. Van Meter the cigarette. She accepted. He lit it for her, amazed at how steady his hand was. He hoped his voice and face were staying as steady and his anger was still well below the surface. He started rolling another smoke for himself. "Perhaps you should be the investigator."

"I could find more than the police did, that's for sure."

Jack stopped rolling. "They didn't find much?"

"They didn't care. They picked up the body and left. Didn't ask no questions or nothing. All they did was tell me to stay clear of the bungalow. Said they'd clean it themselves."

"Did they?"

"They had a woman do it. A little fat Mex. Left the place spotless. I was showing it to renters that afternoon."

Jack twisted the ends of his cigarette, lit it. He inhaled and glanced at the rooming house across the street. "Why do you think her husband may have done it?"

Mrs. Van Meter leaned on the arm of the rocker and tilted her head toward Jack. Passersby could've immediately recognized the gossip pose, had there been any passersby. The block was empty of all living things except a mackerel tabby and the house finch he had his eyes on. Mrs. Van Meter said, "Well, Miss Greene came home that evening drunk as a skunk. The sun had barely set. It was maybe eight thirty, nine o'clock. About twenty minutes later, a car comes rolling down the drive. A Packard so old it looked taped together. The fellow must have known her pretty well because he didn't knock on her door or anything. Just walked right in like he was the one paying me rent. Next thing you know, they're screaming at each other just like a married couple. She comes running out wearing nothing but a bathrobe. It was indecent, I tell you. I looked out the window right over there and saw one of her breasts flopping like mad outside the robe. Bouncing like it wanted to play in the breeze."

"How embarrassing," Jack said.

"Well, she tucked it away soon enough." Mrs. Van Meter tapped her ash onto the porch. She rubbed her house slipper over it until it ground into the concrete. "Anyway, she runs into the street here, and the fellow comes out chasing her. She's screaming bloody murder. He's diving for her left and right. It was a mess."

"Sounds bad."

"Well, she was a drunk. We'd hear her all the time, blasting her phonograph, having little parties, laughing like she wanted the whole world to know something was funny."

"And she screamed a lot?"

Mrs. Van Meter placed a thumb and forefinger on opposite sides of her mouth and rubbed them just below her bottom lip until they met in the middle. If any lipstick had drifted down, this move would've put it back in place. Her makeup hadn't drifted or moved. It was immaculate. She'd put on her face before putting on shoes this morning. "No," she said. "Except for that night I never heard her scream."

"And you said 'we.' You said, 'We'd hear her all the time.' Do you mean you and Mr. Van Meter?"

"Of course. Who else?"

"And Mr. Van Meter was with you on the night in question?"

"I don't like what you're insinuating. Where else would my husband be after the sun sets other than right here with me?"

Jack smiled a gentle grin he'd learned during his early days on the force, when he'd partnered with a cagey veteran named Dave Hammond. Hammond had the best poker face Jack had ever seen. He taught Jack a trick or two. Jack said, "I apologize, Mrs. Van Meter. My assumption was that he was home. I'm just double-checking everything."

Mrs. Van Meter leaned back in the rocker and crossed her arms. "And what else do you assume?"

"These are just guesses on my part, Mrs. Van Meter. Please understand that. But I guess that Mr. Van Meter is either elderly or was in some way incapacitated on the night of July 14, 1944."

Mrs. Van Meter gasped. Her eyes opened wide. She exhaled slowly. "I'll have you know my husband is not elderly in the least. He is my age, and he's healthy as an ox."

"And he sat in his living room while a woman who never screamed was screaming bloody murder in front of his house? He did nothing?"

Mrs. Van Meter tossed her cigarette butt in the weedy lawn. She stood and opened her front door. With one foot inside her house, she turned back to Jack. "Write this down, Mr. Investigator," she said. "Wilma Greene was a drunk and a whore. Whatever she got, she had it coming."

Mrs. Van Meter slammed the door behind her.

Jack left the porch, struggling to banish the thoughts of committing the second murder at this address.

He spent the rest of the morning combing the neighborhood. He started referring to Wilma as Miss Greene, which allowed him to use his father's license more freely, let the neighbors really examine his credentials. The other neighbors were housewives like Mrs. Van Meter, but they were friendlier. They invited Jack inside, offered him coffee or tea, filled him in on local gossip, and talked about each other. And they all had the same story that Mrs. Van Meter had. Wilma had fled into the street screaming. No one came out to help her. A few minutes later, she was dead. The police never investigated.

For a few months after the incident, the neighbors had talked among themselves. This was how they all came to tell the same story, more or less. They were suspicious. It was too coincidental that someone would slip in a bathtub on the same night she ran into the street screaming. But she was a drunk. They all agreed. And she was a whore. There was no doubt about that. That whole "widow" business was just something she told them for sympathy. Quietly, tacitly, they all seemed to get together and agree that, murder or not, it didn't matter and she didn't matter. They didn't say much to anyone and no one came asking until Jack did.

Jack heard this story enough times to keep his hackles down when he heard them call Wilma a whore. He heard it enough to know the rage was coming and hold it back before it could show on his face. Since she appeared to be doing fifty-yard dashes from one side of her bungalow to the other, Jack hit every house on Newland within a hundred yards.

He spoke to his first man at the last house he visited. A fellow who introduced himself as Mr. Lemus. He bypassed the kitchen table and the living room couch and led Jack into a sunny back room. Three or four easels were scattered about the room, all with canvases starting to soak up paint but nowhere close to resembling anything anyone would consider done. The canvases leaning against the walls had enough paint on them to be called finished, but Jack had no idea whether or not they were good. The colors seemed too dull and metallic to him. He couldn't make heads or tails of the shapes or what they were supposed to be a picture of. Sometimes, if he used his imagination, he could see something that might be an arm or a carburetor or a fighting cock. Mostly, they were just blocks and triangles and curves, pictographs in a language he hadn't learned. He raised his eyebrows and nodded with each painting in a mimicry of a man impressed. He asked questions and filled in space with a number of noncommittal wows and isn't-that-somethings.

After several minutes of this, Jack steered Lemus toward the business at hand: the night of July 14, 1944. Lemus laid out the neighborhood version of events. Jack listened and jotted notes like he hadn't heard it a dozen times already that day. When Lemus finished, Jack said, "This Miss Greene must have been a horrible person."

Lemus ran his fingers through the hair on his temples. He'd clearly used henna in it to hide the gray, but the henna was fading and the gray was resurfacing. "Not horrible, no."

"But she was prostituting herself in this, what looks to be a nice, family neighborhood."

"Well." Lemus used his thumbnail to clean the paint from underneath his forefingernail. He looked down at his hands as he spoke. "She wasn't a prostitute. She just had a lot of men over to her place."

"And she had loud sex with them? Could you hear it throughout the neighborhood?"

"No."

"Could you hear it at all?"

"No."

"But it must have been every night, then?"

Lemus raised his eyes into a stare directed out his back windows. Jack gazed back there, also, caught sight of a jacaranda in full, purple bloom. He turned back to Lemus. Lemus took a few seconds to put his thoughts together. "Now that you mention it, I hadn't seen men coming or going for several months before her death. Maybe six, seven months." He picked at dry paint on his pants. "In fact, the more I think about it, the more I think that she only had men over a lot when she first moved in. There was a month or two there when she really cut loose. And after that, it would come in waves. She'd have a wild weekend, going nonstop, then nothing for weeks or months."

"Do you remember when that was? When she first moved in?"

"It was right around the time I had a show over at El Alisal Gallery. I guess that would be sometime around February or March of '43. Does that sound right?"

It sounded right. It would've been just about the time the Air Force had declared Jack dead. Right when Wilma was widowed. Jack flipped through his notes as if that information needed to be written down. "I think so," he said.

Lemus kept staring at the jacaranda blooms, kept digging at paint. He was clearly working toward something in his mind. Jack gave him the time to think. This was something Jack's father had never done during investigations. The old man would charge in, looking to bust heads. Manners and patience were never part of his game. You'd tell him what he wanted to hear or he'd crack you in the jaw. The problem with that, Jack realized as a young man and saw again and again when he worked with cops like that on the force, is that people only tell you what they think you want to hear. Jack could tell himself what he wanted to hear. He was investigating this business to learn what he needed to hear. So he let Lemus gaze and think.

Finally, Lemus came out with it. "I know I should have done something that night. I should have gone into the street and seen what the screaming was about. I should have tried to help." Lemus squeezed his eyes tight and constricted his face, building a dam against whatever emotions were trying to flood his face. He held this for a few seconds. He took a deep breath.

Jack dug a handkerchief from his back pocket—a plain white cotton number—and passed it to Lemus. Lemus waved it off.

"You know she had a twin?" he asked.

"Yeah?" Jack stuffed his handkerchief back into his pocket.

"Birdy or something. I met her at one or two of Wilma's parties. Sharp kid. Looked just like Wilma. She came around after Wilma died. Haunted the neighborhood for a week or two, asking questions, knocking on doors just like you're doing. No one would talk to her."

Jack scooted forward in his seat. This was new. None of the other neighbors mentioned Gertie. "Why not?" he asked.

"Best not to get involved, especially when people are getting killed."

Jack shrugged. Part of him understood. If only he'd felt that way three years ago…. He tucked it away. "Why are you telling me about the twin now?"

"Just to let you know someone put a bullet in her for asking too many questions."

"What?"

"I heard the bullet hit her cigarette tin, get deflected up, and then lodge in her collarbone. Who knows? I got the story from the local knitting circle. They've been known to stretch the truth." Lemus stood and motioned back toward the front door. "Anyway, it doesn't take a whole lot of gunshots before people start to learn what to say and what not to say."

Jack nodded. As he shifted his weight to stand, he realized that his hand was inside his jacket and his fingers were grazing the grip of the Springfield again.

WILMA, 1943

WHEN THE CAR started its descent down the Conejo grade, Wilma caught her first glimpse of Camarillo. It gave her a feeling of sunshine and optimism, despite all the evidence to the contrary. Flat stretches of lush farmland spread across the valley floor to the ocean. Patches of green dotted the golden hillsides as if they'd been painted there in watercolor. It all seemed so crisp and clear and clean, even the little town at the foothill with its white mission-style church next to a humble, rounded steeple. Islands on the horizon cut sharp brown lines into the expansive blue. Wilma had been trying to keep her mouth shut for this whole ride, but the view from this downhill road loosened her up. "It's beautiful," she said.

One of the white coats in the front seat turned to speak to her. "Sure. You'll love it here."

"Nothing like a vacation in the bughouse," Wilma said.

The other white coat, the one who was driving, said, "You better believe it, sister. This place is fantastic."

White Coat One backed him up. "Especially if you like horses. Do you like horses?"

"Who doesn't like horses?" Wilma asked.

White Coat One pointed to the hills off to the left of the car. "Look at those mountain trails. You'll get to go horseback riding on all of them."

It seemed farfetched, but there were trails. Wilma could see those. There were even a few people on horses on the trails. "Really?" she asked.

"Like my partner said, you're going to love it," White Coat Two added.

White Coat One turned in his seat to face Wilma. "If you don't like horseback riding, we have hiking excursions. Not on the same trails as the horseback riders use. We don't want you stepping in anything untoward."

"Lord, no," White Coat Two said.

"And the hills are full of daisies. The girls at the asylum love to pick them after lunch, then lounge in the grass, making daisy chains."

"You're pulling my leg," Wilma said.

"Do you like water sports?" White Coat Two asked.

"Like what?"

"Canoeing," White Coat One said. "There's a river that runs alongside the hospital. We take patients canoeing in it."

"Really?"

White Coat Two kept his eyes on the road but nodded vigorously. "Not just in the river. We have Polynesian boats. You know, the canoes with the floats on either side? If you're good enough in the river, you can paddle around through the ocean."

This seemed like too much for Wilma. Before she could protest, White Coat One said, "It's like being in the South Seas."

"The Marquesas," White Coat Two said. "Tahiti."

"Hawaii," the two white coats said together.

"Yes, ma'am," White Coat One said. "This may be the best two months of your life."

Wait. What? Two months? Was Wilma hearing that right? She asked, "Two months?"

"That's what the paper says," White Coat One said.

"And did we tell you about the springtime productions of Shakespeare in the park the hospital sponsors?" White Coat Two asked.

"Take me back to the two months," Wilma said. "What paper says two months?"

White Coat One dug through a briefcase that sat on the seat between him and the driver. He found a file with only a few sheets of paper in it. He extracted a carbon copy from the file and passed it back to Wilma. She read the form.

It was a notice of commitment, a California 5150. According to the paper, Wilma had waived her right for an arraignment. She refused to speak on her behalf in front of the judge. The judge sentenced her to two months rehabilitation at the Camarillo State Hospital. The arraignment and trial were recorded as happening while Wilma and the white coats had been driving up Ventura Highway. "Look at this time," Wilma said, pointing at a line on the form. "The judge signed this order at noon today. It won't be noon for another half hour, at least."

White Coat One took the carbon copy from Wilma. He read the judge's orders. "Well, I'll be." He turned to the driver. "We better drag our feet dropping this one off."

"You feel like grabbing lunch?"

White Coat One shrugged. "Why not?"

White Coat Two steered the sedan off Ventura Blvd. and into a little roadside café near the St. Mary Magdalen Church in downtown Camarillo. He reached under his seat. White Coat One provided the running commentary. "We're going to duck in for a sandwich. I hope you understand that you can't join us."

Food was the least of Wilma's concern. The booze from her four-day binge had been draining out of her liver since she'd gotten into the car with these white coats. The thought of taking a bite out of a sandwich, chewing, and swallowing it made her even more nauseous than the snowballing hangover she'd been trying to ignore. "It's all right. I'll stay in the car."

"Of course you will. And we'll make you comfortable. Just you sit tight."

White Coat Two took the jacket he'd pulled out from under the seat and came around to Wilma's door. He opened it. He rolled down the window. White Coat One opened the other door and rolled down that window. "You'll get a nice breeze," he said.

"And just to make you comfortable and warm, we'll loan you this lovely camisole," White Coat Two said. He guided her out of the sedan. Wilma stood in the alcove between the car door and the backseat. White Coat Two instructed her to raise both arms. He slid the sleeves down her arms.

"Wait a minute," Wilma said. "You're putting this on me backwards."

Just as she said this, she realized there was no opening at the end of the sleeves. Her hands were trapped. White Coat Two stepped closer, yanking Wilma's hands behind her back before she could think to resist. White Coat One had already slid across the backseat behind her. He buckled the straightjacket in place. The two men forced her down into her seat. They shut the sedan doors.

"We won't be long," White Coat One said.

"No more than an hour and a half, two hours," White Coat Two added.

"Can we get you anything?" White Coat One asked.

"A coffee, at least," Wilma suggested.

To his credit, White Coat One did return about fifteen minutes later with a mug of coffee for Wilma. He explained that he didn't have time to hold it for her while she drank, and he couldn't take off the camisole. So he put the mug between her knees. "Just you balance it there," he said. He went back inside the café.

Wilma spread her legs. The mug tumbled to the floor. Coffee soaked the bottom of her housedress, her nylons, and her mules. The coffee itself stunk like it had been filtered through gym socks. Wilma couldn't take it. She leaned as far forward as she could and vomited everything that was left from her final party with Tom Fillmore: the martinis from the Players, the Formosa Café liver and onions, the red wine to top off the night. It puddled on the floor with the dirty roadside coffee.

Wilma leaned her head against the back of the seat and breathed through her mouth. She waited for some kind of air to move somewhere, for that promised breeze to blow.

The white coats dropped the comedy act on the final seven- or eight-mile drive to the hospital. They left her in the straightjacket and didn't speak other than to curse the stink of coffee and vomit, which had gotten worse over the two hours they spent in the café. Wilma tried to ignore them and angle her head to catch the wind rushing through the back windows. She watched the rows of lettuce and onion and celery crops angle toward her, then straighten, then angle away from her. This nuthouse was in the middle of nowhere. She'd have to be Pheidippides to get away from this joint by foot. And, as well as she could remember, the story hadn't turned out well for him. The way things looked from her backseat perch, Wilma was going down for two months. It was time to reconcile herself to that fact.

When they got to the main building of the hospital, the white coats dropped her off with a burly woman dressed like a cop. The woman wobbled like she'd been thrown off balance by the armory of keys on her belt. A couple of the keys looked big enough to fit the kind of doors you'd find at the top of a beanstalk. She didn't speak. She just pushed Wilma toward a door with a little less iron than your typical bank vault. One of the giant keys opened the door. Wilma had the sense walking through the doorway that she may never walk back out.

A nurse on the inside checked Wilma in. The only words she said were statements of facts, like, "alcoholic" and "two months." She gave Wilma's name as Wilma Chesley. This seemed further proof that the old man had pulled strings to set up this commitment. Not that Wilma needed further proof. Not that it took a lot of pull to get a woman committed these days.

The nurse led Wilma down a long hall. Each door had a sign painted on it. "Dental Clinic." "X-Ray." "Diet Kitchen." "Electroshock." "Secretary." When they reached the door labeled "Hydro," the nurse extracted a key from her giant key ring, unlocked the door, and led Wilma inside.

A row of baths stood along the left side of the room. A woman lay in one of the baths. Heavy rubber blankets covered her body. Only her head rose out of the water.

The tips of her hair were soaked. A fuzzy patch of dry hair rose from the top of her head. She rolled her eyes slowly in Wilma's direction. The eyes focused on Wilma for a split second, then slackened into an unfocused stare. Whatever the woman saw at that moment, she saw it without the use of her eyes.

Wilma had seen some sad women in her time, but this woman was the saddest. Her sallow skin and rubber blankets and empty eyes were enough to make Wilma forget that she was wearing a straightjacket. Someone always seems to have it worse.

The nurse had apparently forgotten about the straightjacket, also. She told Wilma to strip.

"I'll need a little help with that," Wilma said.

"Are you too drunk to undress yourself?" the nurse asked.

"Honey," Wilma said, "if I could've unbuckled myself from this straightjacket, I would've gotten out of that car and found a safe place to hide hours ago."

"Oh." The nurse considered Wilma for what looked to be the first time. "Right." She unbuckled the back of the jacket. Wilma shook herself free. Another woman—a secretary, judging from the formless dress and cracked-leather mules and clipboard in her hand—came into the room. She sat on a bench along the wall opposite the tubs. Wilma stripped to her slip. "Down to the bare skin," the nurse told her.

Wilma took the rest of it off, remembering, oh Christ, her foray the night before with Tom Fillmore. Surely, they'd be able to tell what she'd been up to. Surely, that was one more humiliation waiting to happen.

The nurse led her to the scale and checked Wilma's

weight. "One twenty-eight," she called to the secretary.
Wilma double-checked the weights. Not bad. Say what
you will about these benders, they always brought Wilma's weight down a few pounds. The nurse checked
Wilma's height next. Wilma stood tall, stretching her spine
as much as she could. The nurse called out, "Five-four."

"And a half," Wilma added. "Don't forget the half."

"Five-four," the nurse called.

"Are you sure you can see all the way up to the top of
the ruler, Shorty?" Wilma asked.

The nurse shot her a look. She called out to the secretary, "Five-three and a half."

"Oh, now you're just lying."

The secretary asked Wilma a litany of questions:
birthplace, place of residence, father's name, mother's
name, mother's maiden name, occupation, religion. Wilma figured that the State should have all this information
anyway, and if they were going to rob her of two months
of her life and an inch off her real height, she was going to
make up all her answers. So she did. Birthplace: Kalamazoo. Place of residence: The Doheny Mansion, Beverly
Hills. Father's name: Culbert Olson. Mother's name: Joan
Olson. Mother's maiden name: Crawford. Occupation:
hand model. Religion: pagan.

At the end of this charade, the nurse pushed Wilma
into a tight shower stall. The nurse took a step back and
turned on the water. It felt like it was about two hundred
degrees, and it pummeled Wilma from three directions.
The nurse tossed a bar of soap and a rough washcloth into
the mix. Wilma twisted and contorted, trying to pick up
the soap and cloth without getting her hair wet. "What
the hell are you doing?" the nurse asked.

"You didn't give me a shower cap," Wilma said.

"Get your hair all the way under," the nurse said. "Soap it all down."

After dipping her head, the hot water felt all right. She scrubbed her skin until it was rosy pink, clearing all the crust and old makeup off her face, scouring away any traces of her previous night's transgressions, even opening her mouth to the jets and letting the water wash her teeth and rinse out her mouth. She kept turning and running the cloth over her until the nurse had enough and turned the water off.

The secretary tossed Wilma a towel that wasn't much bigger than the washcloth. It was soaked through before she was done with her hair, much less drying her skin. The nurse pointed to a metal table near the scale. "Hop up," she said.

"I'm still dripping," Wilma said.

"Hop up," the nurse said.

Wilma climbed onto the table. Her dripping skin made it slick. The metal sucked the last traces of warmth from her. The secretary handed the nurse a magnifying glass. The nurse inspected Wilma. She combed through Wilma's pubic patch, parting the wild red hair, checking the roots, pushing Wilma's legs open wider, viewing more of Wilma than Wilma could ever see of herself. The inspection was remarkably and painfully thorough. Had any lice or worms or bacteria found refuge between Wilma's toes or under her arms or within any other crevice, the nurse would have found it. The whole thing seemed to last for weeks. Wilma wondered if maybe this would be her whole two-month stay at the asylum.

Finally, the nurse told Wilma she could stand. Wilma

asked, "Are you sure? You may have missed a freckle somewhere on my ass."

"Enough, Lady Chesley," the nurse said. She pointed to a shapeless cotton dress that must have been hospital property when the joint opened in the thirties. "Put that on." Wilma climbed into the dress. It was big enough to fit the fat lady in a sideshow act.

"Am I supposed to wear this or build a tent with it?"

The nurse hadn't gone for any of Wilma's jokes and wasn't going for this one. She just said, "Wear it."

"Can't I wear my dress?"

"It has coffee and vomit on it," the nurse said. "You'll get it back after it's been laundered."

"Can I at least have something that Dumbo didn't wear in the movie?"

The nurse didn't respond. She walked out of the hydro room. Wilma followed, her bare feet slapping against the cool concrete of the hospital floor.

The nurse rushed down one hallway and into another. Again and again. Wilma trotted to keep up with the nurse's long, purposeful strides. She tried to make note of how many turns she'd taken and which way she'd gone. There was no hope. She was irretrievably lost in the madhouse maze. Some rooms she passed had names of doctors or signs saying things like "Surgery" or "Music Room." Many were dorm rooms. She passed cavernous spaces with thirty or forty beds. Next to them were rooms the size of closets with bunk beds inside. What little daylight snuck into these rooms seemed a cruel mockery. After what felt like a few miles, the nurse stopped at a small room with four beds. "Welcome home," she said.

No patients were in the room. Each bed housed the

exact same style of bland brown satchel. Peeking out of the top of each was a pitiful collection of hairbrushes and photographs and combs and lipstick and paperbacks and knitting needles and yarn. Worn purses and splintered sewing boxes. One bed was empty. Wilma would have to write to Gertie and ask her sister to bring a new collection of sad little lifelines to fill her state-issued satchel. At least one of Wilma's new roommates had a pencil and a notebook there.

The nurse turned to leave. Wilma quick asked, "What am I supposed to do now?"

"Wait. We'll call you for supper in a few hours."

The thought of being alone in this tiny room was too much. "Can I at least have a smoke?"

The nurse took a pack of cigarettes from the pocket of her scrubs and handed it to Wilma. Wilma shook one cigarette loose, stuck it between her lips, and handed the pack back. "Come on," the nurse said. "There's no smoking in the rooms. I'll take you to the Section and light that for you."

The hospital had been so beautiful from the outside. It struck Wilma initially as more of a Santa Barbara resort than a bughouse, with its red tile roofs and iron balustrades and wide, sunny balconies. Wilma pictured the smoking room to be some kind of veranda or garden, like the ones she'd known at Union Station. She couldn't indulge in this fantasy for too long, though. The Section was three doors down from her own. And it was the restroom. The nurse led her inside, lit the cigarette, and left without a goodbye. There were no seats in the restroom, save the toilets and the floor. Wilma chose the floor. The cool tile pressed against the prodigious folds of her cotton

dress. She leaned against the wall, legs splayed out in front
of her, and sucked in the tobacco.

Two months.

JACK, 1946

JACK SPENT the afternoon at the central library, digging up all the news he could on Wilma. Her death was barely a blip. The *Los Angeles Times* had a brief mention: "Local Starlet Dies in Tub." The cub reporter who typed it up made a meal out of the handful of movies you could find Wilma in if you squinted at the right time. They were all B pictures with tiny budgets. Gertie would drag Wilma to the set on Wilma's days off and remake her as a nightclub patron or a pedestrian or a Martian or a doll who elicited a wolf whistle or the world's only red-haired Indian. There'd been one movie Wilma practically carried Jack to so that he could see her perform an actual line. Some mug with makeup for a beard got chased down the street by a dashing fellow. The mug crashed into Wilma. She said, "Saaaay. Watch it!" Jack applauded in the little theater off Figueroa. Someone in the back pelted him with peanuts and told him to can it.

The *Times* thought those movies the key to Wilma. They mentioned she'd been in over a dozen films prior to getting drunk and falling in her tub. There was no mention of her husband who, at the time, was believed to be dead in Germany. No mention of the book she wrote or her family or anything. All of that came out in the second piece Jack found about her. The obituary that Gertie had obviously written. Gertie would've paid by the word for that obit. She'd splurged the extra couple of pennies to add the words "beloved" and "cherished." They caught

Jack right in the back of the throat.

Other than the blurb and the obituary, there was nothing. No mention of a murder, an investigation, of questions raised, of neighbors concerned. Nothing. Just a dead extra and yesterday's news.

Her book was in the racks. Jack climbed four flights of steps and wandered through a maze of shelves before finding the dusty copy. The card inside showed it hadn't been checked out since September of 1944. He climbed back down the steps, brought the book to circulation, and checked it out.

He left the library and headed across downtown toward Cole's. He would have to catch the interurban there and head back this way, past the library again and onto another car up Figueroa, but he needed a walk, some time to think, and maybe some luck at Cole's. He strolled under the shadow of the Biltmore. Somewhere above the high arches and concrete balustrades were the rooms the hotel gave over to officers back from Europe—not the ones with bombardier badges like his. The ones with brass stars. The ones so far away from the action that, if you ran into them, you knew you'd retreated all the way back.

On the next block, he cut across Pershing Square. His father would talk about this being a meeting ground for fairies back in the '20s. If the old man was paid to track down a hood or a thief light in the loafers, he'd come down to Pershing Square and start busting heads until he banged into one with a mouth that talked. By the time the war rolled around, the park was a patriotic site. He'd actually been hooked here, walking a downtown beat, pausing to stop under a palm and take in the statue of a soldier from the Spanish American War. A recruiter found him there, told him that his time with the force would count in his favor if he enlisted. He could be a sergeant, dropping bombs out of planes, fighting fascism *and* taking furloughs on the beaches of southern England.

Well, most of it was a sales pitch. The part about dropping bombs out of planes was true. And he had been a sergeant, for whatever that was worth.

When he reached the Pacific Building, he checked the counter inside of Cole's, looking for a bare head with a bald spot the size of a yarmulke, looking for an arm stuck to a coffee cup that had been refilled a half-dozen times. This was the time of day when he could always find his old partner Dave Hammond here, like it was his office or something.

Jack didn't see him at first. The place was buzzing. Customers flitted around from tables and stools like hummingbirds on bougainvillea, waitresses swooped in with food and out with dirty plates. Jack weaved through the tables to the counter, the place with the only open seats in the joint. A few gray-haired gentlemen lingered over their conversations there. And sure enough, though his arm had grown thin and the hair around the bald spot had turned white, Hammond couldn't be mistaken. Jack took the stool next to him.

Jack didn't address Hammond. He sat facing forward, waiting for the waitress. He pulled out a pouch of tobacco and started rolling his own. The waitress swung by. "Just coffee," he said.

Hammond heard the voice and looked to his right. Jack kept his face forward, his hands on his cigarette. He could feel Hammond's stare, almost hear the internal dialogue. Hammond brought that dialog to the external in no time. "Am I seeing a ghost?" he asked.

Jack slowly turned his head left. When he caught Hammond's glance, he said, "Boo!"

Hammond jumped in his seat.

Jack smiled. It was a cruel joke, but he couldn't resist it when the opportunity arose.

"Jack? Holy cow!" Hammond walloped him in the center of his back. "You're alive!"

"So it would seem," Jack said.

"I was at your funeral, kid. Christ, what happened?"

"At the funeral?" Jack asked. "I don't know. I wasn't there." He pointed a finger at Hammond. "I hope you cried, though. I hope you turned to Gladys and cursed what a waste it was to lose a great man like me."

Hammond smiled. He kept his hand on Jack's shoulder and squeezed hard enough to crush the suit padding. "You son of a bitch. It's good to see you."

"You too."

The waitress poured Jack's coffee. He ordered a slice of peach pie.

"So what the hell happened over there? How'd you get yourself killed and come back to life?"

Jack lit his cigarette, watched the smoke gather around an overhead lightbulb. He gave Hammond the short version. "The plane I was in got shot down. I took a parachute ride followed by a little tour of Germany on my own. Sometime later, I ran into some Nazis who gave me a place to live for a couple of years. Now I'm back."

Hammond scratched his balding head. "A little tour? Were you by yourself?"

Jack nodded. "I was the only member of the crew who made it."

"So you were behind enemy lines? By yourself? For how long?"

"I didn't count the days. A couple months, anyway."

"Jesus, Jack. You must've seen some shit."

Jack waved the comment away. He took another drag and felt the burn down deep in his lungs. "What about you? How's life treating you?"

Hammond smiled. "Good. I got my pension. Little garden in the back. Coffee here in the afternoons to give Gladys a break. It's the life of Riley."

The pie came and Jack ate it. While he did, Hammond thumbed Jack's library book. "I read this," he said.

"Did you?"

"Sure. You know I always liked Wilma."

"She was the best."

"I made her funeral, too. I cried at that one. There wasn't a dry eye in the house that day."

Jack lifted his napkin to his mouth and gave his nose a surreptitious wipe while he was there. "Not many people there to cry, as I hear."

"Oh, there were some. Me. Gladys. Wilma's twin. A host of hash slingers from the joint she'd been working in at the time."

"Did my pop make it?"

Hammond looked down at the linoleum counter. He shook his head.

Jack nodded, pushed away his pie plate.

The restaurant fluttered around them.

"What do you think of that story?" Jack asked.

"Which one?"

"Falling face-first in a tub."

Hammond shook his head. "Hell of a way to go."

"Fishy, too, huh?"

"How do you mean?"

Jack spun his stool to face Hammond the best he could. "Picture it for me, Dave. You're five-foot-four in a four-foot-long tub. There's a wall behind you and a wall next to you. You stand up in the middle. Something makes you slip. And what happens? Somehow, your knees don't go down. They go up. Somehow your arms don't go out. Somehow you contort yourself so that you land on your nose, and with enough force to kill you. What does that fall look like to you?"

"Strange things happen, Jack." Hammond stood from his stool. He dug a handful of change from his pocket and dropped it on the counter next to his half-full coffee cup. "It doesn't have to add up to anything."

"It's suspicious, is all. And you're telling me you didn't ask any questions."

"I asked questions."

"What did you find out?"

Hammond took a step away from the counter. "I found out not to ask questions, Jack."

Jack rushed to fish out enough coin to cover the bill. He didn't want Hammond to slip away this easily. "Hold up, Dave. I'll walk with you."

Hammond placed a meaty hand on Jack's shoulder and pushed him back onto his stool. "Stay and drink your coffee, kid," Hammond said.

"Are you telling me…. You're telling me something. What is it? Were you scared off the case?" Jack asked.

"I wasn't scared. I was just smart enough to know

when to back off." Hammond plopped his fedora onto his head. "Take my advice, kid. Back off."

"Dave, this is my wife we're talking about."

"She's six feet under. You're above ground. Let her stay there and you stay where you are."

"I have to know I'm outmanned before I do that," Jack said, still sitting.

"You're outmanned, kid. I'm telling you this because I love you. Play it smart. You didn't survive months behind enemy lines and years in a POW camp just to get yourself killed over a dodgy story." Hammond waved goodbye to the waitress. He turned back to Jack. "Ask the twin what happens when you stick your nose in the wrong places."

WILMA, 1943

WILMA'S FIRST assignment was in the sick bay. A nurse led her there after breakfast. "It ain't rocket science, doll," she'd said. "You gather up the bedpans and buckets and dump them in the Section. Change the bedding. Wipe down the walls. Mop the floor and polish it when it dries. Do it all in that order. Clean the whole ward. Got it?"

Wilma nodded. The nurse led her to a supply closet where Wilma found the mops and buckets and scrub brushes and polishing brushes and bedding. She dug around for rubber gloves. When she found none, she asked the nurse. The nurse told her that they didn't have rubber gloves for patients. "So I'm cleaning piss buckets and bedpans with my bare hands?" Wilma asked.

"Don't be such a prima donna. You can wash your hands when you're done."

Wilma got to work. She emptied all the buckets and bedpans first, scrubbed her hands raw after she was done, then set to the real cleaning. She'd never been much of a housekeeper. She hated to clean her own home and preferred her place to be more of a nest with clothes and books and projects scattered around. Even so, she knew how to clean. She'd been doing it at restaurants since she'd first started waitressing in her teens. It was the worst, the final hurdle of the night, the time when she wasn't making any real money but was still doing her job. She'd learned to work fast.

She attacked the sick bay with the same fervor. She

changed linens in assembly line style: all the bottom sheets in the ward first, then all the top sheets, then all the blankets, then all the pillow cases. Each motion became mechanical. It seemed to take half the time that changing each bed individually would have. She scrubbed the walls and mopped the floor with the same kind of deliberateness. Before long, she was glistening with sweat. Polishing the floors was toughest. The polishing brush must've weighed fifty pounds. After all the other effort, it took a bit of her reserves to push it around the floor. She got through everything, though.

By ten o'clock, the ward was a showplace. It was the cleanest she'd ever gotten anything in her life. She packed away her supplies and sauntered down to the nurse's station. The same chubby brunette who'd set her to work that morning asked her what she was doing. "All finished," Wilma said. "You could eat off the floors in that joint."

The nurse looked at her watch. She said, "It's not clean enough, yet. Go back and clean it until 11:30."

"Oh, for Christ's fucking sake," Wilma said.

The nurse popped to her feet. "What did you just say?"

Wilma took a deep breath. "I apologize," Wilma said. "I'll go back and clean."

And so she went back through the ward again, rescrubbed the walls, remopped the floors, danced again with that man-size polishing brush. She worked as slowly as she could, sometimes so slowly that she'd stop altogether. She finished her second round of cleaning the ward at about quarter after eleven. She overturned a bucket in the supply closet and sat there for fifteen minutes.

Even with two rounds of scrubbing and mopping

and polishing, with the soap and disinfectant and floor wax, the room still had a sickly insane smell that Wilma couldn't place. It was something noxious, some kind of mixture of alcohol and lighter fluid and industry and decay. And it was in the air, somehow. It made no sense.

The nurse released Wilma for lunch at 11:30.

The dining hall was a long, narrow room with high ceilings held up by wide arches. Daylight flooded in through the side windows to the east. Hanging lamps filled in the rest of the shadows. Four rows of rectangular tables covered the floor, six high-backed wooden chairs per table. Patients were separated by gender, the men occupying the northern quarter of the hall, the women taking up the other three quarters. Wilma carried a muddy brown stew, a hard roll, and a mug of coffee on a metal tray. She searched the table for someone who didn't look too blank, too crazy. Surely, there'd be a host of other drunks just like her. They'd be crazy in a way she could handle.

A woman stood from her table and waved at Wilma. "Yoo-hoo," she called. "Gertie. Over here."

Wilma checked for signs of nuttiness. The woman had perfect posture, shoulders thrown back, chin jutted, head held at an angle poised to balance a stack of finishing school texts. She wore a plain dress of soft cotton, the kind Wilma hadn't seen new like this since before the war started. Even her wave was more of a parade wave than the flopping madhouse arms that looked like they were forever trying to wave a plane down onto a landing strip. She had all the signs of a rich drunk, someone who'd sipped down one too many gin rickeys at one too many debutante balls. Wilma decided to take a chance on her.

The woman welcomed Wilma to an empty seat at the table. "Gertie Greene, is that you?" she asked. "I don't have my glasses, but when I saw those flickering flames of red hair charging from the top of your head, I said to myself, 'I'll be damned if Gertie Greene didn't get sent up for a little dry spell.'"

Wilma set her tray down on the table. She wasn't too surprised at the mistaken identity. She and Gertie had been switching roles since they were little girls. "Looks like you'll be damned," Wilma told the woman. "Gertie hasn't been sent anywhere. She's still down in Hollywood, typing up scripts that some man takes the money and credit for."

"What?" The woman squinted at Wilma. "Are you pulling my leg?"

"No. I'm not Gertie."

"But you know her? And you look just like her?"

Wilma nodded. "She's my twin."

The woman examined Wilma, looking her up and down with the care the nurse had used in the hydro room the day before. "Well, I will be damned. Gertie did mention a twin to me before. Wanda, is it?"

"Wilma."

The woman stretched out a hand to shake. "Nice to meet you, Billie. I'm Carlotta Bell. Folks call me Lottie."

Wilma shook hands. They had a half hour for lunch, regardless how quickly or slowly they ate, so Wilma turned to her stew. She sniffed it.

Lottie said, "Best not to smell. The stew or anything. Just turn that old nose off until you're released from here."

"What is that smell? It's everywhere around this joint."

"Paraldehyde," Lottie said. "I suppose that, if you don't know it, they haven't given you any yet."

Wilma spooned in a mouthful of stew and shook her head.

"Lucky so far. If they try to give it to you, do everything you can to keep it out of your stomach. It's a doozy. It burns going down. Before you know it, you don't know your name anymore or where you are. You get that vacant stare. Your breath reeks. It's the worst."

Wilma sipped her coffee and thought about this. "Is that what I'm smelling? Everyone's paraldehyde breath?"

Lottie smiled and tapped the tip of her straight nose. Wilma couldn't help noticing the perfect manicure on her silver fingernail. Lottie's eyes drifted to catch those of a passing man. He wore cook's whites and had his hair parted straight down the middle like George Raft. Nothing about him told Wilma whether he was a patient or an employee. Lottie winked at him. The man breezed by the table and passed Lottie an apple. Lottie said, "Hey, what about one for my pal, here?"

The man smiled at Wilma. He handed her an apple the way a father passes candy to a little girl on Christmas. Wilma thanked him. He gave her a quick smile, raised his eyebrows, and carried on his way.

"You're a doll," Lottie told him.

The man waved goodbye with barely a glance back.

"Stick with me, kid," Lottie said. "You'll be off that stew and eating real food in no time."

Wilma liked the sound of that. She kept eating her stew, anyway. She asked Lottie, "How'd you know my sister?"

"From pictures." Lottie said that she'd learned to fly

airplanes when she was a kid. Her father had been a hob-byist, flying the earliest, most rickety planes he could get his hands on. He'd take her to the east side of Pasadena, where other men of leisure tinkered with their machines and their lives. He'd come out of the sky with his plane in flames and in pieces a time or two. This convinced Lottie that the Bells couldn't die in the air. She flew with her father and, when she got old enough, flew on her own.

Her father had endowed her with a trust fund, but for a laugh, she started flying for the studios. She took cameramen up around Los Angeles on days clear of smog. They'd capture stock footage, shots that could be spliced into dozens of films. For a while, she worked exclusively with one studio hell-bent on making a Western a week. She'd fly cameramen out east by Bishop and catch sweep-ing shots of the southern Sierras and Death Valley. That's how she'd met Gertie.

Gertie was hired piecemeal by the studio as the script girl for one of their directors. When Lottie would land on the airstrip in Lone Pine, she'd hunt down Gertie and go for a drink. "Only Gertie knew when to quit. I hate that about her."

"You and me both, sister," Wilma said.

"You don't share Gertie's restraint?"

Wilma shook her head. Lottie winked at anoth-er man. He dropped off a couple of prune sandwiches wrapped in wax paper. Lottie slid them both into her handbag. They also exchanged small slips of paper. Lottie smiled and covered the paper with her hand.

"I thought twins were supposed to be identical. How'd you get to be a souse and not Gertie?"

"I'm the evil twin, I guess."

Lottie kept the note under her hand. Wilma wondered about it. She'd noticed this note passing at breakfast. The men and women seemed to flirt through these
little missives. Wilma wanted in on that, or really in on
anything to ward off the boredom.

Lottie asked, "Are you a scribbler like your sister?"

"I used to write a bit."

"Pictures, too?"

Wilma shook her head. "I used to write for the pulps,
under the name William Greene. My husband was a cop.
I'd steal his stories and make some things up and sell them
for sewing money."

"Sell them for drinking money is my guess."

"Can't put one over on you, Lottie."

Lottie opened the note. It read, "shee-roo-koo-dee-
doo." Lottie took a fresh piece of paper from a pocket
notebook and wrote, "bop-bop-skoo-bee-doo-bop." She
passed it to the next man who walked beside their table.
Wilma watched the man cross the dining hall.

"What's your husband now, if he isn't a cop anymore?" Lottie asked.

Wilma shrugged. She wasn't ready to answer. She
watched the man carry Lottie's note to the north end of
the hall and pass it to a dark, broad-shouldered man. Even
in the harsh light of the hall, he was painfully handsome.
He unfolded the note, mouthed the words, and smiled.
Wilma caught Lottie returning the smile.

Wilma said more than asked, "That Negro fellow
over there is your beau."

The smile fled Lottie's face. Her eyes grew wide.

Wilma answered before Lottie could. "It's okay with
me," she said. "Can't any of us start looking down their

noses here. I'm just happy to make a friend."

Lottie rested her silver manicured hand atop Wilma's.

JACK, 1946

JACK SPENT an hour the next morning trying to read Wilma's book. It was called *The Brain Emporium*. It opened with a story about her and Gertie stealing a milkman's horse. She told the story pretty much as Jack had heard it and as he remembered it. He was mentioned by name as the cop who kept her out of the pokey that night. Gertie was changed to "a friend" and given a new name. From there, Wilma wrote about the news of Jack's death, her mourning, and her trip to Camarillo. Heavy stuff.

The rest of the book, presumably, was about Wilma's two months at the nuthouse. Jack would read it later. Maybe. The combination of Wilma's opening chapters and Jack's interviews the day before, the neighbors slagging Wilma, the apathy, the abandonment of the woman he loved: it was about all the pain he could take for the time being.

He watched Highland Park stretch and awaken into the day. He contemplated a jacaranda across the street. It had no leaves he could see but exploded in purple flowers. His second cup of coffee turned into his third, then his fourth.

Gertie's little coupe was parked along the curb in front of his house. He watched her walk up, high heels clomping on the stone path leading up to his porch, her stride purposeful and direct.

Jack called out, "You ever been shot at, sister?"

Gertie flashed a quick half-smile. She strutted up the

porch steps and took a seat next to Jack. "So, you have been investigating?"

"Talked to a bunch of Wilma's asshole neighbors. One of them told me you took a bullet for asking too many questions."

Gertie wore a white knit blouse with alternating red and blue buttons and a red wool coat. She unbuttoned the first blue and the first red, hooked her thumb into the blouse, and pulled the ensemble to the left. She had a .22-size scar on either side of her collarbone, just shy of the shoulder muscle. Jack touched it gently with the pad of his forefinger. Gertie didn't flinch. "Don't read too much into it, Jackie."

Jack stared at the scar. Gertie pulled her blouse back into place and buttoned up. "Who did it? What do you know?"

"Not much. I was leaving Pie Land over on Vermont one night when a Ford sedan swings by. Next thing I know, I'm on the ground and my shoulder's burning. I passed out and woke up in the hospital. Turned out I was lucky. The gunman was downhill and the bullet went up through me. Didn't hit anything that mattered. I was back on the Republic lot before the picture I was working on lost any money."

"And you were shot for looking into Wilma's death."

"Murder. Wilma's murder," Gertie said. "That's all I can figure. Either that or someone was gunning for Rita Hayworth and mistook me for her."

Jack pulled out his notebook and pencil. "Who's Rita Hayworth? Should I go talk to her?"

Gertie set her hand atop Jack's pencil. "Easy there, Dick Tracy. It's just a joke."

Jack didn't know what to make of it, so he offered Gertie a cup of coffee. She declined. She said, "Don't worry too much about that little old bullet. You're so quick to reach for that heater in your jacket, you don't have anything to worry about."

Jack nodded. He picked up *The Brain Emporium* and spun it around in his hands. "I got my old man's Model A running again. I'm thinking a drive up to Camarillo isn't the worst idea in the world."

Gertie smiled. "Ask for Mr. Hughes. He'll give you a tour."

Sometime in the mid-afternoon, Jack found himself deep in the Camarillo strawberry fields that led to the state mental hospital. He pulled over beside a little hog farm on the entrance road to the hospital and pulled himself together. He dipped his comb in his tin of Royal Crown and slicked back his hair. He slid back into his coat and popped his hat back on his head. He took a quick look at himself in the rearview. Everything seemed in order. He couldn't pass for a swell in this dusty green Ford, but he was clean and clean-shaven and presentable enough. He swung back onto the road and approached the entrance gate.

The guard at the gate waved Jack to a stop. "What's your business?"

"My wife sent me up to tour the place," Jack said. "She's thinking of sending her mother here to dry up."

"Living the life, aren't you?"

Jack smiled. "You said it, pal. I've been looking for somewhere to send my mother-in-law since I got married." As he said this, he realized that he wasn't wearing a wedding ring. It wasn't the greatest sin a married man away from home could commit, but it wasn't what a dutiful husband would do. He casually dropped his left arm from the door. His hand dangled low, in a spot Jack hoped would be out of sight for the guard.

"Who'd you set up an appointment with?"

"A fellow named Hughes."

The guard nodded. "Sure." He pointed Jack down the road, told him to take a right and park once he got past the bell tower. Jack gave him a casual salute. The old jalopy sputtered into the hospital grounds.

Jack parked where the guard had told him. He stepped out of the car. Cool breezes floated in from the ocean not too far south and west of here. The midday sun seemed gentle by comparison. Springtime had sprinkled some green on the hills that surrounded the hospital. The administration building was on the north side of hospital grounds. The actual hospital and patients were on the south side. All the buildings on that side seemed to turn their back on the outside world. There must have been grass on the inside, lanais and balconies and windows and recreational facilities. Jack couldn't know. The south half of the hospital was like a fort.

For all the grass and shade trees Jack could see, there were no people. Steam rose from the boiler plant on the west side. The building next to it looked like a factory, with its long sides and high windows. Jack rolled a smoke and watched a few pigeons perched atop the peak of red tile roof.

First, he decided, there wasn't any point in wandering away from the administration building. This place was built to block the view of curious eyes. It didn't leave much room for casual encounters. If he wanted to see anyone, he needed a guide. He lit his cigarette, took a drag, and walked around to the front entrance of the admin building.

He was greeted by a large woman working the front desk. Any intimidation her size or age may have held was buried under her yellow rayon dress and its sunfish pattern. Jack tucked his left hand into his pants pocket. He offered her a friendly smile when she asked his business.

"I have an appointment with Mr. Hughes," he said.

The receptionist kept her fingers atop the appointment book without looking inside. "I'll just get him," she said. "You can sit in that chair while you wait."

Jack sat against the wall and finished his cigarette. It didn't add up. The guard was easy to get past. The receptionist didn't care that he didn't really have an appointment. And now here came Mr. Hughes, ready to show him around, a big grin on his mug and a hand out for a shake. These weren't the type of folks who covered up murders or drew enough water down in Los Angeles to scare Hammond off an investigation. Jack would take the tour with Mr. Hughes, but already he felt like he was wasting both of their time.

It wasn't until after the tour and Jack was back in his car that he saw something worth a look. He'd been driving around the buildings on the south side of the hospital. In the back, he saw a Mercury parked outside what looked to be a dorm. This couldn't be a hospital vehicle. It had chrome enough to blind and style enough to brag. It belonged more on the lots of Republic than parked behind a sanitarium.

A man in a seersucker suit led two women in hospital gowns to the car. At first glance, both women looked a mess: wild hair and naked faces. Despite that, the wind pushing up against their gowns showed them to be young and fit and a bath away from being attractive. None of the three had yet looked up and seen Jack. He turned his glance to the green-splattered hills before any of the trio could make eye contact with him. He rode out of the hospital and pulled onto the shoulder of a dairy road just outside hospital grounds. Sure enough, the Mercury whipped past with the patients in back.

Jack rolled another cigarette. These farm roads were long and flat. It was easy to follow from a safe distance. He twisted the ends, lit the smoke, and lurched out about a mile behind the Mercury.

The Mercury turned left on Ventura and headed north. Jack gunned the Model A until he reached the highway, then crept back several car lengths from the Mercury. The women in the backseat kept their heads on a swivel, as if they were trying to see everything, memorize every row crop and strawberry along the way.

After about fifteen minutes, the Mercury pulled into the Hitching Post, a motor court just north of Oxnard. Jack drove past and circled back into the parking lot of a nearby diner. He parked just in time to see the hospital gowns vanish into a back room. The gee in the seersucker came out in no time flat and hopped back into his Mercury.

Jack had a decision to make: follow the car or bust into the motor court. Shit, Jack was bad at this. He'd been a lousy cop, always quick to turn away from trouble and let the troublemakers go with a warning, always most concerned with watching his ass and getting his twenty bucks a week. He'd never investigated anything. He didn't know which way to turn.

The old man would've known what to do. Jack had been with his father enough times to see the old man bust into places with a shotgun pumped and eyes peeled for an excuse to use it. Or the old man would follow this Mercury to an empty road, pull the driver over, and beat a story out of him.

Jack couldn't see himself doing either. And now the Mercury was taking a left into oblivion. The motor court was the only choice.

Absent a shotgun or his father's suicidal impulses, Jack took a stroll behind the diner. A cook sat atop a garbage can smoking a pre-rolled. Jack nodded to him and approached. "Can I bum one of those?"

The cook tossed the pack to Jack. Jack shook one out, lit it with his own lighter, and handed the pack back to the cook. "Know anything about that little motor court next door?"

"Why do you ask?"

"Just been driving south since San Luis Obispo," Jack said. "Ready to pack it in for the day."

"Where you headed?"

"San Diego."

"Head south to Oxnard Boulevard and take a right," the cook said. "It'll run you through downtown. You'll catch a nice place to stay there. And you can stick with that road down to the coast in the morning."

"Appreciate it," Jack said. He kept walking through

the alley.

With the cook watching, it was too tough to follow the fence behind the motor court. Jack cut across the front of the motor court and kept alongside the road. He didn't even cast a peek at the front office. He went maybe a hundred yards past, then backtracked along a shadow-box fence, stepping carefully over the rugged brush that grew there, keeping his pant legs clear of the thorns on the dried-out bougainvillea. He took a guess on which room the two female patients had entered.

It was tough from the back. The only windows the rooms had on this side were bathroom windows. They were up high. Jack had to stretch just to glimpse over the sill. Inside, he could see a pedestal sink, a claw-foot tub, and a shredded area rug on the floor. He inched to his left in hopes of seeing a sliver of the room through the bathroom door. Just as he got his feet set, he felt a wallop on the back of his head.

Jack turned and raised his right arm to swing at anything behind him. Before he could make out his target, the butt of a gun crashed into his chin and the lights went out.

WILMA, 1943

A MONTH INTO the madhouse and Wilma was settling into a routine. Her job was still in sickbay, but now that she was a veteran, they moved her into rooms that were occupied by patients with tuberculosis. She'd taken to wearing the state-issued dress and hat the hospital provided, saving her own clothes for occasions when spit filled with TB was far less likely to land on her. The hospital also gave her a thin gauze mask to ward away the germs.

Wilma paused, as she did every day, beside the door of one particularly difficult patient named Muriel. Wilma removed her hat and hung it on the end of her mop handle. She paraded the hat in front of the sliver of window at the room's door. There was no glass in the window. Muriel had busted it out years earlier. Every time the hospital replaced the glass, Muriel busted it back out. The hospital had given up replacing it sometime long before Wilma's stay. Now the glassless window was Muriel's only opening to attack the hospital.

When Wilma's hat loped past, Muriel wasted no time throwing a shoe at it. Wilma darted to the other side of the door. She screamed, "Ow. Hey! That hurts."

Muriel cackled inside her room. Wilma trotted the hat and mop handle back in front of the window. Muriel threw another shoe. It echoed against the concrete wall of the hallway. Wilma quickly grabbed both shoes.

Since the nurse didn't want to be bothered with this shoe thrower, she left Wilma to deal with her. Wilma took the key the nurse had given her, unlocked the door, opened it, and flattened herself and her cart against the hallway wall. Muriel raced out of the room as soon as the door was open. Wilma slid inside, dragging the cart behind her. She slammed the door and locked it.

Muriel scurried up and down the hall, looking for the shoes. Wilma started her cleaning. She emptied the bedpan and bucket into a larger bucket she carried on her cart. Muriel returned to the window. "You dirty fucking whore," she screamed. "You're like the blood that drips out of my pussy. You're a yeast infection come to life. Your momma tried to have you aborted. Don't touch my bed."

Wilma pulled the old sheets off Muriel's bed and put fresh linens on. "What else am I, Muriel?" she asked.

"You're the nits monkeys pull off their asses. You're a beard of maggots. You're my next murder victim."

Wilma scrubbed down the concrete walls. They reeked of the paraldehyde that Muriel spit out every time the psych techs tried to force it down her throat. Wilma idly listened to Muriel's threats and obscenities. She was too used to them to find them funny or sad or threatening. She cleaned this room three days a week. Every time, it was the same.

When she finished the walls, Wilma started mopping. As soon as Muriel saw the mop, she spit at Wilma. The TB kept Muriel from being able to spit with any real range or vigor. Wilma mopped everywhere Muriel's lungs couldn't reach. By the time she was finished, Muriel was out of spit. Wilma held onto the back tip of the handle and pushed the mop gingerly into Muriel's range. Muriel kept making the sound of spitting. Nothing came out.

When it was time to polish, Wilma said, "You've said

nothing but nice things about me today, Muriel. I appreciate that."

Muriel stopped spitting and screamed, "You dirty fucking whore. You're the worms crawling out of my ears. You're the corn in my shit."

Wilma polished the floor to the rhythm of this new torrent. When she was finished, she pushed her cart to the edge of the door's radius. This was the toughest part of the room cleaning: getting out of the room and getting Muriel back into it. Wilma had tried a few methods. She'd tried reasoning with Muriel, but that was unreasonable. She'd tried treating Muriel like a child. The problem was, Muriel was crazy, not stupid. The little mental games that work with kids didn't work with her. Once, Wilma had thrown Muriel's shoes at her. Muriel caught them and whipped them back at Wilma. No good. So Wilma went back to her best method. She unlocked the door and threw it open. Muriel raced into the room. Wilma quick dodged her, then kicked Muriel's back leg. She tripped and hit the polished floor with a flop. Wilma grabbed her cart and flew out of the room before Muriel could rise and make another pass.

Once the door was locked, Wilma dropped Muriel's shoes through the glassless window.

She moved on to the next room, the next difficult patient, the next batch of bloody TB spit. The whole routine didn't feel so oppressive on this day, though, because she knew Gertie was coming for a visit at noon.

The café sat on the far north end of hospital grounds, seemingly a world away from the dorms and the baths and the electroshock tables and the iron entry doors and the TB ward and the rooms that required titanic key rings. Only a select few patients—the drunks or junkies or not-so-nutty nutcases who'd proven that they could get with the program—were allowed to see visitors in the café. Since Wilma had been mopping up after Muriel and even worse on the TB floor without making a stink, she made it into the select few. She lined up with the rest of the nurses' pets outside the main hospital, and they set off toward the café.

Wilma hadn't felt sun like this—the kind that lands right on your skin and rubs up against it like a mother's soft hand on an infant's belly—since she'd been committed. From the outside, the hospital did seem like a resort. Lawns rolled out in golf-course green. Red tile roofs and golden hills. Four-story palm trees backed by a blue sky. Had she ever appreciated walking two hundred yards so much in her life?

The patients passed the long laundry building. Steam floated out of the high windows. A patient pushed a cart out of one door, down the lanai, and through another door. Wilma watched her. So that's how it is? The laundry workers get to see these grounds and feel this sun every day. Wilma's mind started spinning, reeling in schemes to get her reassigned to the laundry. She walked slowly, drifting to the back of the line, letting the patients run-walking to the café take the lead. Sure, Wilma wanted to see Gertie, to get as much time as possible with her sister. But something about these four minutes in the sun felt rich, like a moment turning into a memory, like nostalgia for the present.

The café itself looked like a restaurant you'd find in

downtown LA. And not the Bunker Hill part of downtown. The nice part. Over by the Pacific Building, where men in flannel suits spilled out of offices and bought tuna melts cooked to order. A long counter stretched along the far wall. There were workers behind it, actual paid workers, and not just patients, pulling orders from the window and drawing sodas and—could Wilma be seeing this right?—actual beers from taps. Four-top tables with room enough between them for even the fattest of waitresses to waddle between covered the main dining hall. Red vinyl booths lined the walls.

Gertie stood up from a table in the center of the room when she saw Wilma walk in. Wilma waved back. A month at the hospital had taught her to keep her thoughts inside and her emotions off her face. She strolled to the table as if this whole scene were nothing special, just another lunch at Pie Land in Los Feliz. Gertie moved faster. She met Wilma halfway and wrapped her in a hug. "Christ, Sis," she said. A warm tear slid down her cheek and landed on the bare skin of Wilma's neck. Wilma held on as long as she could in front of the prying psych tech eyes.

She let go and wiped Gertie's cheek. "Don't go getting soft on me, kid," she said.

They took a seat. Gertie had already ordered a couple of chicken salad sandwiches. She prattled on about studio gossip while Wilma wolfed down her food. Wilma offered closed-mouthed smiles and head nods for encouragement. She wanted to hold up her end of the conversation, but she couldn't stop eating. She polished off her sandwich and fries and pickle and Gertie's sandwich and pickle. When she finished, Gertie pushed her plate across the table. "Take the fries, too."

Wilma didn't mind if she did.

Gertie asked, "How's my old pal?"

"Lottie?" Wilma asked through a mouthful of fries.

"Of course."

Wilma finished chewing. She looked at the handful of fries on Gertie's plate, resisted the urge to stuff the rest of them in her mouth, and said, "She's okay. She's hanging in there."

"Hanging in?"

"She's not so popular with the other girls, on account of her beau. They put up with her because of me. I won't let anyone say a bad word in my presence. Behind my back, they're picking on her like pigeons on a painted bird."

"What's wrong with her beau?"

"He's a shine. A damn handsome one, too. And talented. You should hear this fellow tickle the ivories. He should be a big star."

"If I know Lottie, he already is. What's his name?"

"Chester Ellis."

Gertie's eyes shot open like she'd been stabbed with a pin. "Chester Ellis? Could it be? What's he look like?"

"I told you, he's handsome."

"Handsome how?"

"Tall and lean. Ropy muscles on his lanky arms. Strong chin."

"Does he have conked hair that's a little bit red?"

Wilma nodded, shoveled in the fries.

"Holy cow! You ain't kidding when you say he can play the piano. He ran the house band over at Al's Continental downtown. Brought the roof down every night."

Wilma took this as her invitation to brag. "I've been playing with him a bit."

"Playing what?" Gertie asked. "You're not double-crossing Lottie, are you?"

"Nothing like that. They have this funny dobro ukulele in the music room. The loudest little thing you ever wanted to hear. I've been strumming rhythm for his melodies. We've arranged a couple of songs. We're playing the bughouse ball at the end of the month."

Gertie smiled. "What I wouldn't give to see you and Chester Ellis playing a set." She gazed off into the distance, as if somewhere outside the big windows of the café lay a picture screen playing a scene of Wilma and Chester doing their best Dixieland routine.

Wilma looked down at her dress, the sharp yellow rayon number Gertie had sent with that first package. It wasn't as nice as Gertie's get-up, but it was the nicest thing Wilma had worn since she got to the hospital. She tossed an idea around her head and let it fly toward Gertie. "You could be in that act," she said.

"What?"

"Sure," Wilma said. "It'll be just like when I used to take math tests for you in school. We'll switch out. You can be me for a while and I'll be you."

Gertie pulled a milkshake close and sucked the thick cream through the straw. She wiped her lips. "What are the doctors telling you, Wilma?"

Wilma shrugged. "I don't have TB. Or syphilis, either."

"Not the medical ones. The shrinks. What does your shrink say?"

Wilma shook her head. "I haven't seen a shrink since

I've been here. Not one. Not once."

"So what kind of cure are they giving you?"

"I like to call it the Unpaid Maid cure," Wilma said. She explained her day-to-day life at the hospital, the dorm she'd been reassigned to with thirty beds, fifteen per side. The smoke breaks in the Section. Storytime in the dorms at night with the girls. A little uke with Chester on weekends. Meals with Lottie. The beans in the cafeteria. The fellows who kept the pretty, flirty ones rolling in cheese and apples and prune sandwiches, though, for some reason, there never seemed to be enough food.

And all the cleaning. The bedpans and piss buckets. Every day, ten hours a day, scrubbing and mopping and polishing. Her life had become mostly just shifts as a maid.

As she said all this, Wilma could see Gertie's ears turn pink, her lips tighten like they'd been cinched by a purse string. To Gertie's credit, she kept her indignation to herself. Wilma launched into her Muriel story. Gertie was graceful enough to act amused.

When the psych tech called time, Gertie hugged Wilma and whispered in her ear, "It's just one more month, Sis."

Wilma felt Gertie's warm breath on her neck and tried not to cry.

Wilma was pulled from mopping at ten the next morning. She wasn't given time to fix her hair or put on makeup or even lip rouge. Even her gauze mask came off on the run. With strands of sweat dripping off her red curls and soaking the underarms of her state-issued dress, she came before a review panel.

She'd heard stories of these review panels from the girls in Unit 6. She'd been told they hate drunks, but Wilma brushed this off as alcoholic melodrama. When she was pushed into the review room, she took the warnings a bit more seriously. Just a bit.

The room was long and wide. A conference table took up the center of the room. Seven members of hospital staff, all men, all wearing suits, sat on one side of the table. Only one chair sat on the other side. Wilma gathered enough to know that was her chair.

She paused for a second to gaze out the three large, arched windows behind the lone chair. The same gentle sun that had caressed her on the way to the café glowed down upon a courtyard. Tall avocado trees mixed in their fair share of shade. A lone bench made of weathered wood and rusted iron nested in the middle, accompanied by a ceramic ashtray striped with light blue tiles. Clusters of flowers lined the four walls of the courtyard. This was a courtyard for the sane, a place for the staff to have a smoke and catch a little fresh air. The thousand crazies Wilma dealt with daily would've trampled it down to dirt in an hour.

Wilma took her seat. She patted her hair enough to know that dreams of being anything close to presentable were hopeless.

The man in the middle of the seven suits asked Wilma, "Do you know why you're here?"

She let the first couple of smart-ass retorts run through her head: *Ah, the eternal question*, and, in the cutest voice possible, *'Cause my mommy fucked my daddy?* She smiled at her ability to resist speaking these responses. The one that came out of her mouth wasn't much better. She said, "Too much drinking and not enough thinking?"

No one laughed. The man in the middle asked, "Are we at an alehouse now, Miss Chesley?"

Wilma glanced at the stone faces to the right of the man and to the left. They looked like busts carved on the side of a city hall somewhere. Wilma changed her tone. "No, sir," she said.

"I'll ask again. Do you know why you're here?"

"I'm an alcoholic, sir."

"And as an alcoholic, do you feel it's prudent to sneak into the café and drink a beer?"

"No, sir."

"Perhaps, then, you'd like to explain why Dr. Harvey saw you doing just that at two o'clock yesterday afternoon."

This blindsided Wilma. All she could come up with was the truth. "Sir," she said, "at two o'clock yesterday I was cleaning the TB ward. Nurse Mendez was overseeing me. Surely, she can confirm this."

The man in the middle leaned forward and caught the attention of the man sitting second from the right. "Dr. Harvey, did you not see this patient in the café yesterday at two o'clock, drinking a beer?"

"I did," Dr. Harvey said.

Seven pairs of eyes glared down at Wilma. She struggled to catch her breath, to make sense of what was happening. "This is ridiculous! I did not drink a beer yesterday or any day since I've been here," she said. Then, a thought struck her. Gertie! Gertie must have stayed back and had a beer after Wilma left. Dr. Harvey must've seen Gertie. Wilma said, "It wouldn't have been me you saw. It would've been my twin sister."

All seven men laughed at this. The man in the middle said, "Your twin sister. Of course. That explains it. You're free to go, Miss Chesley."

It seemed too easy, but Wilma didn't want to push her luck. She stood to leave the review room. The man in the middle barked, "Sit your ass back down. Twin sister! Please, Miss Chesley. Do you think we were born yesterday?"

Wilma dropped into her seat. Her proper posture abandoned her. She slumped back.

The man in the middle flipped through her file. "I see you requested a jury trial. Have you heard back?"

Wilma shook her head.

The man in the middle said, "We have. You've been denied. A jury trial is a statutory right, not a constitutional one. The particular statute you violated does not afford you the right to a jury trial. Do you understand?"

"What statute did I violate?" Wilma asked. Near as she could tell, the only thing she'd done wrong was piss off her father-in-law and live in a state where it's easy to commit a woman to the loony bin. Still, she wanted to see what they saw. She said, "Can I see that?"

The man in the middle snapped the file shut.

"Let me see the denial," Wilma said. "It should be a letter right there in the file. I can read it for myself, right?"

The man in the middle pulled the file closer, well out of reach for Wilma.

"I can also flip to the form that has my next of kin in the file. It'll show that I have a twin sister, won't it?"

"This file is confidential," the man in the middle said.

Wilma could feel a fire building. Her ears burned

pink. Her lips pursed to hold it in. She didn't understand the legal differences, statutory or constitutional or whatever. It didn't matter. The law had nothing to do with this.

The man in the middle said, "Regardless, your actions of yesterday clearly demonstrate that your cure will take longer than the judge initially suspected. Your sentence is hereby extended to one year. We'll see you again in four months."

The seven suits stood to leave the room. Wilma pushed away the shock of it all and started scolding them. "I'll tell you what I understand. I understand that you know good and goddamn well that I have a twin sister, that it was Gertie in the café and not me. You're not as dumb as you look. Not a one of you. You know good and goddamn well I don't belong here. I understand that you fat fuckers are making money off my free labor. You found a maid you don't have to pay and you're keeping me. You're not curing me. You're not helping me. You're helping yourselves."

Six of the men scuttled out of the room. Only Dr. Harvey remained to hear Wilma's tirade.

She kept screaming. "You fuckers took me against my will and are forcing me to work without paying me. You know what we call that behavior in this country, don't you? You know this is fucking slavery, don't you? We fought a whole war against this. Remember it, old man? Remember the Civil fucking War?"

Dr. Harvey didn't respond. He kept staring at her, blank faced. Wilma rose from her chair and pounded the long mahogany conference table. "Is this the freedom my husband died fighting for?"

The door to the review room opened. Two burly psych technicians rushed in, straightjacket in hand. It was all too absurd. Wilma stopped screaming. She closed her eyes and raised her arms in front of her. She knew these camisole fittings hurt a lot less if she didn't resist.

JACK, 1946

JACK WOKE UP on the bed of a motel room. His wrists were bound in leather cuffs with a chain between them; his arms were latched to the headboard above him. He tugged down. There wasn't much room to move. His ankles were in leather cuffs and chained to the footboard. He was completely naked.

He glanced around the room, checked out the louvered closet door, the metal dresser, the nightstands on either side of the bed, the lights seemingly everywhere. He didn't know if it was the knock to his jaw or what, but the room was so bright his head felt ready to split in half. A wave of nausea crashed over him. He took several long, slow breaths until it passed. Vomiting in a situation like this would be deadly.

Nothing happened.

Jack lay on the bed and concentrated on his breathing, the air filling his lungs, his chest rising, the blood rushing from his heart, the gradual exhale. He'd had these experiences in Germany, in the context of a bad situation, on the verge of letting the unknowns overwhelm him, learning to focus on the smallest elements of life to feel the time pass, to give him a chance when the shit storm inevitably struck.

Jack waited and breathed. Time went on without him until the door finally opened. A young woman walked in wearing a maroon satin robe and carrying a large purse. She had the high black bangs and wide-eyed makeup of a pinup girl, but the similarities ended there. She was tiny and dark. Jack couldn't place her: Mexican or high yellow or who knows what. Maybe a refugee from the CBI theater.

She took off her robe, exposing a pair of black garters and garter belts, a black bra, and no panties. Her pubic hair was thick and dark. Jack became suddenly aware of his own lack of clothes. The woman took a riding crop from her large purse. She nodded in the direction of the closet. Jack looked at the closet, too. It was just a closet, near as he could tell. The woman brought the riding crop down on Jack's chest and smacked him twice.

Jack leaned up. "Hey," he said. "Knock that shit off."

The woman sprung onto the bed above Jack, straddled his chest, and punched him in the jaw, right on the spot where the pistol butt had cracked him. He saw stars. Another wave of nausea started to peak. "Okay, okay," he croaked. "Whip me all you want. Just stay away from the jaw."

She stood above him, pulled the riding crop slowly through the open palm of her left hand. Jack focused on breathing, keeping the nausea down. The woman cracked the crop across the soft white skin of his upper arm, just below the bicep. First one arm, then the next. She walked around the bed, sometimes across him, and sought out sensitive spots to attack with her whip.

Jack had been beaten many times in Germany. If he let himself use the proper terms, he'd been tortured. He knew how to survive it, how to take his mind out of his body, find a seat across the room for his spirit to sit and watch what was happening from afar, as if it weren't happening to him. Times like this, the concussions helped.

They kept everything dreamlike.

The woman kept whipping Jack. Red welts rose like rows of strawberry plants across his legs, arms, and chest. It went on for a minute or dozens of them. Jack was too far removed to care. But when the woman knelt beside Jack's legs and took him into her mouth, his spirit was yanked back into his body.

He was going to feel this whether he wanted to or not. He did his best to see the scene from a distance.

Something was going on here, obviously. Something didn't make sense. It could've been a dream. Jack had to acknowledge that. His brain had taken a beating that he maybe hadn't recovered from yet. His thoughts were floating in and out like a dream, sometimes leaving his body, sometimes rooted inside it. The situations around him were too different from ordinary life. He couldn't figure out why this woman was doing what she was doing.

And he felt like there was a third person in the room.

Jack closed his eyes and listened. He couldn't hear any breathing save the mechanical moans of the woman on top of him, any movement besides the creaking bedsprings. The more he focused, the more he could hear some type of whirring. It could've been the knock to his head and the blood pumping through his brain. It could've been a fan or a film camera or anything.

That's when Jack realized: *Oh shit, it is a film camera. There's a cameraman right behind me.* That's who she'd nodded to in the closet right when things got started. That's who she was looking at above his head.

Jack closed his eyes. Just as he'd learned to do in that POW camp, his mind abandoned his body. Let whatever would happen to it happen.

After an impossible amount of time, he opened his eyes again. Both the woman and the cameraman were gone.

He could've made himself believe it was all a dream if not for the welts all over his skin and the discharge stuck to his leg hairs. Jack still had the leather cuffs on his hands, but the woman had unhooked them from the bedpost. He sat on the middle of the bed and pulled his feet up. The ankle cuffs were secured by a simple belt buckle. He freed his legs and swung around to sit on the edge of the bed. He let his hands rest on his lap. The wrists cuffs were secured by a belt buckle, too, but they were chained too closely together for him to unhook it. He thought maybe he could use the edge of a dresser to work the buckles loose. When he stood to try, a wave of nausea flooded him. He vomited on the carpet beside the bed.

Maybe this wasn't the best time to try an escape, he decided. Even if he could get the wrist cuffs off, he didn't have any clothes or car keys or any way to travel the sixty miles home. He lay back down on the bed and waited.

The wait took so long that he dozed a little until he finally went to sleep. He slept for several hours.

He awoke this time to someone slapping his head and stars flashing across his field of vision. Before even opening his eyes, he threw a two-armed punch at whoever was slapping him. He felt the knuckles of both hands slam into a sternum. He opened his eyes to see the thug flailing backwards across the room. He sat up on the bed, fought off the dizziness, and scrambled to his feet. The thug caught his balance first. He threw a pair of plaid, flannel pajama pants at Jack. They landed at Jack's bare feet. "Cover yourself, tough guy," he said. "And follow me."

Jack picked up the pants and stepped into them. The thug opened the door. Night had fallen outside. It looked pitch black against the bright lights of Jack's room. The thug led Jack into the black, across the patches of brown and green grass that passed for a courtyard, and into another motel room. This one had been outfitted as a screening room, with a handful of straight-backed chairs facing a blank white wall. A projector sat on a tiny kitchen table against the opposite wall, just below the window. A woman stood next to the projector. The thug nodded to her. Jack could barely make her out in the darkness. He could tell she wasn't the woman who'd molested him. This one was taller, fuller, whiter, and older. She was also dressed to the nines.

The thug pushed Jack to a straight-backed chair. "Sit there and look forward," he said.

Jack abided.

The woman flicked on the projector. The screen lit up with Jack's afternoon partner walking in the motel room. Her maroon robe came across as dark gray on the film. The camera panned over to Jack, naked and bound on the bed.

Jack said, "Okay, you made your point."

"What point is that?" the woman at the projector asked.

"You got me. You filmed it. My face is clear as day and you own the film. What do you want?"

The woman flipped on a lamp next to the projector.

The image on the wall looked faint. The scene still played itself out in front of Jack. As much as he wanted to turn to look at the woman, he couldn't peel his eyes off this film.

"I want to know who you are."

Jack thought about making up a name, but he knew they had his suit, which meant they had his father's PI license and all his father's business cards. Jack's driver's license would've been in his wallet, also. No point in lying. Jack said, "I'm John Chesley."

The woman walked over to meet Jack. She grabbed a chair, swung it around, and straddled it. She rested her arms on the back of the chair. The film flickered out of focus across her face. Jack studied the face: the hard eyes, the tight lips, the grooves of her forehead meeting above her eyebrows. This was the face of someone in charge. He may not know much about what she was in charge of. He just knew she was boss. She said, "Bullshit."

This confused Jack. "What's bullshit?" he asked.

"You're not John Chesley," she said.

"I'm not?"

"You're not," she said. "I knew John Chesley. Knew him for years."

"Did you, now?"

"Sure," she said. "I knew that old son of a bitch well enough to get a little frog in my throat when I heard about his death, what was it, eight, nine months ago?"

Oh, shit, Jack thought. *She's talking about my father*. He said, "Six months ago. October. Just shy of Halloween."

"And now, what? You're trying to tell me you're him, back from the grave, forty years younger?"

Jack tried a smile. His swollen jaw hurt too much for that. He loosened his face. "I'm his son. John Chesley, Jr."

The woman looked back at the thug. "Hey Dimples, didn't Johnny say that his kid died in the war?"

The thug nodded.

Jack couldn't resist. The name was too perfect. He said, "Is that right, Dimples?"

Dimples launched at Jack, bringing a fist into his head before Jack could dodge one way or another. The message was clear. Only she got to call him that.

The woman grabbed Jack by the cheeks and stared at his face. She turned his head to the right, then to the left. "If you're Junior, how'd you come back from the grave?"

"I never died. I was in a POW camp. The Air Force made a mistake."

The woman kept her fingers on Jack's face. She looked past him to her thug. "Dimples, holler out to Paddy. Have him make some calls. See if Junior is telling us the truth."

Dimples stuck his head out the door and yelled, "Paddy." He stood in the frame, keeping one eye on the courtyard and one on Jack and the woman.

The woman focused back on Jack. "What were you doing looking in the bathroom window of my motor court?"

"I'm a peeping Tom," Jack said.

The woman slapped him. "Bullshit. Try again."

"It's the truth," he said. "If Dimples had come along a minute later, he might've found me in a compromising pose."

She slapped him again. "Dimples didn't knock you out. I'm not some petty crook that has only one muscle man. I got enough men around here to find out what I need to know."

"And what do you need to know?"

"Who you are and what you were doing looking in my bathroom window."

"I'm John Chesley, Jr.," he said. "I'm a peeping Tom."

The woman exploded from her chair and threw Jack backwards in his. He landed head first against the floor of the screening room. His legs were still tangled in his chair. His ears started ringing. The woman stood over him. Something about this latest blow made her look like a pair of tough queens. Everything in the room had a double.

She knelt on his chest and spoke through gritted teeth. "Quit fucking around. If you're carrying John Chesley's license, you're posing as a dick. You're looking into something. That something has something to do with me. That's what we know. You fill in the story from there."

Jack figured that weaving a lie into a mostly true story would help get him out of this. "I really am John Chesley, Jr. When I was in the war and my wife thought I was dead, she went on a bender. She was sent to Camarillo for an alcoholic cure. I went up to the hospital today to see what that was all about. When I was there, I saw a Mercury loading up two broads. I thought to myself, that's peculiar. So I followed him here. I reckoned, if you were doing something with those crazy broads, I might be able to lean into you, make myself a little shut-up coin." Jack lifted his bound hands to point at the faded film wrapping up on the wall in front of him. "Now it looks like I don't have anything on you that you don't have on me."

Paddy showed up at the door. Dimples told him to make some calls, see if John Chesley, Jr., was still alive.

The woman lifted herself off Jack's chest. "Dimples, lift this son of a bitch up."

The thug came across the room and propped Jack back up into his chair.

The woman righted her chair and straddled it again. "There's still one question you haven't answered," she said. "Why are you pretending to be John Chesley?"

"I just told you. I am John Chesley."

She shook her head and let loose a deep breath. "Why are you pretending to be John Chesley, Sr."

"I'm not."

"You had his PI license in your suit."

Jack nodded. "It's not my suit. It's my father's. My suit was dirty, so I borrowed one of his this morning." Jack stared the woman in the eye. "Not like he was going to use it."

The woman stood and walked to the doorway. Dimples followed. She whispered, "What do you think?"

"Hell, he's ugly enough to be Chesley's kid."

The woman shook her head. "Chesley was never ugly." She stepped into the courtyard. Dimples followed. He shut and locked the door behind them. Jack gazed straight ahead and watched the end of his film with the same sense of nausea and shame and arousal he'd had when he made it. When the movie was over, the loose strap of film flapped around the projector reel.

Jack walked over to the camera. He stopped the reels from spinning. He pulled the film out and held it to the projector bulb. The bulb was still hot enough to melt the film. He melted frame after frame until the whole roll caught fire. He tossed it into a steel trashcan, where it smoked and burned.

The door opened again. Dimples and the woman walked into the cloud of film smoke. "Look at this," Dimples said. His grin was wide, his dimples deep. "Boy genius thinks we didn't keep the negatives."

The woman tossed Jack's suit at him. He caught some of it. The rest fluttered onto the floor. "That's your copy you're burning, Johnny," she said.

Jack squatted down to inspect his suit. The jacket and shirt had been cut along the sleeves and down the sides. The pants were cut down the legs. They must have cuffed him first, then undressed him with a knife. Even his belt had been sliced into three pieces. Jack dug through the pockets for his lighter, his tobacco and papers, his wallet, and his keys. They gave his Springfield nine millimeter back to him. Jack checked the clip. It was full. He glanced at Dimples and the broad in charge. If they were brazen enough to hand him back a loaded gun, then he knew someone somewhere was pointing another loaded gun at him. He dropped his effects in his fedora, slid his bare feet into the socks and shoes, and left the rest as a pile of rags. "So you're calling me Johnny now," he said. "You must believe I'm alive."

"We know who you are and where to find you," the woman said.

Dimples walked over and unbuckled Jack's cuffs. Jack knelt to pick up his fedora.

The woman kept talking. "You just stay out of our hair and you'll be all right. But you mention anything about this motor court to anyone, and suddenly copies of your little movie will find their way to your wife, your mother, your boss, everyone. Got it?"

"Got it."

Jack started to walk for the door. Neither Dimples nor the woman stopped him. He stepped into the court-yard and across the weedy lawn. Some of the rooms had lights on behind the curtains. Some glowed in a fainter light. Some leaked grunting and moaning, or whip cracks and commands, or a combination of everything. Jack walked past the front office and into the next-door diner parking lot.

He placed his hat on the fender of the Model A. His keys were at the bottom of his hat. He dug them out and opened the driver's door. Out of the corner of his eye, he saw the cook closing up shop. The cook recognized Jack, made note of the pajama pants and crop welts. "I told you to go downtown for a room," he said.

Jack nodded. "You did at that."

WILMA, 1943

EVERY NUTCASE who wasn't stuck in Hydro or drooling from electroshock or otherwise bedridden and incontinent was primping for the bughouse ball. The girls in Unit 6 fought for space in front of a mirror to build their bangs into structures of architectural interest. Makeup fluttered out of forgotten cases and pasted onto faces. Elbows flew in front of sinks. Those who were pushed aside retreated back against the wall, where they slid into dresses their families had sent from home or the State had issued recently enough to keep them free from madhouse stains. In between, the women weighed their chances. They outnumbered the men at the hospital two- or three-to-one. On top of that, some of the men were there for dancing with other men. One woman pointed out that there were probably an equal number of women patients who'd been committed for dancing with other women. Her wardmates dismissed the optimistic viewpoint. The odds were bad. That couldn't be denied.

Lottie stood behind a drunk so short that the top of her head barely reached Lottie's shoulder. Lottie could see well enough to put on makeup from the second row. By and large, she stayed out of the gossip. One bitter patient said, "Lottie's not worried about the odds. Dinge or not, she has a beau to fill her dance card."

Lottie folded her hair into a bun and didn't offer her antagonist so much as a wince or sidelong glance.

✦ ✦ ✦

Because she was a musician, Wilma had gotten ready much earlier. While the girls in Unit 6 fought for mirror space, Wilma sat outside the hospital dance hall with Chester Ellis and a host of other musicians. Camarillo was, it seemed, overflowing with Hollywood talents whose antics landed them an involuntary stay here. There were enough of them to field a full band for tonight's party and to have replacements for most of the chairs. Wilma and Chester would perform together, but not for the whole night. Loud as Wilma's dobro ukulele was, it couldn't match the volume of horns and drums. And Chester didn't play much background. Not for free. He'd play for this ball, but only front and center. The one exception was a little number Wilma had written for the girls in Unit 6. She charmed Chester with it during one smoke break. He agreed to back her up, and even in that, he insisted Wilma add a break in the song for him to solo. Wilma was more than happy to accommodate.

The musicians had tuned and sound-checked and even run through a few warm-up numbers in preparation. Now, they were ready and there wasn't much to do except pull some wooden chairs onto the lawn of the south quad and watch that lazy orange sun dip down behind the hills westward. There were about a dozen of them sitting in a half circle facing the sunset. For a while, no one talked. A guitarist everyone called Tappy finally broke the silence. "This ocean breeze reminds me of a gig I had in Hawaii back in '27. A two-month stay at the Royal in Honolulu, playing for all the swells. The honcho from Dole had his own table near the bandstand. A couple of the members of the old royal family had tables in back. Celebrities filtered in and out. Old Doug Fairbanks and Mary Pickford came in for a few nights. Even that cute little kid from the Chaplin picture. What was it called?"

"*The Kid?*" a drummer suggested.

Tappy shot a squinty-eyed stare at the drummer. He shook his head. "I guess it was. Anyway, he was a little older, a little less cute when I met him. Hell, though, they all came out for that stay. It was a union job, too. We had money and rooms to share down along Waikiki."

"Sounds like heaven," Wilma said.

Tappy nodded. "It should've been. But I got off that boat from Los Angeles at night. I was already drunk. I caught a trolley to the Royal and kept the drunk going with my guitar and bags at my feet. I could play all right with a head of booze on me, so I only slowed down when I played. If my fingers weren't on the fret board or didn't have a pick in them, they were wrapped around a drink. And not just that first night. The whole damn two-month stand. Drunk the whole time.

"Finally, we get through the contract. The band leader doesn't have to worry about the union covering my back, so he fires me. Tells me to stay off his fucking island. I didn't even know he was unhappy. I played fine the whole time. It wasn't my playing that bothered him, he said. It was my shenanigans. I thought back on it. Which shenanigans would that be? How the hell was I supposed to know? The whole trip was shenanigans. I was barely alive at the end. Too close to dead to wonder what stuck a thorn in his britches, anyway. So I go back to my room, pack my bags, take the trolley to the docks, and that's when I take a look around at the island. I was seeing it for the first and last time. Christ, it was beautiful. More than that. Beautiful doesn't cover it. I'm just not smart enough to find the right word to put on that place. It's as close to God as I've ever been. And I spent the whole time ignoring it, holed up in hotels and bars. Shit."

Well, that story did the trick. It hit every member of the dozen somewhere deep. They traded their own tales of wasted days and lost nights. Wilma, for sure, had hers to add. Chester did, too. All of them sat in the waning daylight trading regret and shame and, well, bragging a little on top of it.

The dance started without a hitch. Since Wilma and Chester played together, they took breaks at the same time. Chester spent his breaks twirling around the dance floor with Lottie. Wilma mostly chatted with the Unit 6 girls. She took a turn or two on the floor with another recovering drunk but, truth be told, after her recent widowhood and that little tryst with Tom Fillmore, she wasn't much in the mood for love. A Camarillo affair just didn't seem to be in the cards for her. She sipped her virgin punch and waited for her turn on the stage.

At about ten o'clock, the guards told the band to start winding down. They'd all promised Wilma the chance to do her number, so they put down their instruments and called her up. She cradled her dobro uke and stepped to the microphone. Chester took the piano behind her. Most of the nutcases were danced out. They gathered around the stage for Wilma's song.

Wilma leaned into the mic and said, "This goes out to the women in my ward. Where are my Unit 6 girls?"

The very ones who'd been fighting in the mirrors four hours ago were loose and sweaty enough to surrender dignified airs and give Wilma a cheer.

Wilma turned to Chester. She counted the time. One. Two. Three. Four. She ran through the chorus chords two times. Chester started the melody. On the third measure, Wilma sang her song.

When I'm at Camarillo
(an original number by Wilma Greene)

Now I'm at Camarillo, I never would've thunk
of such a lovely place, for such a hopeless drunk

Oh it's a place that just suits me
A bughouse case you would be
If you could see what I can see
When I'm at Camarillo

Spending nights with the daft
Sometimes I spank them in the aft
And act as if I were the staff
When I'm at Camarillo

The docs and nurses, they work hard
To get us off the sauce
They shock and drown and beat us
To get their point across

The highballs, they have gone away
No beer or wine for me today
I won't be out there making hay
When I'm at Camarillo

I get free cheese with flirty stares
Steal Section smokes from unawares
Paraldehyde wipes away my cares
When I'm at Camarillo

I dish out floor wax by the crate
Wear lingerie from the State
And eat gooey beans from my plate
When I'm at Camarillo

The docs and nurses, they work hard
To get us off the sauce
They shock and drown and beat us
To get their point across

I shower weekly with the nuts
In the stalls with weird-shaped butts
Sally falls, my favorite klutz
When I'm at Camarillo

At this point, Wilma paused for Chester's piano interlude which, in practice, had run through two measures of the chorus. With a laughing and raucous audience of nuts inspiring him, he kept it running for six full measures. Wilma was all right with that. She danced and strummed rhythm until he had his fill, then brought home the final verses and chorus.

There's a jazz pianist trying to kick
A talkie queen whose head is sick
And all of you taking in my shtick
When I'm at Camarillo

I miss all this spring's afternoons
Stuck in here, singing tunes
And cleaning up after all the loons
When I'm at Camarillo

The docs and nurses, they work hard
To get us off the sauce
They shock and drown and beat us
To get their point across

And here I dance, cheek to cheek
With madhouse cases who really reek
Worse than the breath of a circus geek
When I'm at Camarillo

By the final verse, everyone in the hall—guards, nurses, doctors, psych techs, and patients—were singing "When I'm at Camarillo" with Wilma. She gave Chester one more piano interlude at the end, then they both finished with a flourish. Wilma let that sheepish smile glow on her face. She brought her lips close to the microphone, just shy of kissing it, and said, "Thank you. Goodnight."

Two days later, the lyrics to Wilma's song made it into nearly every satchel and wallet in the asylum. Patients sang it when they mopped or cooked breakfast. Nurses hummed it through the rounds. Wilma became a madhouse celebrity. Her cafeteria time was filled with notes and apples from admirers, male and female alike. Wilma let the good feelings glow down on her, but she also knew that they didn't mean much. She still had to clean

Muriel's room and the rest of the TB ward. She still couldn't swing a transfer to the laundry. She still had ten and a half months of her yearlong sentence to go.

At least, that was the case until one of the guards pulled her aside on the way to supper. His last name was Giroux. If he had a first name, Wilma had never heard anyone use it. Giroux was tall and lanky. He wore a pencil-thin mustache and enough pomade in his hair to choke out the perpetual aroma of paraldehyde. He was Canadian and had come to Camarillo by way of London and the Royal Air Force. He did almost no work at the hospital. If a ruckus erupted, you could find it by going to the space Giroux had just vacated. If you wanted to escape, you did it through Giroux. At least that's what the bughouse gossip said.

Giroux placed a gentle hand on Wilma's elbow just outside the dining hall and steered her along a sidewalk that was supposed to be out-of-bounds for patients. Wilma hesitated. Giroux said, "Don't worry. You can't get in trouble when you're with me."

Wilma followed him down the path strewn with morning glories.

Giroux kept his hand on her elbow. He said, "Your song has become quite the hit."

Wilma smiled. "Folks seem to like it."

Giroux gazed forward as if, somewhere up ahead on the path lay his thoughts. He walked into them. "The tune was familiar. Was it George Formby?"

"On the nose," Wilma said. "I just changed the words to 'When I'm Cleaning Windows.'"

Giroux snapped the fingers on his left hand. "I knew it. Not many folks know Formby on this side of the

Atlantic. How do you?"

"My sister works in pictures. A British cameraman gave her the 78 as a gift."

"Do you know any more of his ditties?"

"All the good ones." Wilma listed the songs on the 78. Giroux nodded along. "What else can you play?"

"You name it. Benny Bell. Tin Pan Alley numbers. Dixieland. Everything. What do you want to hear?"

Wilma and Giroux reached the end of the dining hall. The sidewalk turned to the right and followed along the southern wards. Patients could look out the windows at these grounds, but never walk them. Giroux turned right. Wilma walked along under his protection.

He paused again, walking toward his next thoughts. Wilma waited. He asked, "Have you played much for audiences?"

"Some," Wilma said. "Not much."

"I have to ask you something." Giroux's voice grew small, tender. "Have you ever, or, let me rephrase, would you ever. No. One more try. Could you possibly be coaxed into playing numbers at affairs that reflect, let's say, less than traditional values?"

Wilma had seen enough men beating around enough bushes to guess what idea he was trying to scare up. "Are you asking me to play a burlesque show?"

"Now we seem to be close to an understanding."

"We also have a problem, that being the fact I'm a patient here until the spring of 1944. There are no burlesque theaters in the bughouse."

Giroux nodded. He adjusted his hold on Wilma's arm so that he seemed to be cupping her elbow. "Arrangements can be made. Your sentence can be commuted."

Wilma didn't want subtleties. She asked, "You can get me out of here?"

"It depends. How do you feel about nudity?"

"Why, Officer Giroux, I'm nude under this state-issued dress." Wilma tried to catch his eyes and bat her lashes. Giroux continued to face forward.

"How do you feel about performing your ukulele in the nude? For a small, select audience."

Wilma stopped walking. Giroux turned to face her. Wilma ran a fingernail along his jawline. "Honey, you get me out of here legally, a select audience can watch me sing and dance my bare ass all the way back to Highland Park."

Giroux looked down at Wilma's feet. A wolfish smile crept across his face. He let go of Wilma's elbow and offered his hand to shake. Wilma, not exactly sure what she was agreeing to, shook. They started back down the path toward the dining hall.

"Of course, you'll keep all this under your hat, both before and after I make arrangements."

"Of course," Wilma said.

Good to his word, he secured her release one week later.

JACK, 1946

JACK GREETED the sunrise the next morning from the porch of his parents' house. He had a cup of coffee and a copy of his wife's book. The book rested on his lap. Jack rubbed his thumb over the smooth front cover. He did this unconsciously, as if the book were a kitten. Now and then, he'd lift his mug of coffee to his lips.

The neighborhood gradually woke up around him. Lights came on in bedroom windows, then in kitchen windows. Soft rumblings grew slightly louder at a sloth's pace. Men emerged from doorways with hats on heads and briefcases in hands. On one or two porches, an aproned wife kissed her husband goodbye. Cars floated down Avenue 52 and merged into the bigger streams of York and Figueroa. The city got down to the business of staying a city.

Through it all, Jack refilled his mug a time or two and caressed his wife's book without looking at a word inside it. When the clock struck eight, Jack went back inside, ran a comb through his hair, dressed in his last remaining suit, and strolled a half dozen blocks down York to the police station there.

Word must have gotten around that Jack was once again among the living because no one treated him like a ghost when he walked in. Old coworkers rose from their desks, shook his hand, patted his back, asked questions that they didn't want answered about the war, and tried to convince him to come back to the force. A few made jokes about the egg the Oxnard thug had planted on his jaw the day before. Jack smiled and goofed through it for as long as he had to, then he excused himself to head downstairs to see Stacchi in Records.

Stacchi worked alone in the basement of the station, filing away old or cold cases, answering the phone, mostly loafing. He'd been a patrolman like Jack until he was caught taking one too many bribes. The higher-ups liked Stacchi, so instead of firing him, they stuck him where he wouldn't have much to sell.

Jack found him with his nose in a filing cabinet. A cigarette was burning on his desk. The ash was less than a quarter inch long. A desk drawer hung slightly open. The chair was spun away from both the aisle where Stacchi stood and the desk itself. Jack pointed out this evidence and the story it told. He said, "You heard my footsteps and quick made like you were working, huh?"

Stacchi smiled. "What happened, Jack? They made you detective?"

Jack stepped forward for the handshake and pleasantries. Afterward, Stacchi invited Jack to take a seat on the other side of the desk. "What really brings you here?" he asked.

Jack pulled out his wallet and set a twenty on the blotter. "I'm wondering if you can get some information for me."

Stacchi looked at the bill. He nodded.

Jack said, "I'd like to know the names and current addresses of women who were sent to Camarillo for the alcoholic cure between February and May of 1943."

"And that's worth only twenty bucks to you?"

Jack knew Stacchi was a master of the bribe. There

wasn't a whole lot of money to play with, especially since Jack didn't have a job and would have to buy a new suit before too long. Twenty seemed generous to him. It was a lot of goddamn money. He said, "When I started out before the war, twenty was just about a week's pay. It's nothing to sneeze at."

"I'm not sneezing," Stacchi smiled. He'd lost a few teeth since Jack had worked with him. The front four were still hanging in there, but his fangs were gone. "I just want to know what you're looking into loony girls for."

Jack weighed the truth and found it a little heavy. In all likelihood, these records would be downtown at headquarters, not at the York station. Stacchi wouldn't see them, wouldn't see Wilma's name on the list. He'd just be the go-between. Jack said, "Wandering daughter job."

"What? You take over the old man's business?"

Jack shrugged. "Not really. Just this one case. The girl's parents were close with the old man. They came crying. I got soft."

"You always were soft," Stacchi said. He pulled the telephone close and dialed direct to the central station. He chatted briefly with his buddy, then asked for the list. "I'm sending a plainclothes guy to pick them up. Name's Jack Chesley. You'll know him by his cheap corduroy jacket." Stacchi paused, laughed. "Will noon work?"

Apparently, noon was soon enough. Stacchi hung up the phone and made the twenty disappear. "You got that, kid?"

"Noon at Records downtown," Jack said. "I got it."

Stacchi shook Jack's hand. "Don't be a stranger," he said.

✦ ✦ ✦

A few hours later, Jack picked up the information from records, easy as pie. They were handwritten on three sheets of white paper. No envelope. Jack glanced through them only long enough to find Wilma's name. It was there, right next to the word "deceased." Jack folded the papers in half and in half again. He stuck them in the inside pocket of his corduroy jacket, thanked the clerk, and headed out.

Jack heard his name when he hit the street in front of the central station. He turned to find his old partner Hammond trotting down the steps. In his police blues, with his hat covering the balding grays, he looked years younger than he had in Cole's a couple of days ago.

Jack waited for him to approach. "What's with the buzzer?" he asked. "I thought you said you retired."

"Retired?" Hammond sent a friendly punch into Jack's forearm, harder than it needed to be but not hard enough to raise Jack's hackles. "I'll never retire."

Jack held Hammond's glance for a second. He knew the guy. Hammond wasn't lying now, which meant he was lying at Cole's.

Hammond offered a third interpretation. He said, "You must be losing it, kid."

Jack shook his head like a dog trying to dry himself. "A couple years in a prison camp will do that, I guess."

Hammond started down the steps. "Come on," he said. "Let's go into Little Tokyo and jaw."

Jack followed.

They walked down First Street, past the city buildings and into the Japanese section of town. Jack had known this neighborhood well when he was stationed around here. It was a place to take a break, to hide out from all the madness up around Bunker Hill, maybe get a bite to eat if you trusted the waitress to bring you something good even though you couldn't read the menu and she couldn't speak English. He liked the idea of that kind of meal today: the soups with thick noodles and soft meat, something easy on his aching jaw.

A block into Little Tokyo, Hammond pointed out what Jack had already noticed. "Not many Japs around here. You see that?"

"I do." Jack nodded. "What happened to them?"

"What do you mean, what happened? We shipped them out."

"What? Where?" Jack hadn't exactly had the opportunity to read a newspaper for most of the past four years. Any news the Air Force or prison guards didn't see fit to give him, he didn't get. He'd heard plenty about the Japanese, but not about the Japanese in America.

Hammond filled him in on the internment camps and the changing shape of Little Tokyo. He waved a hand in front of him. "As you can see, it's mostly dark meat now."

A passerby stepped to the side to avoid Hammond's hand. He shot a sideways glance at Jack and Hammond. Jack greeted him with a head nod and kept walking.

Hammond led Jack into a dive with all the food laid out cafeteria style. Jack picked what was soft: stewed greens, blackeyed peas, cornbread. Hammond piled a plate full of boiled meat. They carried their trays to a cashier. Hammond nodded toward Jack. "He's with me."

The cashier waved them both through. They sat at a small table.

Through a mouthful of meat, Hammond said, "You

ain't playing it smart, are you, kid?"

"What do you mean?"

"I hear you've been going up and down Wilma's old street, asking questions."

"I did," Jack said. "What of it?"

"That's not backing off, is it?"

"No," Jack said. "But it was before you told me to."

Hammond stuffed some more meat into his face. He chewed it enough to allow himself to talk, but not enough to allow him to swallow. "What are you telling me? Make it clear."

Jack set his fork down. He crumbled some cornbread into his beans, where it gradually sunk into the juice and ham fat. "I went down to Newland Street and asked some questions. No one told me anything except that my wife was a whore. I started to think that she really did just get drunk and fall in a tub. Then I went to see you, and you told me to back off. I took that to mean that Wilma was into some kind of business I don't want to know about, so I stopped asking around. Clear enough?"

"Sure," Hammond said. He took another bite and chewed longer this time. "One more question. What did you do yesterday?"

"Got the old man's flivver running again."

"Did you?"

"I did. It's parked back at the clubhouse. I'll show you after lunch."

"And what happened? A wild wrench flew up and gave you that knot on the chin?"

Jack lifted his beans close enough to sniff. They seemed safe. Salty, but safe. He dumped a heavy spoonful into his mouth and used the chewing time to think.

His jaw didn't like all this teeth grinding business. Jack kept at it until he could fashion a response. "I'm not too smart about any of this, Hammond. Suppose you tell me what you think it is that I need to be protected from. You think I'm going to find out my wife started sleeping all around town once she thought I was dead? I already know that. You think I'm going to find out about her time in the bughouse? Hell, she wrote a book about it. So what could she have been doing that you don't want me to find out?"

Hammond raised his knife. He hadn't used it on his meat, yet. He hadn't needed to. The beef had been boiled down into soft strands. He pointed the knife at Jack. "You're stupid, kid, but you're not that stupid."

Jack figured he'd lay a face card down, just to see how Hammond would play the hand. "Wilma was murdered, wasn't she?"

"Of course, Jackie. We all know that."

It seemed time to call Hammond, so Jack tossed his hand onto the table. "And you know who murdered her?"

Hammond put the knife down. He shook his head. "I don't know. I have ideas, but I don't know."

"Why don't you tell me your ideas, then?"

Hammond dropped his eyebrows and stared at Jack. He held the eye contact far beyond the point of comfortable. Jack didn't look away. If they were playing a game, Jack wasn't going to give in easily.

After nearly a minute, Hammond looked down at what remained of his plate of boiled meat. He shoveled the last of it into his gullet. "If you get too close to this, there'll be another murder that I don't want to know about."

Jack chewed on this for a second. "You think I'm going to kill whoever killed Wilma?"

Hammond pushed himself back from the table and stood to leave. "No." He plopped his hat back on his head. "That's not at all what I'm worried about."

WILMA, 1943

IT WAS NO burlesque theater: no stage, no costumes, no comedians, no dances, no dressing room, no props. Giroux brought Wilma to a ground-floor suite decorated to look like the penthouse on a B movie back lot. The room was long and thin like a dining hall. A beat-up baby grand sat in the corner, wood warped and legs wobbly. You didn't need to plunk the keys to know it was out of tune. A hallway beside the baby grand led to a bedroom and bathroom. On the other side of the room, eight men were gathered around an octagonal poker table. Just beyond them stood the bar. A bartender with thick, hairy forearms shook a batch of martinis. Cheap chintz loveseats and armchairs swallowed most of the room. The men in attendance had gathered the furniture in front of a portable movie screen. Nothing showed on the screen. Most of the men had vacated the seats and were drifting toward the bar.

Giroux had somewhat prepared Wilma for this scene. He'd rescued her dobro ukulele from the bughouse. He'd given her a dark indigo dress—formfitting, but absolutely the wrong color for her pale, freckled skin. "Don't worry so much about the dress," he'd told her on the drive north from Camarillo. "You'll take it off after three songs." And he'd explained the deal: she'd sing and play, stripping a little between each tune. By the sixth song, she should be topless. By the seventh, bottomless. She'd only do an eighth if they called for an encore. Afterwards, she'd stay and entertain the gentlemen. When Wilma asked, "Entertain? Like how?" Giroux waved it off with his slender fingers.

He hadn't prepared Wilma for the oily feeling in the room, like a crop duster had just coated it in DDT. These men had something about them, some weird cocktail of anger and lust and desperation. They didn't do or say anything specific. Wilma just felt it. It's okay, she told herself. You're just out of the bughouse. Everything will feel weird for a day or two.

Giroux led her to the area between the portable movie screen and the horseshoe of furniture. A chubby fellow came over to meet them. His red suit had wide shoulders and pegged pants, something like a zoot, only tailored with wartime wool rations in mind. He looked at Wilma and asked Giroux, "This her?"

Giroux nodded.

The chubby fellow called out, "Gentlemen, gentlemen, your attention please. We have a very special treat for you, flown all the way from the British Isles—and boy are her arms tired—this little butterfly of a beauty, this dazzling dame, this wild Irish rose...."

One of the men at the poker tables hollered, "Make up your mind, Pozzo. Is she English or Irish?"

The men wandered over from the bar, fresh martinis in hand. Wilma watched them as they watched Pozzo. The other thing Giroux hadn't prepared her for was the makeup of the party. These fellows weren't your everyday stags. They were Hollywood folk. Some of them Republic contract players. Wilma recognized a few actors who'd taken front stage on films she'd been in the background of.

Pozzo carried on. "This lovely limey lass, this magnificent mick maiden is here to woo you with her voodoo. Gather round, don't be shy, put your pud in your hand and your mud in your eye and get ready for the mind-blowing, fine-glowing, time-slowing lady of the hour. The one. The only. The world's greatest ukuleleist. The irrefutable. The inscrutable. The unshootable. Gee Gee Gillicuddy and her magical ukulele!"

Pozzo windmilled his arms and pointed to Wilma. One or two men set down a martini glass and clapped. Wilma figured that was enough of a round of applause to warrant her, "Thanks, fellas." She kicked into a version of Benny Bell's "Everybody Loves My Fanny."

The eyes of the audience bore into her. If they had any appreciation for Wilma's ability to run through the finger-tangling e-flat key, nothing in their faces betrayed it. If the song's double-entendres tickled them anywhere inside, they kept that feeling from slipping outside. Before the last verse, she gave her pipes a rest and treated the men to a Formby-style split stroke. It was met with yawns and one rake calling, "Take it off, already!"

Well, Wilma reckoned, these folks know entertainment. If they felt this act needed to kick up its tempo, she'd oblige. She skipped the last verse of the song, stopped strumming when she hit the home chord, and segued into her best Gypsy Rose Lee impersonation. She didn't have the poetry or grace of Gypsy. It was Wilma's first strip show. What did she know? She said, "I see all you fellas with your little ukuleles in your hands. The friction is making the room warm. I hope you don't mind if I make myself more comfortable." She rolled the skirt of her dress up her leg.

Pozzo raced over to the baby grand and pounded through an out-of-tune Tin Pan Alley number. Wilma unhooked her garters in time with the song. She gradually slid off one stocking and tossed it to a yawning character actor—a pock-faced gink who typically played the rat in gangster pictures. He sniffed it and tossed it over his shoulder. Wilma repeated the scene with the other stocking, tossing this one into the pot of the poker game. She picked up her ukulele, said, "Cut it, Pozzo," and launched into "O'Brien Is Trying to Learn to Talk Hawaiian." It was the longest song she knew. She'd play the shorter numbers when she had less clothing on.

As promised, Wilma accompanied her set with a gradually diminishing outfit. The men took a bit more interest when she was completely bare. Their leering eyes made her understand for the first time that she wasn't nude—she was naked. A room full of horny men stood between her and the door. Giroux stood to the corner, holding her dress. She had little confidence in his willingness to return it to her. Wrong color for her skin or not, she wanted that awkward indigo rag back in her possession.

The men did call for an encore. With her final number, she played, "Ain't She Sweet." The story behind the song, Wilma knew, was that the songwriter wrote it for his daughter. It was supposed to be innocent, paternal, lovely. She played it as such. She smiled through it like a little girl and danced along as a kid might.

The men didn't seem to get the hint. Their stares grew in intensity.

Wilma finished the song, bowed to a smattering of applause, and turned directly to Giroux. Giroux handed her a martini instead of her clothes. "Drink this," he said.

What the hell? Two months at the nuthouse and thirty minutes of a stag party left her with a thirst like she'd
never known. She tossed the drink down her throat so
fast she couldn't taste the gin. That warm feeling settled
into her empty stomach. That old gin flame set fire to her
throat.

"Can I have my clothes now?" she asked Giroux.

Giroux hugged the dress like a child with a teddy
bear. "You're a wonderful musician," he said.

"Thank you." Wilma reached for the dress. Giroux
stepped back. The combination threw her off balance. She
caught herself on Giroux's shoulder before she fell. "Wow,"
she said. "I used to be able to handle this stuff better."

"You're a natural at the striptease," Giroux said.

Wilma nodded. Something about Giroux seemed off.
He was doing a trick with his face, making it drift in and
out of focus. He kept talking, and in English, too, but
Wilma could only catch every third word. She squinted
her eyes to concentrate. Her ukulele slipped out of her
hand and landed on the hardwood floor with a clunk.
"Say," she said. "What's going on here?"

"You should pick up your ukulele," Giroux said.

Wilma wasn't falling for it. Something was beyond
her comprehension. She didn't need to figure it out. She
just needed to get out of the room. Giroux could keep the
dress. It didn't matter. She needed air. A little air would
prop her back up. She stumbled as well as she could toward the door, reaching for the backs of loveseats and
chairs for support, sometimes falling into the arms of
men who steered her in the wrong direction. I have to
get outside, she told herself. If I can make it outside, I'll
be all right. She focused on the door. It was right there.

Seven, eight steps away. She could make it. She counted the steps. One. Two. The door swelled and shrunk. She kept walking. Three. Four. The director screamed cut. The film faded out. Wilma flopped.

✦ ✦ ✦

She woke in the back room who knows how many hours later. Whatever they'd slipped into the drink, it was too much. Near enough to kill her. Even so, she didn't feel exactly lucky to be alive.

She was still naked. She lay on top of the sheets. The night had grown cold. She wanted to crawl under a blanket but wasn't sure she could move. Whatever had happened while she was passed out, it left her feeling like she'd been thrown from a train. A little warmth came from the man passed out next to her. In the faint light of the room, she recognized him. He'd been a Hollywood heartthrob back when lollipops were still innocent to her. He, too, lay atop the sheets. He still wore his slacks and dress shirt. His tie had been loosened. His shriveled member hung from the zipper hole of his pants.

Surely, he'd done something to her when she was passed out. Of all the sore parts screaming for attention in her brain, none were more sore than the parts between her legs. She felt raw and sticky and didn't want to try to figure out what had happened.

And of all the thoughts racing through her head, one took center stage: *Get out!*

Wilma collected whatever strength was left in her leaden muscles. She pulled herself to her feet, felt around the floor for the heartthrob's sportcoat, and put it on. Luckily, he'd worn a high-buttoned number. It was enough to keep her breasts inside and to cover her ass. This coat would do if she couldn't find more clothes on the way out.

No sounds but snores drifted through the place. The poker and stag flicks and martinis and rape had all finished for the night. Wilma tiptoed into the main room. Men slept on floors and loveseats and armchairs. She stepped carefully over and between them. She cut a path as direct to the door as she could. No one stirred.

Quiet as a mouse, Wilma opened the door and stepped into the grass courtyard. A full moon cast a bit of light down on her. The rest of the motor court seemed to be asleep. Wilma had no way of knowing what time it was. Judging from the slight glow far to the east, she pegged it as closer to early morning than late night.

Her bare feet crunched across the dry grass of the courtyard. Cool, damp air coated her bare legs. She could smell the ocean somewhere not too far away.

She walked past the office to the motor court. No one stirred inside. She kept going, out to the sidewalk, checking the road north and south, weighing her options. Hitchhiking seemed a bad idea. She didn't want to climb into a stranger's car smelling of sex and wearing nothing but a sportcoat. A faint light glowed from the kitchen of a nearby diner. She decided to take her chances there.

She banged on the back door for nearly a minute before the cook finally opened. He was a tall man with thin shoulders and beefy forearms. His skinny legs held up a prodigious belly. He looked at Wilma through dark, deep-set eyes. "Oh, Jesus," he said. He scratched the thick black stubble on his face and took a step back. "Come in."

The cook walked away from Wilma. He rooted

through the metal shelves filled with sacks of potatoes and cans of lard until he found a small pair of checked cook's pants. He tossed them to Wilma. "You can wear these," he said. "I have some T-shirts in the cabinet over the sink. Take one. Phone's next to the cash register out front. Reverse the charges."

Wilma stepped into to the pants. "Thank you," she said. He waved a hand in the air and set to cutting up vegetables and storing them in metal containers.

Wilma found a shirt, turned her back to the cook—who wasn't looking anyway—pulled it on, and put the coat on over it. She looked ridiculous, sure, but she was fully clothed again.

As instructed, Wilma called collect. Gertie picked up on the ninth ring. She accepted the charges and got right down to business. For what this call would cost by the minute, Wilma couldn't blame her sister for being brusque. "Where are you?" Gertie asked.

"I'm at a diner on Ventura Boulevard. Somewhere north of Camarillo, next door to a clip joint called the Hitching Post."

The cook called out from the kitchen, "It's the Golden Egg. North end of Oxnard."

Wilma told Gertie the same thing.

Gertie said, "Did you bust out of the nuthouse?"

Wilma wasn't ready to explain anything. The last thing she wanted to do was break down crying in this greasy spoon. "Don't ask."

Thankfully, Gertie didn't. She said, "Give me a couple hours. It may take a bit to find a car."

"The Golden Egg on Ventura Boulevard," Wilma repeated. "North end of Oxnard."

The cook invited Wilma to help herself to coffee. She poured a mug and sat at the far end of the counter. The cook didn't seem to be in a talking mood. Wilma appreciated that. He worked through his setup. She sipped coffee. The day gradually broke around them. The two opening waitresses came in, chatting with each other, ignoring Wilma, getting dressed in their uniforms, wiping down the tables, and laying out silverware. A cashier came next. She opened the safe in back and set up the register. A bus boy was next. He put ice under the cook's vegetable bins and moved the evening's dishes from the drying rack to above the cook's line. Wilma haunted the far end of the counter. The staff treated her like a ghost.

At some point, just before the first customers came in, the cook pushed a plate in front of Wilma: two eggs up, two slices of bacon, and two pieces of sourdough toast. He said, "Eat something."

If pressed, Wilma would've said she had no appetite. But after two months of barely enough food at the mental hospital and no dinner the night before, she was hungry. She put the eggs and bacon between the pieces of toast and ate it like a sandwich. A waitress silently refilled her mug while Wilma chewed. She nodded her thanks.

When she was finished, Wilma felt around her clothes out of habit, checking to see if she had any money. She felt a lump on the inside pocket of the sportcoat. She'd accidentally stolen the heartthrob's wallet. It was full of cash, too. Three or four large, easy. She peeled out a twenty to stick under her mug just before she left. That ought to cover the food and clothes and hospitality.

✦ ✦ ✦

The diner was nearly full and bustling by the time Gertie arrived. Seeing her sister walk through those diner doors so much like a better version of herself, Wilma started to well up behind the eyes. It was all she could do to stuff the twenty under the coffee mug and cross the restaurant to meet Gertie.

The floodgates opened as soon as Wilma was safe inside the old, battered Packard that Gertie had borrowed. She cried all the way back to Highland Park. A time or two, Gertie rested a hand on her leg or rubbed her shoulder. Mostly, she left Wilma to work through her pain.

Gertie took care of things back at the bungalow. She explained something satisfactory to the Van Meters. It was enough to get them to open the door to the bungalow. Gertie opened the windows and let the stale air drift out. She ran a bath and helped Wilma into it. She started cleaning up around the place when Wilma finally came to her senses and said, "Please, God, Gertie. Quit fussing around here and go to work. I want to be alone."

Gertie fought. Wilma insisted. Finally, Gertie left.

Wilma spent the next hour scrubbing her skin until it felt like a complete layer had been removed.

JACK, 1946

MAYBE HAMMOND'S warnings were hanging too heavy in Jack's head when he got home. Maybe they were just right. Jack noticed something was off. A few clumps of mud lingered on the porch steps he'd swept that morning. They could've come from a mailman or salesman or anyone. They didn't lead to the front door, though. They drifted left and faded away by the dining room window. Jack didn't approach the window. If someone had gone in that way, they might be sitting right by it, looking out at him.

Jack reached inside his coat, unlatched the shoulder holster, and slid out his Springfield 1911: the same type of pistol that kept him alive in Germany during those months between bailing out of his plane and winding up in a prison camp. With the little automatic in his right hand and the house key in his left, he tried the lock. Still locked. He turned the key and the knob, pushed the door open, and sprung himself to the side of the doorway. He crouched low on the porch, shoulder tight to the siding of his house. A gunshot rang out into the Highland Park afternoon. A bullet whizzed out of Jack's open doorway.

He leaped from his crouch, over the porch rail, and hit the grass beyond the thorny hedges. He stayed low. With his belly flat against his front steps, both hands on the Springfield, and his head peeking just above the porch floor, he stared into his open doorway. A faint light came in through the window in the kitchen door, way in the back of the house. It wasn't enough to light up the dark hallway. Jack checked the archway leading into the dining room. No one seemed to be casting a shadow from that side. Other than that, Jack just saw his parents' house: the bare walls and old furniture and fraying area rugs, the crown molding on the edge of the ceiling leading down into wavy plaster. Nothing overturned. Nothing out of place.

Jack listened. A faint clicking emerged from the living room: hard shoes on pine floorboards. The shooter approached the back of the open door. Jack could see the shooter's eye through the door crack, just below a hinge. Without enough time to really aim, he pointed his Springfield at the eye and shot. Blood splattered through the crack between the door and the frame. Jack leapt to his feet and ran into the house. He found a body flopped in the foyer. It was missing an eye and part of the back of its head, but still twitching and gurgling, coughing blood and trying to claw its way back up. Jack stuck the Springfield into the gaping mouth, angled the barrel into the palate, and shot again. That put a quick end to this guy.

Jack didn't take it for granted that the shooter was alone. He ran throughout the house, kicking doors, knocking over chairs and couches, checking under beds and inside closets. When no one else turned up, he checked the yard, behind trees, in the tool shed, under the house, everywhere. If the shooter hadn't been alone, he was now.

Jack walked across his front yard. He checked his neighbors' houses. No one seemed to be peeking through cracks in drapes or dips in Venetian blinds. He seemed to have Meridian Street to himself.

Three gunshots will do that to a neighborhood.

Back inside, Jack checked out the shooter. Even with the bullet holes and mush, enough of his face remained for Jack to know he didn't know the guy. Nothing was familiar about him. He was short. Even sprawled out like that on the floor, the shooter couldn't have been five and a half feet long. He wore a sharp green worsted wool suit, double-breasted with baggy, pleated pants. Nice as it was, it played second fiddle to the shooter's silk, pinstriped shirt and wide silk tie. This was a getup to be buried in. If not for the small size and the blood soaking into the back of it, Jack may have considered stealing it. He didn't want to live his life in corduroy.

Jack set his little automatic down on the floor. He dug through the shooter's pockets. A claim ticket to Clark's Camera Shop on Fountain. A fresh pack of Chesterfields. A box of kitchen matches. Two quarters and four dimes. A Cadillac key. A pocket watch. Jack dragged a match across the hardwood floor and used it to light a Chesterfield. Even with the knowledge that he was smoking a dead man's cigarette—and not just a dead man, but a dead man whom he killed, who tried to kill him—the ritual calmed him. He dove into the moment of taking that long inhale, swishing the smoke through his lungs, and letting it creep back out. The pause gave him enough sense to pocket the claim ticket and put everything else back.

Last, Jack reached under the corpse and dug a wallet out from its right hip pocket. He found seventy-four dollars and a driver's license that said the guy's name was Herbert Parker. The name didn't ring a bell.

He righted an armchair next to the telephone. He sat down and asked the operator to connect him with the Hitching Post. When someone at the front desk answered, Jack said, "This is John Chesley, Jr. I want to talk to the broad in charge."

The guy at the desk told him to hang on. A little rumbling came through the line, something like a drawer opening, a receiver being set inside, and a drawer closing. After that, there were no sounds. Jack had enough time to smoke his Chesterfield and drum a Dixieland song on the end table and take off his hat and jacket and comb his hair. Finally, the gravelly voice of a tough older woman came on. "What's shaking, Johnny Boy?" she said. "Are you looking to buy a film from me?"

"Nothing of the sort," Jack said.

"Good thing. That's a popular little scene already. A stag party here last night watched it three times."

This struck Jack as a lie. He'd left that clip joint too late in the evening for a stag party to come in and watch movies. At that hour, stags stop watching movies and either get a girl or go home. Even so, Jack felt his face heat a little at the suggestion. He tried to stay focused. He said, "I have a package for you, if you want it. It's called Herbert Parker."

"What's a Herbert Parker? How big is his package?"

If the lightness of her tone was a put-on, this old broad was a hell of an actress. Jack cast the darkness. "Herbert Parker is a corpse right now. I think you sent him to make me one."

"Make you one what?"

"A corpse."

"Wait a minute," the woman said. "Let me see if I'm getting this straight. Someone named Herbert Parker tried to kill you?"

"That's right."

"And you killed him first?"

"Right."

"And you think I sent this guy to kill you?"

"That's exactly what I think."

"Oh, sweetie. You are the worst detective I've ever known." She let slide a little laugh. "First off, if I wanted you dead, I wouldn't have gone to all the trouble of getting that blackmail material on you. I would've just killed you last night when you were up here. Second off, if I sent someone to kill you and you killed him first, and then you called me to brag about it, I'd know right away to send a few more someones to get the job done right." She paused. Jack could hear her take a long steady inhale followed by a beat and a long steady exhale: the familiar sound of a smoker taking a drag. "Does that make sense to you?"

Jack didn't respond. His breath got short, like someone had pinched his nose and stuffed a wet rag in his mouth. He covered the mouthpiece and gasped for air. He felt himself grow dizzy, lightheaded.

While this happened, the broad in charge's voice came through the earpiece like she were planets removed from Jack. She said, "Take it from me, sweetie. You need to find another line of work."

Jack hung up the phone. He stayed in the chair, shaking and sweating and gasping for breath. The black-eyed peas and corn bread and greens wrestled with each other in his stomach until they all came racing out and splattered into a pile on Jack's mother's old area rug.

When it was all out, Jack took the chairs and end table off the rug. He rolled it up and carried it to the backyard. A scrub jay perched in the avocado tree sang a song to the afternoon. A passenger jet flew across the blue sky above. Gentle breezes blew through a honeysuckle bush not yet in bloom. Jack flopped the rug over his clothesline. He unraveled his hose and rinsed off the vomit. He washed himself while he was at it, pouring the cool water onto his face and hair. The wet pomade dripped down onto his collar.

He sipped the cool water. It tasted like rubber.

This break was enough for him to pull it together a bit. He went back inside, toweled off, changed into a clean shirt, combed his hair, and sat again in his armchair by the phone.

"What do you know, Jack?" he asked himself. Sometimes speaking aloud, even if only to himself, helped.

"You know big shit is happening here. It's big enough to bury Wilma's murder and hire out yours. You know that you don't know enough to be careful. You know there's a weird little motor court in Oxnard that could be involved but probably isn't. You know Hammond won't make with the information you need."

Jack took another drag and lingered in the pause. He answered his own answer. "In other words, you don't know anything."

He shrugged. As lousy a detective as he was, he felt pretty confident that it would be smarter to report this murder than to hide it. He picked up the phone and rang the York station. Homicide. As luck would have it, Detective Winston picked up the call.

"Hey, Frenchy. It's Jack Chesley."

"Jackie. I heard you were among the living."

"I am," Jack said. "But I got a problem with someone who isn't. He's lying here in my living room, bleeding all over the floor."

"Dead, you say?"

"From here on out."

"Murdered."

"Shot dead, anyway."

"Know who did it?"

"Yeah," Jack said. "I did it."

Winston laughed. "All right, kid. I'll be right over."

"I'm at the old man's house," Jack said. "On the corner of Meridian and Avenue 52."

"I know where you are."

Not five minutes later, Winston walked up the front steps. He wore a wartime suit of tweed cut close across the jacket, no extra material for pleats on the pants. Years of dropped cigar ashes colored the thighs of his slacks. Hair oil and sweat carved a ring around his hatband. Maybe it was just the afternoon sun sneaking below the hat brim, but Winston looked like the years were catching up with him. His skin had grown slack and sallow since Jack had seen him last. Jack thought, this must be how my old man looked in his last days.

Jack met Winston on the porch. The two shook hands. Jack led him through the open doorway. He sidestepped a puddle of blood. Winston followed suit. He took a glimpse at the floor. "Jesus, Jack. That's a lot of daylight coming into the back of this guy's head."

Jack nodded, searched his brain for a thought and said the best one that came to him. "Yep."

Winston knelt beside the shooter. "What happened here?"

Jack stuck with the truth. "Looks like this guy picked his way in through my dining room window, then waited for me to get home. When I opened the door, a bullet buzzed by my ear. I didn't wait to ask questions. I put one in his eye and another in his brain."

Winston grabbed the shooter's head and lifted. One bullet hole carried through the floorboards. Sticky blood dripped down it. "So you won the gunfight, then finished the job."

"How do you win without finishing the job? I thought all gunfights were to the death."

Winston dropped the head back down. He snagged the shooter's silk handkerchief and wiped the blood off his hands with it. He patted all the pockets, reached under the shooter, found nothing, then stood. "You got his wallet?"

Jack nodded. He picked it up off the end table and tossed it to Winston. It flapped and spun through the air. Winston caught it.

He said, "Come on, Jackie. Let's figure this out somewhere else."

Winston took a seat at the linoleum kitchen table. Jack grazed his hand over the coffee maker and reconsidered. He dug a bottle of the old man's rye out of a high cabinet. He grabbed a couple of glasses better suited for lemonade. "Have a drink with me, Frenchy?"

Winston waved him over. Jack set the glasses on the table. He poured himself five fingers of rye, drank it down, and refilled his glass. He pushed the bottle and empty glass toward Winston. Winston poured a smaller belt. He kept his right hand on the alligator skin wallet. His fore and middle fingers tapped on it arrhythmically. "Did you know Parker?"

"The stiff?"

"Yeah."

"No."

Winston kept his fingers going. "But you knew him well enough to know that was his name?"

"No," Jack said. "I read his driver's license, just like you did."

Winston shook his head. "I didn't read his license. I haven't opened the wallet yet. I just know old Herb."

Jack felt his breath getting tight again. He'd slid into the bad habit of trusting his father's friends—Hammond, Winston—when even the old man didn't trust them. And his time in the prison camp should've taught him to trust no one. Damn it. He was a lousy detective. He hadn't even noticed that Winston had kept the wallet closed the whole time, hadn't even considered that the shooter could've been LAPD related.

Jack threw a little more whiskey at the panic.

Winston said, "He was a shamus. Like your pop."

"The old man was never a shamus like that. Did you get a load of that guy's shiny Luger and bespoke suit?"

"Parker traveled in more well-heeled circles. Hollywood, mostly. The studios. Almost exclusively."

A studio dick? Jack needed a few seconds with this information. He pulled out his tobacco and rolled a cigarette. He offered it to Winston.

Winston shook his head. "I have store-bought."

Jack bit the end and lit up. Since all of this brought no bright ideas, he just asked. "I don't get it. Why would the studios send someone to kill me?"

"That's the thing, Jackie. Herb isn't a hit man. He's on the up and up as much as any of us."

Jack looked as far down the hallway as he could see from the kitchen table, which wasn't particularly far. The body was snug in the other room, but also lodged in Jack's mind's eye. "You call breaking into my house and taking a shot at me square?"

"I didn't say he was square. I just said he was on the up and up as much as any of us. Anyway, I don't think he meant to hit you."

Jack felt the heat rise inside him. "What is this? Gentlemanly gunfights and warning shots? I just got back from a war, Frenchy."

Winston got hold of his whiskey then, tossed it down his gullet. He nodded. "Fair enough, kid. Parker picked the wrong playmate today. We'll chalk it up to that."

"But why? Why was he coming to get me?"

Winston dug a dirty fingernail into a chip in the linoleum tabletop. "I was about to ask you the same damn thing."

WILMA, 1943

THE BATH INSPIRED Wilma. The old skin was gone. New skin could grow. She could be reborn.

She dressed, walked down Figueroa to a little stationery store, and picked up a ream of white typing paper. She stopped at the little market, too, and picked up some basic groceries: bread, peanut butter, honey, fruit, eggs, milk, cereal. It would be enough to keep her going for days. In another moment of inspiration, she ducked into the drugstore on her way home. She picked up a handful of sinus inhalers.

When she got home, she cracked open an inhaler. She popped the gooey inhaler tab into her mouth. It tasted awful. She washed it down with a gulp of milk. That coated her mouth with a sour, rotten taste. She stashed the groceries and brushed her teeth. By the time she was finished, the inhaler had done its job. Her heart raced. The blood in her veins felt like the water that had flooded this side of the city back in '38: tumbling over itself, washing away everything in its path.

Wilma slid a piece of paper into the typewriter and started banging away. She'd let everyone know what was going on up there in Camarillo, how a woman could get trapped there if her husband or father or even her son-of-a-bitch ex-father-in-law wanted to get her out of the way, and how the patients were indentured. She'd tell all about the dirty dealings from the staff—the hydro, the electroshock, the TB ward, the rumors of the mass grave just beyond the southernmost housing units, and the pipeline to brothels like the Hitching Post.

She wrote with fire and anger, channeling her best Upton Sinclair. At times she even paused and thought about Sinclair living right up the road in Pasadena. Maybe he could help her get this thing published.

Wilma didn't sleep for four days. She didn't leave the bungalow. Save a quick conversation with Gertie, who checked in every day after work, Wilma talked to no one. She popped inhaler tabs and ate peanut butter honey sandwiches and grapes by the bushel and typed her manifesto. She felt the soapbox grow under her feet.

On the fourth day, the Hitching Post came calling.

Wilma didn't answer the knock on the door. She kept typing. The knock lasted for a couple of minutes. When it stopped, Wilma could hear a knife working its way between the doorjamb and lock. Her friends would've called her name. Her landlord would've used a key. Wilma grabbed a pair of scissors and raced toward the door just as it swung open. She didn't recognize the punk busting through her doorway. She jabbed her scissors into his midsection. They hit a button on his sportcoat and glanced to the side, harmless. The punk grabbed her by the lapels of her robe and flung her backwards into the arm of her loveseat. She flopped over it and landed sprawling on her area rug. The punk stepped outside, grabbed a bulky cube of a suitcase, and came back in.

"Stay down and shut up, Wilma," he said.

Wilma propped herself up on her elbows but didn't try to stand. The punk stepped over her. He pulled the coffee table to the side a couple of feet, set the bulky cube on it, unlatched the buckles, and took a small film projector out. "Ma Breedlove sent me," he said.

"Who's Ma Breedlove?"

The sharper jabbed the pointy toe of his wingtip into the soft flesh below Wilma's ribs. "Don't play dumb with me. Get your ass off the floor and take a seat. Face that wall."

Wilma climbed onto her loveseat and took a mental inventory of her bungalow. She had a few knives in the kitchen, a baseball bat beside her bed, and a few glass ashtrays that could do some damage if she threw them the right way. This punk had a piece jutting out of the back of his pants. No weapon she had was any match for that. She could never get under his coat and grab that gun herself. She sat and waited to find out who Ma Breedlove was and why she sent this flat-nosed middleweight to find Wilma.

The punk clicked the full reel on the front arm and the empty reel on the back and strung film through the camera. Wilma didn't move. The punk circled the bungalow, closing all the curtains. When it was sufficiently dark, he flipped on the projector.

The flickering images on her bare plaster wall brought to life the bedroom of the ground floor penthouse at the Hitching Post. Four men carried a naked and unconscious Wilma onto the bed. Two men stood at the foot of the bed. The film had no sound. Black shadows haunted the edges. The middle of the picture came in clear. A group of men gathered around a passed-out Wilma. One of them spread her legs wide.

Even with a system full of inhaler tabs, Wilma's heart rate doubled. Her blood caught fire. The punk watched

Wilma instead of the movie on her wall. "Look at you," he said. "You're such a fucking whore."

Wilma gathered a mouthful of spit and sent it into the punk's face. He smiled.

Two men on the film argued over Wilma's prone body. The camera panned behind them. A line formed. One of the arguing men pulled his shirt off.

The punk wiped the spit off his face and smeared it onto Wilma's robe. Wilma shot him a look from the side of her eyes. He slapped her. "Watch the film."

On the wall, the line of men had been interrupted by the ex-heartthrob. He whipped off his sportcoat and pushed aside the shirtless guy, who was at the front of the line. The shirtless guy stumbled.

Wilma closed her eyes. The punk slapped her again. "Watch this," he said. She kept her eyes closed. He slapped her again. She started to scream. Raw. Guttural. Tearing her throat. The punk didn't do anything until she paused for breath. He whispered, "Scream all you want, Toots. No one is coming to save you."

This just made her cry. While she did, the punk whispered a play-by-play from the film on her wall, explaining exactly what was happening, down to the tiniest detail, pausing occasionally to lick a tear off her cheek.

Finally, through watery eyes, Wilma saw the film go black.

"Okay," the punk said, turning to face Wilma. "Ma Breedlove wants you to come back and work for her. You still have a debt to pay her and Giroux. You come back, we'll forget all about you running away."

"And if I don't come back?"

The punk shrugged. "We call up Camarillo. You

finish your sentence there. Plus time added for your escape. You'll spend the rest of your life up there, cleaning
lungers' bedpans and spittoons. Your choice." The punk
walked past Wilma and opened the door. A gash of midday sunlight cut across the bungalow. "We'll give you a
week to decide. Bring the camera and film with you when
you come back."

JACK, 1946

AFTER FRENCHY had cleared out and the coroner picked up the body and Jack had scrubbed all the blood off his floor, he decided to take a break from the case. He piled furniture in front of his windows and doors so no one could come in. He found a warm and welcoming bottle and buried himself in it for a few days.

The whiskey was harsh and plentiful. The days were dark inside the house. Jack drank until he passed out. Whenever he came back around, he stayed conscious only long enough to throw booze at that problem.

Something like this had happened in Germany, only without the rye. Just after dropping its payload onto a small German city, Jack's plane had been shot and was going down. The crew gathered their packs and kits and bailed while they could. Because of his position in the plane and his bizarre politeness in a moment of crisis, Jack was the last to get out. He parachuted down into enemy territory—territory he had just bombed. He could see the survivors of the town chasing the parachutes. He expected gunshots, but these poor bastards didn't have guns. As he got closer to the ground, he saw they had pitchforks and shovels and pickaxes and fence posts and kitchen knives and whatever else they could pick up. It was enough. As soon as each member of the crew landed, they swarmed him. From Jack's vantage point, these weren't swarms humans could survive.

Jack fumbled through his kit and dug out the .45.

He floated down toward a waiting mob. One woman in particular seemed to be leading the group coming after Jack. She was a sturdy broad. Wide shoulders. Wide hips. Greasy overalls. More of a factory foreman than a house-wife. She waved a cleaver at Jack. Jack picked her, first. He took careful aim and fired. He'd been doing this all war: picking a target from above and firing down. Killing from the air. His aim was true again. The woman dropped. A boy, maybe fifteen on the old end, picked up the cleaver and kept running for Jack's landing space. Jack took aim again. Dropped the kid.

By the time he landed, the mob was looking for other crewmen to swarm. Jack was out of his head. He dropped his parachute and looked to spend his other seven bullets on German townspeople. He plucked an old man off his navigator. That mob scattered. It was too late for his buddy.

Jack sought out another mob in this potato field. Most of his crewmates had landed before him. Out of reach. He could only find a couple of townspeople near-by. One kid gathered a handful of rocks and threw them at Jack. He dropped to his knee and shot the kid. And that was the last one. He didn't know where the mob went. He only knew it was away from him.

Jack ran back to his navigator and took his bailout kit. He found a compass inside. All he knew was that safe-ty was several hundred miles of occupied territory to the north and west. He'd have to find a way across a channel or a sea, too.

There was also the matter of the town he'd just bombed, sitting immediately between where he was and where he wanted to go.

Jack headed for the cover of some woods south of the potato field. No one seemed to pursue. He threaded through the trees for a couple of hours until he found a bombed-out schoolhouse. He went inside.

Not much remained. A few torn books, splintered desks, about a third of the floor. If there'd been kids inside when it was bombed, their corpses had been removed. Everything of any value had been removed. All that was left was Jack and some rats. And his realization: I am the one who dropped the bombs on these towns. Sure, there was a whole plane and a whole war effort, but on Jack's bomber, there was only one guy who took aim and dropped the bombs. Jack. Just like there was only one guy in the crew willing to keep shooting to stay alive.

The weight suddenly settled on his shoulders. He'd killed four human beings that day. One woman. Two kids. One elderly man. No soldiers. No one with guns. More than that, he'd killed everyone his bomb landed on in that small German city right before he parachuted down into it. Him. Jack Chesley, the grubby kid from Meridian Street. When the time came to kill, he was the killer.

Oh, Christ.

Jack curled up into the corner of the schoolhouse and wallowed. He stayed there for two days, not eating, not drinking, barely moving, crushed under the weight of his actions. If not for the overwhelming thirst that became more painful than his conscience, he may have let himself die there.

Now Jack threw whiskey at that thirst and wallowed again. How many days did he lie around his parents'

house? Four? Five? How many times did the phone ring? Christ, it seemed to be going every time he snapped back awake. Would he let himself die in these bottles of whiskey? Maybe this time, yes.

Only Gertie didn't let that happen. She showed up at the front door on the fourth or fifth morning, banging and calling for Jack. He had to weigh his options—he'd crawled inside this bottle so that he wouldn't have to talk to anyone, and Gertie was someone. Talking with people would be difficult. Even Gertie. But all that door banging hurt his head more than the prospect of ending his bender did. He pushed the armchairs out of the foyer and opened the door. Gertie took one look at him and said, "What a mess."

Jack stepped aside and invited her in. "I need to pick up around here."

"I'm not talking about the house. I'm talking about you. Jesus, Jackie, I've known urchins to crawl out of a ditch looking better than you do. And you stink, too."

Jack looked down at the front of the T-shirt he'd been wearing for days. Was that...? Yep. That was crusted vomit on his chest, right where it would've dripped down from his chin. Jack looked lower. At least he had pants on.

Gertie said, "Pull yourself together. I need you."

"What for?"

"We're shooting a gangster picture, and we need an extra. A yegg. You're just ugly enough."

Jack rubbed his stubble. "Should I keep the beard?"

Gertie laughed. "You look too awful for movies, Jack. Clean yourself." She glanced at her wristwatch. "You have ten minutes to shit, shower, and shave. I'll make coffee."

Jack abided.

✦ ✦ ✦

They arrived at the studio at eight o'clock on the dot. After the triple S and coffee and a quick egg sandwich from an automat, Jack felt something like a human, even if he was still drunk from his brannigan and dressed like a clown. He'd been sleeping in his best pair of slacks during the bender. His other suit had been sliced into strips at the Oxnard brothel. His only remaining choices were in his father's closet. The old man had carried around forty pounds that Jack hadn't yet packed on. Couple his natural leanness with two years in a POW camp and another year not trusting anything he ate and four days of a whiskey diet, and Jack was turning into a beanpole. The old man's pants had been flat across the waist, but once Jack pulled the belt tight, they looked pleated. He could've smuggled watermelons under the shirt. The jacket fit all right across the shoulders, then ballooned out. The whole ensemble came across like a reverse zoot.

First thing Gertie did once they hit the soundstage was holler over to the wardrobe girl. "Ethel, this is Jack," she said. "Put him in something decent. Pinstripes, if you have it." She lowered her voice. "And if he could walk off the lot wearing it today, all the better."

Ethel winked and led Jack by the hand to a nest of portable garment racks. She pulled two of the racks into an L that blocked off the rest of the soundstage. "You got on clean underwear?" she asked. Jack nodded. "Good," she said. "Strip down to it."

Jack slid out of his jacket. Ethel stepped forward, grabbed his shirt in the middle, and pulled it apart. Buttons flew everywhere. "Don't get any ideas," she said. "I'm just in a hurry. I got seven other lugs like you to dress this morning." She took out a measuring tape and ran it along Jack's arms and torso. She nodded. "The pants you'll take off yourself."

Jack worked his belt loose. Ethel dug through a rack of suits until she came across a forty-two long of dark blue gabardine. No pinstripes, but double-breasted and wide shouldered. Matching pants. "You wouldn't be Jack Chesley, would you?"

Jack dropped his pants. The still, soundstage air was cool against the hair of his thighs. "I am."

Ethel tossed the jacket and pants across a rolling bureau. She turned to the shirts, flicking her hands across a row of white, cotton numbers. "I knew your widow."

"Wilma?"

Ethel's fingers stopped moving. She lowered her brow and glared at Jack. "Were there others?"

Something about that look and question made Jack aware that he was standing on a huge warehouse floor wearing only his T-shirt, boxers, and a fallen pair of black socks. He glanced over the garment racks for Gertie. She was on the other side of the soundstage, passing around the day's shooting scripts. Jack said, "Nope. Just Wilma."

Ethel smiled. "She was a hoot, that gal. I could tell you stories, but you probably don't want to hear them."

Ethel pushed a dress shirt against Jack's chest. He slid into it while she ran a tape along his inseam. "I'd love to hear your stories," he said.

Ethel tossed the blue, double-breasted jacket to him. Jack pulled it on. Even without the mirror, he could tell he looked smart. Ethel measured the inseam of the pants on her bureau. She marked them with chalk, dug a pin cushion out of a drawer, and folded up the cuffs. She pinned them in place. "Later, maybe. I don't even have enough time to hem these rags for you." You can get someone to sew them after the shoot." She tossed the pants to Jack.

Jack caught them, turned them around in his hand. Hemming was no big deal. He'd grown up poor. When she'd been alive, his mom had been some swell's domestic, which meant she didn't do any of the domestic stuff at home. He'd learned how to do for himself. "You got an extra needle and thread? I can take care of this."

Ethel dug both out of the bureau and handed them to him. "Knock yourself out." And, in the same kind of low-voice move that Gertie pulled before, she added, "By the smell of things, you might need a nip or two to get through this shoot. Talk to Hayles. He's always holding."

Jack pasted on a sheepish smile. He took the needle and thread and retired to a wooden folding chair in a corner of the soundstage. Not a bad setup. He could check out the whole scene from this vantage point: the burly guys toting cameras onto hulking tripods, the furniture movers pushing desks and couches and sometimes whole walls wherever the pretty boy told them to put them, the dolls glowing in their makeup chairs, the lugs glowering in theirs, the barking to-and-fro of it all. The stale air, the growing clouds of smoke on the high ceilings, the buzz of voices threatening to escalate to a roar: it all gave the place a ringside feel. Jack sat in the one and only cheap seat, socks sagging, legs bare, boxers catching occasional gusts from a fan or an open door, his needle and thread making his cuffs jake.

He was almost sorry to finish the work and have to fold himself back into the picture.

At least there was a food table piled with donuts and

coffee. He met Roderick Hayles there. Hayles had been in
pictures since Jack was in diapers, and the wear was getting the worst of him. From a distance, he still looked like
a leading man. Get closer and details told another story.
He had ridges running into his eyes too deep to cover
with makeup. His nose seemed to be growing its own
little red bulb of burst blood vessels. His teeth were the
kind that sleep in a glass at night. He still had posture like
his spine was made of a flagpole, and he kept his chin up
literally, and his deep voice vibrated every letter in every
word he spoke. The combination of tatters from a hard
life and manners from a Pasadena childhood made him
seem all the more aristocratic. Not typically Jack's kind of
guy, but when Jack caught Hayles sneaking a little whiskey into his coffee, Jack slid his own mug close. Hayles
splashed a shot Jack's way and offered a sideways smile.
They tapped mugs. The morning got rolling.

Gertie caught up to both of them and led them onto
the set. It was decorated like a dingy office. Cheap brown
wallpaper in a fleur-de-lis pattern covered the three walls.
A dented metal filing cabinet leaned against the left wall.
A fake window hung on the back wall. It opened to a
painting of downtown Los Angeles. A splintered pine
desk stood in front of the window. It was battered enough
to match the filing cabinet and wallpaper. A frayed chintz
loveseat sat against the right wall. Striped linoleum covered the floor, with a dusty area rug on top, in front of the
desk, where chairs normally would've been.

A kid in overalls taped Xs onto the floor in two spots
in front of the filing cabinet and beside the rug. Gertie
told Jack and Hayles to stand on these. Jack looked for a
place to stash his coffee. "You can keep it for now," Hayles

told him. "This is just lighting."

The kid taped another X on the area rug. A short, lean carpenter stood on the X. Hayles said to him, "What's the matter? Fillmore's too big to stand in his own light?"

The carpenter shrugged. Jack asked, "Who's Fillmore?"

Hayles laughed, raised his coffee to Jack. "I like you, kid. Who's Fillmore? I only wish he were around to hear that."

Jack let it lie. He was enough of a detective to gather that Fillmore was the guy who'd be standing on that spot once the shooting started. Hayles apparently didn't like him. Fillmore probably thought himself a big star. Jack doubted Fillmore was much of anything. Gertie typically worked B pictures. And the title of this picture, *No Good from a Corpse*, was as B as they come.

A man in a tweed suit approached Jack and Hayles. He said to Hayles, "You know the score?" Hayles nodded. The man handed Jack a skinny .22. A Browning, maybe. From the weight of it, it was unloaded. Jack turned it over. The clip had been ejected. The man said, "Roderick's playing Beauvais. You're playing the yegg what gets dropped. I'll be Clive. Got it?"

"Got it," Jack said.

"Good," the man said. "You'll listen to Beauvais and Clive jaw for a while. You can look at either one of them while they're talking." He pointed at a camera placed near the right wall. "Don't look at that camera." He pointed behind Jack. "Don't block that camera."

Two cameras? Jack reckoned Gertie was moving up in the world.

The man kept instructing Jack. He explained that,

when Beauvais said, "That's enough," Jack was to step forward and jab the gun at Clive's chest. Clive would slap the gun out of his hand and take a poke at Jack's chin. Jack would drop from the punch and lay there while the actors played out the rest of the scene. Jack nodded. Easy enough.

The man looked to someone standing by the cameras. "Lighting good?"

"It's good, boss."

The man told the carpenter to scat. He stood on the X and said to Jack, "Give it a try."

Jack set his coffee down behind his X. He stepped toward the man and poked the gun in his chest. The man slapped it out. Jack let go of the gun and turned with the slap. The man threw a punch in the general direction of Jack's chin. Jack acted like he'd been hit and fell. The man helped him back up. "Looks like you got it, kid," he said.

"Easy as pie, Mr. Fillmore," Jack said.

The man said, "I ain't Fillmore, dipshit. Fillmore's Clive once we get rolling." He looked at Gertie. "Where'd you get the rube?"

Gertie said, "Did he take a punch and drop?"

"Yeah," the man said.

"Then what the fuck are you bitching about?"

The man shrugged and walked away.

Hayles picked up Jack's coffee and handed it back to him. Jack finished the cup. Hayles said, "You really don't know who Tom Fillmore is, do you?"

Jack shook his head.

"Where have you been these past four years?"

"Overseas," Jack said. "Mostly in a German POW camp. We didn't get any movies over there."

"Wow." Hayles bowed slightly with his head the way a king might acknowledge a knight's return from the battlefield in a historical epic. "What does one do in a POW camp for four years?"

"It was only two," Jack said.

Hayles laughed. "Only two?"

"And I learned this." Jack raised his right eyebrow while keeping the rest of his face perfectly still. Then he lowered the right eyebrow and raised the left one. Then he led his two eyebrows in a little waltz: right, right, left; right, right, left. He wiggled both ears, then only the right ear, then only the left, then another waltz.

Hayles watched the whole performance with his jaw slightly agape. When Jack finished, he said, "Now that's talent."

✦ ✦ ✦

Jack and Hayles chatted while the rest of the crew hustled around them, getting everything square. At one point, Gertie stopped by to make sure Hayles knew his new lines. "Like I wrote them myself," he said. He reached out to tap Gertie's ass as she walked away. Jack casually swung his arm down and blocked Hayles's grope.

When Gertie was out of earshot, Hayles asked, "You know her?"

"I do."

"Did you know her sister?"

This surprised Jack. "Her sister?"

"Sure," Hayles said. "She had a twin. A real dynamo. Dead now for a couple years, but I bet that ass of hers still hasn't quit."

Jack froze his face muscles into a blank expression.

Inside, a war raged between his desire to slug Hayles and his need to find out all he could about Wilma. Hayles didn't seem to notice at all. He told the story of running up to a little clip joint in Oxnard, an all-in-one kind of place. You could get your dirty pictures and dirty films and whores and doms and whatever you needed. He said Wilma had been there back in the spring of '43. She'd done a performance for a stag party he was at. It was mostly naked ukulele songs. But she kept drinking with the fellows and danced for a song or two playing on the Victrola. She either drank too much or someone slipped her something. Before too long, she was passed out and the guys lined up to run a train on her. "I got to go first, on account of being in pictures," Hayles explained. "And she was such a sweet young thing I didn't let any of the other guys have a turn. I stayed with her, slept right by her side that night. In the morning, she was gone. I drove up to Oxnard every day that week looking for her. It's not a short drive."

Jack cleared his throat. "It isn't."

"She split that joint, but you better believe I found her when she got back down here."

Jack both wanted to ask more and couldn't. He wiggled his empty cup. Hayles told him to bring it close. Jack did. Hayles used one side of his coat to hide the cup from prying eyes and poured Jack three fingers of scotch. Vat 69. Jack recognized the burn as it went down. This is a soundstage, he told himself. Play it like it's all a movie. Act like you can get through this.

✦ ✦ ✦

A new guy broke into the scene. He had flecks of gray on

his temple and a chin carved in marble and the kind of eyes you don't want looking at your wife, ever. Okay, Jack thought. This is a movie star. Two cameras and a guy who looks like this? This ain't no B picture.

The director called everyone into place. Hayles and Fillmore stepped off their Xs. The kid peeled them up from the floor. Jack stepped back and the kid took his X, too. Someone yelled, "Rolling." Another man with a clapper stood in front of the three men, called out the scene and the take, and clapped the wood. Hayles and Fillmore argued about some business. Jack watched them like he would any conversation. Hayles said, "That's enough." Jack stepped forward with the gun. Fillmore swung at the gun with the wrong hand and barely touched Jack. Jack let the gun drop. Fillmore threw a sorry excuse for a punch at Jack's neck. Jack let the tap drop him.

The director yelled cut and started cussing. "For Christ's fucking sake, Fillmore. Are you a little girl playing patty cake on the schoolyard? What the fuck is this, you little pillow biter?"

He went on for so long that Jack felt bad for Fillmore. He felt responsible. He said, "It's my fault, sir." He put the pistol in Fillmore's right hand. "I expected him to swing at me with his right hand, like this." Jack demonstrated. "So that he'd push the gun away from his body, not toward it. That way, my head would follow the gun and he could take a poke at my exposed jaw with his left hand." Jack slowly mimed the actions.

Fillmore's face turned red. He gritted his teeth and glared at Jack.

Jack took the gun back. He grabbed Fillmore's right wrist and carried his arm through the proper actions.

When his chin was exposed, Jack said, "And you can really hit me. You don't have to fake it. I know how to roll with a punch."

"You're fucking right I'll hit you," Fillmore said.

"Let's try it," the director said. Everyone returned to their marks. The film rolled again. Hayles and Fillmore argued again. Hayles had enough. Jack stepped forward, threatened Fillmore, and let himself be disarmed in the world's gentlest display of toughness. He dropped. Hayles and Fillmore finished the scene with Jack flat on the ground.

The director acknowledged it was better, but Fillmore was still too soft. They ran through it all again and again. Fillmore hit Jack with all his might each time. Jack let the blows come. They were nothing compared to the slaps his father had given him out of love or congratulations when Jack was a kid.

Ten or twelve tender pokes to the jaw later, Jack was done with his day. He knew he should linger, press Ethel to tell her stories, find out more about Hayles, talk to Gertie. Gertie knew more than she was telling. This whole day felt like another script she'd written, like she'd set up Jack to meet Ethel and Hayles, like she was dropping clues. The only bad take of the day was Jack slipping out early instead of playing it like Fillmore's character would've, digging deeper, finding something leading to the truth.

That was too much for today. Jack checked out. The production company gave him thirty bucks for his trouble. No one mentioned the new suit he walked away wearing.

✦ ✦ ✦

Halfway across the lot, on his way to the interurban, a golf cart swung up beside Jack. Hayles sat at the wheel. He stopped the cart and stood up. "I want to shake your hand, kid." Jack put his hand out. Hayles shook it. While still holding it, he said, "That was some dozen blows you took across the kisser. Didn't even leave a mark, did it?"

Jack slid his hand out of the shake. He looked around the alley between soundstages. Nothing but old movie props and sunlight and Hayles and him. "I knew they were coming and rolled with them," Jack said. "Didn't hurt at all."

Hayles leaned in and inspected Jack's jaw. Jack stood still. This tenderness, the intimacy of being so close, of knowing this man fucked Wilma while she slept: it unhinged something. Jack kept his voice cool. "Funny thing about those scenes," Jack said, "is that it's damn near impossible to knock someone out with one punch."

Hayles leaned back and squinted. "Can't be that tough," he said.

"Ever watch a boxing match? How many blows do those guys take from the toughest lugs around? How many does it take to drop them?"

Hayles shrugged. "I guess. But those guys know how to take a punch."

Jack said, "Conditions have to be almost perfect." He placed a gentle finger just to the left of Hayles's chin. "You have to land your second knuckle here, exactly. That forces the jawbone up into the brain." Jack dropped his hand and repositioned himself. "You have to be on the balls of your feet, swing your hips, throw the punch with your whole body. Like this."

Jack hauled off and cracked Hayles in the jaw, just

like he'd telegraphed. Hayles didn't have time to be surprised. He dropped. Jack fished the flask of Vat 69 from Hayles's coat. He took a couple of gulps. Then he hopped into the golf cart, parked it so it looked like Hayles had fallen out of it, and tucked the open flask into Hayles's hand.

"And that's how you do it with one punch," he said to no one but himself.

GERTIE, 1943

GERTIE BURST into the bungalow without knocking. The room was dark. Wilma slept on the loveseat with her head cocked back, jaw hanging slack, and a little string of drool sneaking out of her open mouth. The film projector cast a white light against the wall. The back reel spun. The tail of the film flapped with each revolution.

Gertie opened the curtains and a couple of windows to let a breeze in. She turned off the projector. She ducked into the kitchen and found the place a mess. She washed the plates and bowls and knives and spoons and mugs from what looked like a four-day diet of peanut butter sandwiches and cereal and coffee. She set a new pot of coffee brewing and smoked a cigarette while she waited. From the kitchen doorway, she could see the back of Wilma's head resting on the loveseat.

Busted sinus inhalers told Gertie a more complete story about Wilma's mood for the last few days, how jumpy she'd been, how much energy she'd had. Okay, Gertie decided. If the kid needs to sleep off all that speed, let her do it.

Gertie poured herself a mug and sat at the Formica dining room table. The typewriter sat there with her. She picked up the first pages of Wilma's manifesto and started reading.

✦ ✦ ✦

An hour later, Wilma woke up screaming. Gertie rushed

over to her and wrapped her in a hug. Wilma twisted and squirmed out of Gertie's arms. There was something feral about Wilma's eyes, something that couldn't comprehend what they were seeing. "It's okay," Gertie cooed. "It's just you and me, safe and snug here."

Wilma's eyes focused in on Gertie. She stared for a second, those blue eyes burning. Then the floodgates opened. Gertie pulled her close and patted her back. Wilma cried it out.

It took some time for Gertie to get the story: the escape from the bughouse to the Hitching Post, the rape, the film, the punk, and the threat. Wilma told it in fragments. Gertie pieced them together into a chronology that she could understand. It took time, not only to get the key details, but for the rage to well up inside Gertie and for her to find a way to let it subside to a manageable level. Wilma had a lot of crying to do, also.

After all that, Gertie said, "What was Jack's old partner's name?"

"Which one?" Wilma asked.

"The old timer. The one who was at the funeral with his sweet little wife."

"Hammond. Something Hammond. Dan, maybe. No, no. It was Dave. Dave Hammond."

Gertie sat next to the phone and started making calls. She started with the York station. The dispatcher there told her to call someone at the downtown station who told her to call his wife who told Gertie to call Cole's P.E. Buffet. The waitress at Cole's brought Hammond to the phone. Gertie introduced herself and said, "Wilma has an emergency. I wonder if you could come over and lend a hand."

Hammond asked for the address, took a second that Gertie interpreted as him scribbling it down, and said, "I'll be there in ten minutes." He hung up without another word.

Gertie went into the kitchen and wrapped ice in a towel. She brought it out to the loveseat and pressed it against Wilma's eyes. Wilma took hold of the towel. "Play a record," she told Gertie. "It's feeling like a funeral home in here."

Gertie opened the lid of the Victrola. A new 78 sat on the turntable. She read the label. Chester Ellis. The guy Wilma had been in the bughouse with. Gertie worried it would trigger more crying. She lifted the record off the table and started to put it in its sleeve. "No. No. Play that one. I want to hear Chet's piano."

Gertie turned the hand crank to wind up the spring, released the catch, dropped the needle on the record, and gave the room over to the music. Neither she nor Wilma spoke while the side played. When it finished, Gertie flipped it and played the other side. She brewed another pot of coffee. Hammond knocked on the door just about the time the coffee finished brewing and the needle reached the matrix of the B side.

"I'll do the talking," Gertie said. Wilma nodded. Gertie opened the front door.

Hammond's right hand rested on his service revolver. His chest ballooned like a rooster's. His glance darted around the room behind Gertie. Before he stepped inside, he asked, "What's the emergency?"

"Wilma's been raped."

"By who? Is he still here?"

Gertie stepped back from the door. "No. He's not here."

"Is anyone in danger?"

"We all are," Gertie said. "But not right this minute."

Hammond took a second to process this, then slackened. His hand slipped off his gun. He walked inside.

"Coffee?" Gertie asked.

"Please." Hammond walked over to Wilma and kissed her forehead. He sat in the armchair next to the loveseat.

Gertie came back from the kitchen with three mugs of coffee. She set them out on the table.

Hammond took a sip without waiting for it to cool. "What's all the fuss about? Who did what when, and how do we nail this son of a bitch?"

Gertie said, "You know Wilma was in Camarillo, right?"

Hammond nodded.

Gertie said, "Well, she got stuck there. They kept adding time to her sentence. It seemed like she wouldn't get out. So she cut a deal with a guard named Giroux. She'd play some ukulele at a stag party and he'd get her release papers."

"And that was it?" Hammond directed his question to Wilma. "Just play ukulele and you get sprung? That doesn't sound right."

Wilma started to speak. Gertie put a hand on her knee. Wilma stopped. Gertie said, "There was a catch. She had to do a striptease."

"So there was no ukulele?"

Gertie looked to Wilma. Wilma raised her head slightly. Gertie said, "No. There was a ukulele."

Hammond chuckled. "A ukulele striptease. Okay. I'll try to buy that."

Gertie clenched her jaw and stared at Hammond

for a second. "The ukulele's not important here. What's important is that, after the striptease, Giroux dropped a mickey in Wilma's drink. When Wilma passed out, one of the guys at the party raped her."

"Do you know who he was?"

"Roderick Hayles," Gertie said.

"The actor?" Hammond sipped his scalding coffee. He scratched the gray shadow of a beard creeping onto his face. "I don't know." He shook his head and kept running his fingers across the bristles on his cheek. "I just don't know. It's a hard case to make, Wilma. There's no evidence. It's your word against his."

Gertie cut him off. "It's not," she said. "We have a film of the whole thing."

Hammond took a quick breath in. This turned into a coughing fit. It sounded like he was yanking half his lung up into his throat. He went out the front door and spit in the gravel driveway. When he came back in, he said, "You have film? Is that what this projector is all about?"

Gertie nodded.

Hammond shrugged. "Well, let's see it."

Gertie wound the film from the back spool onto the front one. No one spoke while the two reels whirred. Once the tail started flapping again, Gertie threaded the film into the projector. Hammond closed the curtains. Wilma didn't move through it all. Gertie told her, "Why don't you go in the back room for this, sweetie?" Wilma shook her head. "Please?" Gertie said. Wilma remained adamant. She'd stay and watch.

Gertie started the film, watched the men carry Wilma into the room and line up to rape her. After Hayles got started, Gertie said, "That's probably enough."

Hammond kept his eyes fixed on the images on the wall. "No," he said. "Keep it running." He dug a pack of cigarettes from his pocket and lit one without taking his eyes off the wall.

Gertie inspected the men who were gathered around the bed or lined up behind it. They were all Hollywood guys. Gertie recognized a DP she'd worked with when she was doing piecework at Warner. A couple of the men were under contract at Republic. They were back-of-the-stage guys, not exactly extras but not exactly swimming in their own lines, either. She didn't know their names off the top of her head. Given a little time, she could figure them out. Everybody knew the guy who was doing the deed. He looked his real age without the makeup or soft lighting or finishing school dignity. Still, he was unmistakable.

When the film ended, Hammond said, "I remember Hayles when he was just a kid. Back in the days of silent pictures. He played the boxer what got killed in the ring." He took a deep drag from his cigarette, filling his lungs and letting the smoke seep out. "That was a good picture."

Neither Wilma nor Gertie weighed in. Gertie turned off the projector.

Hammond said, "That's evidence of something, ladies, but it's not evidence of a crime."

"You got to be kidding me," Gertie said. "It's film of a famous actor raping my sister."

Hammond shook his head. He took another drag and tapped his ash into a square glass tray on Wilma's coffee table. "It's film of an actor fucking your sister. Not raping. Fucking."

"How is that not rape?" Gertie asked.

Hammond leaned back in the armchair. He patted down a patch of gray hair over his ears. He turned to speak to Wilma. "Look," he said. "You went to a stag party. You got naked. You got drunk. You were asking for it."

Gertie leaned close to Hammond and raised her voice regardless. "So if you, and I'm talking about you personally, Dave Hammond, go to a stag party and get drunk, are you asking for Roderick Hayles to fuck you in the ass?"

"It's different. I don't get naked. I don't tease men. Tease a man and you got to expect the consequences."

"So how about this, then? All those bastards in Pasadena are teasing me with their money. They go and build their big houses on South Orange Grove and I know they have bundles of cash inside. They're teasing me with that. So if they get drunk and pass out, it's okay for me to rob them, right? They're asking for it, right?"

Hammond took a long drag from his cigarette and blew the smoke in Gertie's direction. When the cloud dissipated, he said, "It's different."

He started to say more, but Gertie exploded from her seat. She kicked over the table. Three mugs went flying. Coffee sprayed. The arm of the projector dented on the hardwood floor. The projection bulb popped. Wilma wrapped herself into a ball on the loveseat.

"It's the same fucking thing," Gertie screamed. She picked up the hot projector and flung it at Hammond with all her might. It looped through the air and crashed down onto Hammond's brogans, crushing his big toe.

Hammond sprung to his feet. He whipped his .38 from its side holster and pointed it at Gertie.

Speaking without thinking, Gertie said, "You know, your partner told his wife everything. Wilma knows. She

knows everything you've been up to. If you don't help her
in this, so help me God, I'll bury you."

Wilma locked a stare onto Gertie with those blood-shot blue eyes. Hammond kept the gun pointed at Gertie's face. Gertie tried to keep her cool. It was all a bluff, but she could tell from both of their reactions that Hammond had been up to something and Wilma did know what it was. Hammond took several deep breaths. Gertie stared down the wavering gun barrel. Wilma said, "Enough. Enough. Christ. I'll go back to the Hitching Post if it keeps us all alive."

JACK, 1946

JACK PARKED in front of the Bell house on South Orange Grove. It was one of the richest old boulevards in rich old Pasadena. Even so, the Bell house stood out. It was a kind of ultimate bungalow, seven or eight times the size of Jack's parents' house, exponentially bigger than the bungalow Wilma was murdered in. The front porch had more floor space than most dance halls. Long eaves adorned with fir rafters cast enough shade to keep this side of California cool. The first two stories took up enough of Jack's field of vision to obscure the third story peeking up in the middle of the roof. Everything was expensive wood: cedar window frames, redwood shake shingles wrapping the house, teak window boxes with rows of white and golden flowers, a mahogany front door just wide enough to squeeze through a grand piano and the twelve men carrying it. Before Jack could walk up to all that, he had to contend with the wide, rolling lawn.

Since he'd spent those months alone in Germany, trying to walk his way back to Allied territory, open spaces made him nervous. He'd learned to stick to tree lines, dense forests, places with rocks to duck behind or bushes to dive into, places where snipers couldn't take a clean shot at him. Even now in peacetime, he couldn't walk across this lawn without scanning the row of pines separating the Bell house from its neighbors, convinced a soldier was in there somewhere, looking at Jack through the sight of a Karabiner 98k. He kept his eyes on the redwood shakes of this opulent monument in front of him and pushed aside the memories.

Jack tapped on the front door. The dense mahogany swallowed the sound of his knock. Far to his right, he found a doorbell and pushed it.

He brought his nose close to the cedar door jamb and inhaled. He could still smell the tree it had once been.

A burly Filipino in a butler's coat opened the door without unlatching the chain. He looked Jack up and down in a way that made Jack aware of the Hollywood gangster suit he'd stolen the day before and was still wearing. The butler said, "Yes," in a way that suggested he wasn't agreeing with anything.

"How do you do, sir?" Jack started. He dug one of his father's business cards out of his suit pocket and handed it to the butler. "I'm an investigator working on an insurance claim." The butler took the card but didn't look at it. He kept his glare locked on Jack's eyes. Something about this triggered Jack's impulse to say way too much way too politely. "It has to do with a young woman's untimely death. According to my sources, she was close friends, for a time, with Carlotta Bell. I'm hoping to speak with Miss Bell briefly, if that's possible. I assure you that she's not under suspicion of any sort. I don't wish to take up much of her time. If she could answer just a few questions, I would greatly appreciate it."

The butler kept staring at Jack. Silence settled between the two of them. Jack had nothing more to say. The butler offered nothing. He looked at the business card, took a step back, and shut the door.

Jack stood alone on the brick front porch. A spring breeze fluttered through the flowers blooming in the planters. A bee settled on a pink hydrangea flower. Jack watched it crawl along the petals. He thought about ringing the doorbell again and decided it could wait, so he watched the bee and drank in the breeze instead.

After a minute or so, the butler opened the door. "Mr. Chesley," he said. "Miss Bell is not currently here. Her father, Mr. Leslie Bell, would like to see you."

Jack nodded. He followed the butler into the foyer, across the soft Turkish throw rugs, and into a small dining room where a man sat peeling a hardboiled egg. The butler pointed to the empty, high-backed chair across from the man at the table. Jack sat down. The butler walked to the edge of the fireplace and stood against the wall, still as a palace guard.

Jack watched the man peel his hardboiled egg. The man had thick gray hair in a horseshoe around his head. He was bald on top, the skin smooth and delicate, as if he'd never left the house without a hat on. He wore a worsted brown suit and a wide tie that was mostly lost under the matching vest. His focus locked on the egg until it was peeled. He set the egg on a bone china plate and said, "So, you're looking for my daughter."

"Yes, sir. I am."

"What's this all about?"

"A young woman died prematurely two years ago. Now her husband has returned from the European theater and he's looking to collect on her death. I'm investigating the nature of the death. My sources claim that your daughter was friends with the deceased. I'm hoping she can help me understand some of the circumstances surrounding the final days of the young woman who passed," Jack said.

"Who's the chippy?"

"Excuse me?"

"The chippy? Who's the dead broad?"

Jack couldn't tell if this whole scene was for real or not. He looked at the egg, white on a white plate, then up at the man, his furry gray eyebrows, his dark, close-set eyes. What kind of guy lives in a museum like this and calls a young woman a chippy? Everything about Bell felt like a performance, like a director had told him where to sit and what to do, like a screenwriter had fed him lines. Jack kept his face neutral and said, "Wilma Greene."

"Sure. Wilma Greene. Took a face plant in a bathtub a couple three years ago. I remember." Bell spun the egg with his manicured fingers. "What's to investigate?"

"Accidental-death policies tend to pay up to three times more than homicides. There has been some suggestion of homicide in this case."

Bell nodded. "Could be, what with the circles she ran in."

Jack rested his elbows on the heavy mahogany table and leaned closer to Bell. "What circles would that be?"

"Oh, you know. Hollywood folks get to playing gangsters in pictures and come to think they can act like one in real life. And you never know what you can run into in the bughouse."

"The bughouse, sir?"

"Sure. The dame spent a couple months in Camarillo. Wrote a book about it and everything."

"And you read the book?" Jack asked.

"Renny did." Bell pointed a thumb at the butler. "Isn't that right, Reynaldo?"

The butler didn't move. His stare remained fixed on a

curtain rod behind Jack and to the left. Bell said again, in a louder voice, "Isn't that right, Reynaldo?"

"Excuse me?" the butler said.

"We're talking about the bughouse book. I'm telling Mr. Chesley you read it."

"A fine book," the butler said. "Quite illuminating."

"So there's the lay."

"If I'm not mistaken, sir, your daughter was in the facility at Camarillo at the same time Miss Greene was. Though, in what capacity, I don't know. Based on your social standing, I'm assuming Miss Bell was a volunteer at the hospital."

Bell sat straight up in his chair. He popped the whole egg in his mouth. Jack watched him chew. All the money in the world, and this guy would send his daughter for a state-sponsored stay at Camarillo. It didn't make sense to Jack. Nothing about this guy did. He must have had a first-rate boarding school education but he talked like a lug. He could've snacked on caviar but he chewed on a hardboiled egg. Still, he lived in a museum and wore bespoke suits around the house. And, though Jack hadn't seen it, this butler was surely packing a roscoe somewhere under those tails.

Bell finished chewing the egg. He pulled a decanter close, poured a drink, and threw it down in a lump. Not that Jack wanted a brandy on the heels of his most recent bender, but it would've been nice to have an offer he could turn down.

Bell said, "Now, about my daughter. She's an interesting case. Her mother raised her to be a real debutante. Piano lessons. Finishing school. The works. The kid had no interest in any of it. Then I got the big idea to take her out to an airfield and up in my little twin Jenny. The kid was hooked. I taught her to fly. After a while, I picked up an old Jenny from a Canuck in Alta Loma and gave it to Lottie. Nothing too fancy; just a trainer. Next thing I know, the boys at the airfield are coming to me with stories about stunt flying and wing walking. So there's Lottie in a nutshell."

"A daredevil?" Jack asked.

"A spoiled brat is more like it. I give her the moon and she builds a cottage on the dark side."

"And that's where she is now? Living on the dark side of the moon?"

"On the nose, shamus." Bell poured a second brandy and dumped it down his throat. "That's why I let you in here. I want you to find her for me. Bring her back to the warm bosom of her mother and me." He stood from the table, dug a kidskin wallet from his back pocket, and peeled out five crisp Jacksons. "This ought to get you started. Drag her ass back here within the week, I'll throw a Franklin on top."

Jack folded the bills and tucked them into his pocket before Bell changed his mind. It seemed like a sucker deal. Jack was going to find Carlotta, anyway. Bell didn't have to pony up anything. Before Bell could realize this, Jack said, "I'll find your daughter for you, sir."

Bell wrinkled his brow. "Find her?" he said, shaking his head. "I'm not paying you to find her, chump. Finding her is easy. I'm paying you to bring her back."

Jack stood to shake on the deal.

Bell waved away Jack's hand and said to Renny, "Make sure you write out a receipt."

Reynaldo nodded.

Bell walked out of the room, his soft alligator wingtips gliding over a carpet worth more than the house Jack had inherited. Reynaldo took his seat across from Jack. "To the best of our knowledge, she's living on West Adams, near the university. You might begin your search there. But be careful. She's cohabiting with a jazz musician who shot at the last man her father sent to retrieve her."

GERTIE, 1943

THE TWINS HATCHED a plan to keep Wilma out of the Hitching Post. It was the same one that got them through tough tests in high school and out of bad relationships in their teens: they switched places. Gertie moved into Wilma's bungalow. She rigged all the windows and doors with cowbells. If anyone should try to sneak in while she slept at night, he'd sound like Bessy clomping through the pasture. When she wasn't sleeping, Gertie steered clear of the bungalow and Highland Park. Her shooting schedule kept her on the lot for long hours that month, anyway. The director lived in South Pasadena. He was happy to drive Gertie to and fro. It got him an extra forty minutes of free Gertie labor a day.

Wilma, for her part, holed up in Gertie's room at the Studio Club in Hollywood. The matron—hired by Will Hays himself—made sure no men got beyond the courtyard of the dormitory. Wilma spent her days inside the room, typing a new version of her bughouse story. She left the soapbox and the first draft in her bungalow. The new version had a sense of humor to it. If Hammond's visit had taught Wilma anything, it was that no one cared about the problems of women in this world. A fiery tale of a woman wrongfully committed wouldn't change anyone's mind. And if the popularity of her bughouse ballad had taught her anything, it was that people were best reached through humor. The more gallows, the better. So she spent her days in Gertie's room turning two of the hardest months of her life into a comedy.

Five weeks passed.

✦   ✦   ✦

Gertie stepped out of the afternoon sunlight and into the foyer of the Studio Club. Two women sat in the high-backed chairs in front of the large windows overlooking the courtyard. Both women appeared to be reading, but Gertie couldn't be sure. Since the chairs faced the courtyard and not the front door, Gertie could only see the platinum crowns of their heads angled down. Neither of the women were Wilma despite the fact that Wilma promised to be sitting there waiting for Gertie. The matron behind the reception window to Gertie's right said, "Hey, Wilma. What's the good word?"

"Hey, Virginia," Gertie said.

She'd greeted Virginia nearly every day for nine months prior to pulling the switcheroo with Wilma. Gertie wondered if Virginia knew the score. Surely, she could tell the sisters apart. They may have been identical coming out of the womb, but twenty-five years stamp a lot of individual characteristics on a person. They weren't identical anymore.

"Your sister's taking a break from typing up *Gone with the Wind*. She's in the courtyard with Rhett and Scarlet."

"Thanks, doll," Gertie said. Virginia winked at her.

Gertie felt like she wasn't fooling anyone. She headed outside.

The Studio Club was a fortress in the middle of Hollywood, a rectangle of brick walls lining the streets, imposing and seemingly impenetrable for any swashbuckling types who might wish to corrupt the chaste studio girls living within. All of the windows and most of the activity were geared toward the long courtyard in the center of the rectangle. Women sunbathed along the second floor verandas and lounged about on the soft green grass. On sunny, early-summer days like this one, the dorm rooms emptied out and the courtyard filled. Gertie meandered through the lawn chairs, over women napping on blankets, past a card game, through a low-lying cloud of gossip, and over to the fountain, where Wilma liked to catch the afternoon shade.

Wilma sat beside the fountain with her two new Studio Club friends, Meta and Bill. Meta was a script girl over at Columbia. Bill was a novelist when he was in Mississippi and a screenwriter when he was in California. He had a wife and daughter back there, and he had Meta out here. Their affair was one of the more open secrets in town. When Gertie first moved into the Studio Club, Meta gave her one of Bill's books to read. Gertie couldn't get through it. It was too Southern. The sentences went on forever. All the characters were men except for one woman for who, Gertie just knew, it was going to end poorly. She told Meta how wonderful it was and let the book gather dust in the back of her closet. When Wilma moved in, she found it and fell in love. The girl, Wilma told Gertie, ends up at a party she never should've gone to and gets raped. "Lovely," Gertie had said. "I'm sorry I put that down."

"No, no. There's more. She redeems herself at the end."

Redemption seemed like the wrong idea entirely. From Gertie's perspective, Wilma didn't need to redeem herself for anything. Gertie kept these thoughts to herself. She let Wilma work through problems in her own way.

Meta, Bill, and Wilma were talking about writing when Gertie came up. Bill had just started outlining a new novel. Meta and Wilma argued over who'd get to read it first. "I can offer you a trade," Wilma said. "My bughouse book for your new one."

A reticent smile crept out from under Bill's narrow mustache.

"Don't you even entertain the thought of giving that manuscript to anyone but me, Bill. You know who butters your biscuits," Meta said.

Well, don't give it to me, Gertie thought. *I don't have all day to read one goddamn sentence.* She kept the sentiment to herself, said hello and goodbye to the couple in short order, and dragged Wilma off with her. They weaved back out of the courtyard, through the foyer, and onto Lodi, where they started walking south toward Santa Monica Boulevard.

"No one is fooled by our ruse, are they?" Gertie asked.

"Well, I had to tell Bill and Meta. They've been so much help with my writing."

"You should pull Bill's trick and just have Meta write the whole damn thing for you," Gertie said.

Wilma stopped walking. A breeze sputtered down Lodi Place. Gertie could feel it creeping up under her long printed skirt. Wilma grabbed Gertie's wrist. "That's not true, is it?"

Gertie shrugged. "It's a rumor, kid. Believe what you want."

"But Meta isn't a writer, is she?"

"What do you think a script girl does?"

"I don't know. Get coffee for the director. Pass out scripts."

Gertie rolled her eyes, yanked her arm away from Wilma's grasp, and stormed down the street.

Wilma hurried after her. "Come on, Gertie. Take it easy."

"How long have I been at this?" Gertie didn't look over her shoulder to see Wilma's response. Wilma knew good and goddamn well. Seven years. Gertie had been working in pictures for seven years. She'd gone to the studios right out of high school, started in the typing pool, and was there for only a couple of months when a producer noticed that she'd been revising more than typing, actually sprucing up the dialogue, and, well, changing a scene or two that needed it. Pretty soon, she'd been bumped up to rewriting entire screenplays before they went to production and making changes on the fly once filming started. She explained all this to Wilma.

Wilma cocked a hand on her hip. "I know all that, Sis. I'm teasing you."

Gertie stared at her twin. In a low, growling voice, she said, "It's not funny."

Before Gertie could see it coming, Wilma wrapped her into a hug. It was another old trick from childhood: the hug to end the fight. Gertie felt the tension in her back and shoulders unwind.

"Okay, kid," she said. "Truce."

The twins started walking again.

Herbert Parker sat waiting for them at the back table of a café on Santa Monica Boulevard. He was easy to spot, even in the shadows. He wore a canary yellow, wide-shouldered suit with a green silk shirt and an orange tie. A matching yellow fedora sat on the table next to him. His dark hair was slicked back.

He stood when the twins approached the table. The thick soles of his roach killers were just enough to make him the tallest of the three. He kissed Gertie on the cheek, then stretched his hand out to Wilma. "You're the sister in trouble, eh?"

Wilma nodded. She scanned Herbert's suit and said, "Christ, where does a man get that much wool in wartime?"

"It's the same amount of wool as a tall man's suit. Just cut in different places." He swept his hand in the direction of the two empty chairs at the table. "Please."

The twins picked chairs and sat. Gertie said, "Dish."

Herbert got right down to business. "I sent one of my boys up to Oxnard to find what he could about the Hitching Post."

"One of your boys?" Wilma asked.

"Yeah. Problem?" Herbert asked.

"You don't do your own investigations, Mr. Parker?"

Herbert lifted a sweaty glass of iced tea to his lips. He drank it down to the ice, showed the empty glass to the waitress, and held up three fingers. "Mrs. Chesley, your sister can't afford my rates. I kicked it down to contract work."

Wilma looked at Gertie. Gertie nodded.

Herbert said, "It's like this. The Hitching Post is untouchable. They pay out to the local police department. They're tied in with the mental hospital, as you know. And all the power in that county goes through the cops and the nuthouse. A broad who goes by the name of Ma Breedlove runs the joint. Her real name is Myrna Laurie.

She's from an old money Oxnard family. Her father owned all that farmland out there when he was young, lost it all by the time Myrna was out of high school. She came down here and started running with a wild crowd. Remember Bambina Delmont?"

Gertie shook her head. Wilma said, "Sure. The tart who framed Fatty Arbuckle."

"Exactly. Well, she and Myrna were boon companions."

The waitress approached the table with three iced teas. She passed them around. Wilma took a sip, scrunched her face, and dumped sugar into it. She stirred the sugar in a futile attempt to get it to dissolve in the cold tea. The tinkling of ice and her spoon against the glass provided the soundtrack for Herbert to continue his story.

"So Myrna learned to hustle. Blackmail was her specialty. She ran a little scam in the twenties where she'd hire Bambina and a few other girls to have sex with married men. She'd pop out of the closet in the middle of the grunting and snap photos. Got so prolific at it that married men were scared to cheat on their wives for most of the fall of '21.

"Then she catches a fellow named Leslie Bell with his trousers around his ankles and his ass in the air. Only Bell goes one better than paying off the blackmail. He recognizes a certain kind of fearlessness and entrepreneurial air about young Myrna. He offers to back her in a whorehouse. Myrna says, 'No. Too risky to have it all in one place.' Bell says, 'Easy. I'll send my boy to pay off the law.' Turns out he works with your pal Dave Hammond there in the LAPD. Hammond goes up to Ventura County, gets the sheriff on the payroll. Everything's jake."

Gertie let out such a heavy breath that it stopped Herbert's story. How the hell was she supposed to blackmail these fuckers to leave Wilma alone if all their crimes were paid for and protected by police departments in two counties? She said, "I can't use any of this."

"You could use the scam," Wilma said. "Hire a hooker to fuck Hammond and snap a picture."

Herbert shook his head. "You can't touch Hammond. He's too big."

"Damn it," Gertie said. "He's the smallest of the three."

"We need a new plan," Wilma said.

"Only one way I see out of this," Herbert said.

Gertie finished the thought for him. "Go to Ma Breedlove and pay her."

Herbert nodded.

Wilma threw her glass at the empty plaster wall of the café. Tea splattered across the white paint. The glass dented the plaster and fell on the hardwood floor without breaking. The five or six patrons and employees in the front of the café turned to look at the back table. Gertie and Herbert didn't react. Wilma muttered, "This is bullshit."

Gertie couldn't sleep. She lay in bed, chewing on the information Herbert had passed on earlier that afternoon. A midnight cowbell rang through the bungalow. Someone was letting himself in. Gertie reached under her pillow for the pistol Herbert had loaned her. She sat up on the edge of the bed wearing nothing but her flimsy nightgown and felt the weight of the pistol in her hand. Cold, steel death.

She'd never fired it and wasn't at all sure she could fire it at a man. Footsteps clomped across the hardwood floor. This was no thief. Whoever was in the front room was happy to announce himself.

At least there was only one of them. A lucky shot and Gertie could be in the clear. She looked at the pistol again. She'd seen dandies in the B pictures she worked on wield these things with such ease. She'd held them by the half dozen when carrying them back to a prop bin. But this was no prop. It was a real gun with real bullets in her hand.

It did have bullets, right? She just pulled the trigger, right? That's all it would take?

The footsteps got closer. Gertie told herself, "Act, goddamn it. Do something."

She held the gun like the molls in the movies and put her free hand on the switch of the lamp beside the bed. A silhouette emerged in the doorway to the bedroom. Gertie clicked on the lamp. The room flooded with light.

The man standing in the doorway squinted. Gertie tried to place him. He looked like her brother-in-law Jack: tall frame, slightly hunched shoulders, hands like a couple of baseball mitts at the end of stocky forearms. Only Jack was dead somewhere in Germany and this guy looked like he'd dug himself out of a grave. Instead of Jack's long, straight nose, this guy's cartilage had been busted enough to meander and flatten at the end. His hair had long ago gone to gray and his skin was about halfway cured and ready to be made into a handbag. Everywhere Jack had looked kind, this guy looked vicious. All the warmth Jack had projected turned to ice in this goon.

"I know you," she said to him. "You're Jack's dad."

"No shit, Wilma. Put the peashooter down and let's talk."

He took a step forward into the doorway. Gertie raised the gun and followed Herbert's directions: just point it like it's your finger. Aim for the chest. It's a bigger target.

John Sr. said, "You know how to use that gun, Wilma? You even know how to turn it on?"

Turn it on? Gertie looked at the gun. Herbert never told her how to turn it on. As soon as the gun was lowered, John Sr. took a couple more steps in her direction. She got wise and raised the gun. John Sr. kept walking toward her. She said, "Take one more step and I'll shoot."

John Sr. cracked a sideways smile. "Sure you will."

Gertie exhaled and pulled the trigger. A bullet flew out and went somewhere. John Sr. didn't even flinch. He kept walking toward her. Gertie fired again and again. Nothing. The shots didn't even slow the man down. She thought maybe Herbert had given her a gun full of blanks. She paused for just a second to look at the damn thing. John Sr. launched into this pause. He grabbed the gun with one hand and smacked Gertie's temple with the other. A fireworks display erupted across Gertie's eyes. Next thing she knew, John Sr. was picking her up off the floor.

"Come on, you little whore."

Gertie squirmed under that meat hook of a hand digging into her upper arm. There was no room to move. She resorted to her second line of defense. "I'm not Wilma," she said. "I'm her sister. I'm Gertie."

"And I was born yesterday." John Sr. flung Gertie onto the bed face first. He climbed on top of her, digging a knee into her tailbone. The fireworks started again.

John Sr. gathered her wrists behind her back and slapped a pair of handcuffs on her.

"I'm serious," Gertie said. "You got the wrong girl."

John Sr. climbed off and yanked her to her feet. She stumbled, her bare feet slipping across the dusty floor, seeking some kind of purchase there. John Sr. pushed her toward the doorway.

"Can't I at least get dressed?"

John Sr. stuck his meaty hand on her neck and steered her across the bungalow. "You don't need clothes where we're going."

JACK, 1946

AL'S CONTINENTAL CLUB looked like it had gone to Germany for the extent of the war and then come back to downtown Los Angeles with the rest of the GIs. The plaster walls had been painted a dark red that wasn't exactly blood red, but was close enough to camouflage blood should it spill there. The dents and chips of the heavy oak chair rail and paneling told stories of beer bottles broken so the neck could be turned into a weapon, of chairs flying back and whoever had been sitting in them racing away, of men tapping along to the rhythm section with their keys against the wall, and, maybe in the smooth worn sections, of lovers pressing against it in a vain attempt at getting closer than possible. The tables were no better: pockmarked and scarred from high heels dancing on them, bare wood darkened by cigarette ash, legs wobbly from giving out and being haphazardly repaired. This was not what Jack expected.

Before the war, Al's had been more upscale. It was never so swell that Jack couldn't afford to walk in, but it had been clean and bright. The maître d' had looked right in his tails and tie. The bandstand would boast a seven piece, all union musicians, professionals who played and went home to families after their final sets. Expecting this type of scene, Jack had taken twenty of Leslie Bell's hundred bucks to a tailor he knew on York and picked up a gray summer suit hanging on a dummy in the window. The wool was so soft and thin it could pass for flannel in indoor lighting.

Gertie, too, had gotten dressed for the occasion. She wore a blue fit-and-flare dress and a white angora cardigan. She'd been to a stylist who'd tamed her wild curls into something soft and wavy and pulled off her forehead with a blue silk bow the size of the smallest hair combs.

If they were overdressed when they walked into Al's Continental, no one seemed to notice. Patrons huddled together at tables. Two waitresses weaved around the joint with trays full of cocktails. A Chesterfield girl peddled smokes. A four piece plucked strings and checked tuning and wet reeds and stocked enough drinks to get them through the set. A lean, dark man at the piano uncapped a milk bottle and poured himself a glass with nothing added. Jack said, "Get a load of this joint."

Gertie flashed him a smile. "The ambiance will seduce you."

They took a couple of seats near the stage. The waitress caught them before the chairs got warm. Jack ordered a rye for himself and a gimlet for Gertie. The waitress took the order running. Gertie scanned the room and said, "Well, there you go, Jackie. We found Carlotta Bell for you."

"Where?"

Gertie pointed out a woman sitting alone at the table nearest to the piano. She had a candle pulled close to her and was reading a paperback in the flickering light. She wore high-waisted slacks and a flowing cotton shirt with the shoulder pads missing and her muscular arms filling the fabric.

"That's her?" Jack asked. "Just like that?"

"I told you I knew how to find her."

Jack nodded. "I just have to decide how to approach her."

"Even easier," Gertie said. She made an "O" of her forefinger and thumb, put it in her mouth, and blew a whistle just loud enough to get the attention of the people at the four or five closest tables. She waved her hand to Carlotta Bell and called, "Yoo-hoo. Lottie. Over here."

Lottie closed her paperback. She put it in her purse, hooked the purse in the crook of her arm, picked up a fizzy drink, and walked over to join Jack and Gertie. Jack stood and pulled out a chair for her. She sat in it. Jack sat back in his.

Gertie introduced them and said, "Lottie, your father gave Jack a hundred bucks to find you. He promised him another hundred to bring you back to Pasadena."

Lottie looked at Jack and smiled. "I don't know. Pasadena's a long way from downtown. They had to build a new road to get there and everything."

"Don't worry about Jack," Gertie said. "He grew up in Highland Park. He knows all the roads on that side of town."

The waitress brought the drinks. He hadn't ordered a double, but the rye looked to be just about that. Jack paid and dropped a dime on her tray for the effort. The pianist tickled a warm-up riff. Gertie and Lottie kept with the banter.

Lottie asked, "Has he thought about how he was going to kidnap me and drag me back to my daddy?"

"I think he brought a club that he bought off a caveman."

"Very nice. He could drag me by the hair after he knocks me out."

"Every girl likes to be pulled by the hair."

Lottie scanned Jack from head to toe and back to the head again. "I don't know, Gertie. He doesn't look like much of a caveman."

"Wait 'til a few of these ryes settle in. He'll be dragging his knuckles with the best of 'em."

Jack smiled. He led his eyebrows through a little dance, downed his first rye, and raised his empty glass to the waitress. She responded with the slightest of nods.

Lottie asked, "Has he thought about waiting until I get on the red line home and sitting on my lap so I can't move until we get to the Pasadena stop?"

"That's a capital idea," Gertie said.

Jack pulled out his tobacco pouch. He made a canoe of a rolling paper and rolled the first of three cigarettes. "It won't work," he said. "Too many transfers between here and Pasadena."

"You could slip me a Mickey Finn," Lottie suggested.

"You could sweep her up in your arms like what Rhett Butler did to Vivien Leigh."

Jack passed two of the newly rolled cigarettes to Lottie and Gertie and kept the last for himself. He struck a match on the scarred table and lit all three. He waited for more kidnapping ideas from the pair. Wilma and Gertie used to razz him like this. They'd had a better rapport than Gertie and Lottie, but that could only be expected. The twins had been working together since they'd shared a womb.

Before the next kidnapping joke could slip out, the drummer brushed a cymbal. The man at the stand-up bass thumped a rhythm. The saxophone joined in, soft and smooth. Everything nice. Everything predictable.

Then the piano started and the whole room was awash. Jack's memories of Gertie and Wilma were swept up in the notes.

Christ, he missed being married to her.

The pianist had a wild style about him. He'd pound along to the rhythm with his left hand, just enough to open up some quiet spaces in the song, then seek to fill those spaces with his right hand. And his right hand was mesmerizing. The fingers would flicker across the keyboard in a blur that seemed too fast to be intentional, too fast to be real, but all the notes were right and in the right place. He'd settle into a catchy little melody, play it two or three times, then fly away again into some kind of dazzling harmonies. It all crashed together into a complex flurry of moods: somber heavy notes followed by some whimsical right-hand twinkling, blending into a happy little rag that would race forward until it got too fast and could only be reined in by the same melody slowing down to settle into a melancholy air.

The whole room stopped everything to listen to him. He carried the band through all his mood changes, telegraphing just enough to let them know what to do with the tempo, keeping just enough up his sleeve to surprise everyone now and then. The guy was amazing.

Jack wasn't a fan.

He had enough mood swings on his own to deal with. He wallowed too much in melancholy nests. He had enough trouble trying to quiet his mind without this guy throwing him into a pensive place. Where were the simple waltzes? Hell, even a foxtrot would've done. It was a Saturday night. He didn't want to be wowed by a virtuoso. Gertie had her dancing shoes on. Jack would much rather spin the dame than sit here stewing.

Gertie took her eyes off the pianist's fluttering fingers and said, "That's Chester Ellis. He was up at Camarillo with Wilma."

"Really?" Jack said.

Gertie nodded. "Lottie, too. The three of them palled around."

Jack looked at Lottie. She watched Chester play like there was only one man in the band, one man in the whole damn room. Chester, for his part, kept spinning that piano through a spectrum of moods.

When the band's set ended, Chester refilled his glass of milk and brought it with him into the crowd. A few patrons patted him on the back and shoulders as he crossed the floor. He didn't turn or talk to any of them. He pulled out the fourth chair and joined Lottie, Gertie, and Jack. Without hellos or introductions, he said to Gertie, "I heard you was dead, Wilma. Glad to see you ain't."

Lottie placed her hand on Chester's forearm and said, "Uh, Chet."

Chester didn't respond. He said, "You got your ukulele? Want to do a number tonight?"

Gertie smiled like a schoolteacher. "I'm not Wilma," she said. "I'm her twin. We met at the funeral, remember?"

Chester let out a heavy breath. "I must have been pretty high that day." He sipped his milk. Lottie lifted her hand off his arm. The fabric of his shirt stuck to his sweaty forearm in the shape of Lottie's hand. "Goddamn,

I thought I was looking at a ghost through that whole set. I thought I was playing for a dead woman." He looked at Jack for the first time. "I don't think I know you. I'm Chester Ellis." He stretched out his gifted right hand.

Jack shook it and said his own name.

Lottie said, "Chet, this is Wilma's ex-husband."

"The dead one?" Chester asked.

"Yep," Jack said.

Chester shook his head. "Goddamn room full of ghosts. We all just haunting each other."

The waitress came by. Jack ordered a second gimlet for Gertie and a fourth rye for himself. Chester still had his lukewarm bottle of milk. Lottie hadn't touched her soda water since she sat down more than an hour earlier. Jack pieced together a brief biography of the two from the evidence he had at hand. They'd met at the madhouse, probably both there trying to kick a habit. Lottie's ornamental soda water was nothing more than a signpost to a waitress to leave her alone. This suggested to Jack that she must've been a drunk. Chester's lean physique and the fact that he must spend almost all of his time seated in front of a piano suggested a different habit to Jack. Dope, probably. That would explain the man keeping his sleeves down while he sweated through a set. Jack was willing to bet the farm that Chester's forearms were decorated with scarred track marks along the veins. The couple must have bonded through a shared history of addiction and madness and all the things that lead up to it, all the things it led them through. Now they were in love and Leslie Bell didn't like it.

The fourth rye came along. Another double. Jack took a sip. It wasn't enough to drop his knuckles all the way to the floor, but if he'd done the math, he'd know that three and a half doubles put him on his seventh drink. His tongue loosened a bit. He pointed back and forth between Lottie and Chester. "This little love affair is what has your rich daddy all upset, huh?"

Lottie didn't answer. Chester locked eyes with Jack. He didn't shoot Jack a glare, exactly. He seemed too tired for that. Still, there was something of a warning behind Chester's eyes. "It ain't so little."

Jack did the quick math. "So you would've met, what? Two, three years ago? Passed those little cafeteria notes that Wilma wrote about in her book. Helped each other out of the bughouse. Got straight. Fell in love. Only thing is, if this candlelight doesn't deceive me, Mr. Ellis is what we call a Negro, and California Civil Code 60 prohibits the two of you from getting married, if that's what you want. And even if it weren't law, old Leslie Bell don't like it. How close am I to right?"

Lottie and Chester exchanged glances. Chester said to Jack, "Mister, you got a problem with us?"

Jack leaned back in his chair. He knew he'd tripped a wire inside Chester and didn't want anything to explode. He wasn't sure what to say to keep everything calm, and he didn't know if he did have a problem with Chester and Lottie. Like every white boy in Highland Park, he'd grown up to believe that the only things lower than white trash like himself were the Mexicans down in East LA and the blacks who lived alongside the factories south of downtown. A couple of years imprisoned in Nazi Germany made him think hard about everyone who'd taught him about a master race. Losing his wife and then hearing all she'd been up to once she thought she lost him made him think even harder about love. He didn't know how to add all these things up or how to explain them in a dirty downtown jazz club with a head full of rye. The best he could come up with was, "I'm just being nosy, I guess. Trying to hear a love story."

This last comment flew like a zeppelin across the table. No one responded to Jack. They just looked at each other. Jack rubbed the condensation along his new glass of whiskey and ice. He wanted to drink it and also knew that he was the only one drinking at the table and that was part of the problem. Without a band to play and with all the other patrons carrying a low-level din throughout the place, there was nothing to break the stalemate among the four.

Gertie was the first to speak. She said, "Lottie's dad offered Jack a hundred bucks to drag Lottie back to Pasadena."

"What?" Chester said.

"It's true," Lottie said.

"But that don't make sense, honey. You was just out to his house last week."

This time, Gertie said, "What?"

"I only go out there when he's not around," Lottie said. She shrugged. "I still like to see my mom."

"Wait. So..." Gertie paused. She picked the lime out of her gimlet, twirled it around her fingers, squeezed the juice into her rocks glass. All the while, she mumbled words Jack couldn't catch. After a few seconds of this, she said, "This smells like a setup, doesn't it?"

Jack went ahead and downed his rye. He didn't understand.

Gertie explained it to him, slow and easy. Leslie Bell

had to know how to find Lottie. She was in the same place every night. He could've done what Gertie'd done: opened the paper to see where Chester Ellis was playing and go there. And Bell couldn't have thought Jack would really kidnap Lottie. They'd already explained to him how absurd that was. Even if he did kidnap her and take her to Pasadena, she could just hop in one of the several cars in the garage and come back downtown. She could catch the red line back to her apartment. Hell, she could call a cab. He couldn't keep her there. "So what could be his motive?" she asked.

"I don't know," Jack said.

"What's his beef with you?" Lottie asked. "You owe him money?"

"No. He gave me money. I didn't even ask for it."

"Sounds to me like he just wanted to know where you'd be tonight," Gertie said.

"You gonna get jumped when you walk out of here," Chester said.

Jack looked at the naked ice in his rocks glass. Now this all made sense. He stood and slid into his sharp new gray jacket. The bill was paid. He pushed the keys to his coupe toward Gertie. She scooped them off the table. He asked Chester to lead him to the back door. Chester lifted himself out of his chair, took one last sip of milk, and nodded toward the stage. Jack followed him between tables, through a swinging kitchen door, and past a square grill and expo station and racks of canned food and a small, greasy refrigerator. Only one cook was still on duty. He sat smoking by the back door. Chester nodded to him. He nodded back. Chester pointed to the back door. "Take a right in the alley and head out to Traction.

Run west to Alameda and catch a red car. Don't play. Ain't nowhere to hide around here."

Jack nodded. He shook Chester's hand again. The skin was soft and meaty. Chester looked down the whole time. Not shifty. Just with the tired eyes of a man who'd played two sets already and had two more to go. Jack buttoned his coat, took a deep breath, and raced out the door.

He stuck tight to the brick walls of the alley, dodging trashcans and scaring a shaggy white cat. At Traction Avenue, he paused to look right, look left. A dark, empty street too close to Skid Row and too far from the swells. A lamppost cast a circle of light down around Hewitt, where he'd parked. Moonlight reflected in the barbed wire along the roof of a nearby warehouse. No one seemed to be around. Jack ran for Alameda, which would be three blocks away if he stayed on open, obvious Traction Avenue, under the moonlight and streetlights, no doorways to duck into or cars to hide behind. He could also turn left on Third and take the shortcut, maybe find some people he'd blend into. His hard soles clomped on the concrete.

He turned as soon as he hit the intersection at Third, flew past a recessed doorway, and snagged his foot on something he hadn't seen. He fell sprawling to the sidewalk. Footsteps raced toward him. Jack rolled over and dug into his jacket for his Springfield. Before he could reach it, a brogan stomped down on his right wrist. Jack looked up to see the wrong end of a nine-millimeter barrel. He said to the gunman standing over him, "Hello, Dave."

Hammond looked down the barrel at Jack. "I told you to keep your fucking nose out of this."

GERTIE, 1943

GERTIE SAT in a straight-backed wooden chair. Her hands were cuffed behind her back. If the room had a radiator, it wasn't on. The cold ocean air from outside the room seemed to have drifted inside in a cloud of fog. Waves of shivers crept along Gertie's bare arms and legs. Her nipples were hard as gun barrels. Gertie couldn't help feeling like they made her flimsy nightgown a moot point.

John Sr. stood behind her. She couldn't see him but she just knew he was plenty warm in his wool suit. His son would've stripped off that wool jacket and wrapped it over Gertie's shoulders. No. Check that. Jack wouldn't have crashed into a bungalow at midnight, cuffed the twin sister of the girl he was looking for, or dragged her up to a whorehouse in Oxnard. But Jack was dead in Germany and his old man loomed in the shadows nearby.

Ma Breedlove walked into the room with two lugs. They both looked like kids, couldn't have been more than eighteen or nineteen. One had a wispy mustache. The other was either clean-shaven or too young to need a razor. Gertie didn't doubt for a second that either one would put her in a hospital if Ma Breedlove ordered it.

Ma spun a hard-backed chair, straddled it, and sat in front of Gertie. She ran a fingernail down the length of Gertie's cheek. "Why'd you run off on me, Wilma?"

"I'm not Wilma," she said. "I'm her twin sister Gertrude."

Ma raised her eyes to John Sr. She said, "Chesley, slap

this bitch."

John Sr. stepped forward and cracked Gertie across the back of her head. His heavy ring dug into her crown. A cool drop of blood made its way out of the wound. Gertie could feel it weaving through her hair.

Ma said, "Let's start again. Why'd you run off on me, Wilma?"

Gertie stared into Ma's eyes. They were cloudy and brown like a palooka who's taken one too many blows to the temple. Gertie said, "Don't matter how many times you slap me, Myrna. I ain't gonna turn into Wilma."

Ma stood from her chair. She straightened her long, woolen slacks. She spun the chair so that it rested behind her. "What's the story, Chesley? Does the dame have a twin?"

"Don't buy this stupid shit," John Sr. said.

"I'm not asking for advice. I'm asking for information. Does Wilma Greene have a twin sister?"

John Sr. looked to the dirty throw at his feet. He mumbled, "Yeah."

Ma stepped closer to him. Her young muscle followed, flanked on either side of her. "What do you know about the twin?"

"Nothing," John Sr. said. "Don't matter. That's Wilma sitting in that chair. I dragged her dumb ass out of bed and brought her straight to you."

Ma grabbed John Sr. by the cheeks and squeezed. His mouth puckered like a fish's. "Chesley, I don't hire you to think." She let go and turned back to Gertie. The two lugs stepped between John Sr. and Ma. Ma paced in front of Gertie. "Okay, let's say you're the twin. What difference does that make to me? I don't care what whore I'm selling. One warm body is just as good as another. Either you or your sister gotta pay off that debt."

Gertie did her best to stifle the shivers. "What debt?"

"You made a deal with Giroux. He gets you out of the bughouse and into here. I pay Giroux for you. You work off the debt."

The cold seemed to come from within Gertie. She held her jaw half open to keep her teeth from chattering. Tough as she could sound, she said, "Sounds to me like this Giroux sold you a false bill of goods. You should get your money back from him."

Ma shook her head. "Someone sells you a car and it gets stolen, you don't go after the car dealer. You go after the thief. Right?"

Gertie shrugged.

"Same as with a whore. Someone sells me a whore and she absconds, I don't go after Giroux. I go after the whore."

"My sister's not a whore."

Ma smiled. "She is. I have a film to prove it. Wanna see?"

Gertie shook her head. She never needed to see that film again. She didn't need to be sitting in this clip joint office, freezing her ass off, either. "Sit down, Myrna," she said. "Let's look each other in the eye and cut a deal like real women."

Ma looked at her two lugs and John Sr. standing behind them. She nodded to herself. No one in the room moved. Ma sat in the straight-backed chair. "Start talking."

"What's Wilma's debt?"

"Fifty dollars a week. Five weeks out. Two-fifty. Plus

ten percent for the knucklehead that brought you here."

Two hundred seventy-five dollars! It was like Ma had looked into Gertie's bank account and totaled the life's savings. Shit. Gertie painted on a poker face and said, "I can get you that." She looked down at her flimsy night-gown and bare legs. "I don't have it on me, but I can put it together by tomorrow evening."

Ma slung an arm over the back of her chair and crossed her legs. "Plus fifty bucks a week."

Impossible. Gertie didn't make fifty a week. If Wilma went back to work and the two of them pooled all the money they earned, they couldn't come up with an extra fifty bucks a week. Gertie tried to keep these facts off her face. She asked, "For how long?"

"For as long as you or Wilma have that sweet little ass I could sell."

Gertie chewed the inside of her bottom lip. This deal couldn't be indefinite. She ran figures in her mind. *How much does a whore really make in a week? How much does it cost to feed and house her? What does that life look like?* She laid it out for Ma. "Okay, let's be realistic. Let's take you at your word that you could make fifty bucks a week out of Wilma. How long do you think you can get that much money? How consistently? You have to figure that, if she escaped once, she's going to escape again. You'll keep a closer eye on her, but even that costs money. So you'd have to get her hooked on something. It can't be booze. Wilma on booze is too hard to control. You'd need some-thing stronger. Morphine or something. And that's pric-ey. Cuts your fifty a week down to twenty-five, at best."

Ma shrugged. "Thirty-five."

"Okay. Let's say thirty-five. But you have to get her

hooked right away. And that eats up a woman. Wilma's sweet little ass gets all skinny and bruised in no time. She gets that vacant junky look. At best, you're getting a dime a turn out of her from the sailors down at Hueneme. And if you're doing that kind of volume, someone's gonna shoot syphilis or something into her. You'll have to kick her out on the streets to die within a year from now. Right?"

Ma twisted her mouth. She locked those muddy brown eyes onto Gertie. One of the young lugs tapped a waltz with his foot. Bum-bum-bum. Bum-bum-bum. Ma said, "You're right. More or less. I'd get two years out of her."

"That last year, you're not getting thirty-five a week."

Ma nodded. "True. It'll be down to twenty-five."

"Fifteen, tops."

"No," Ma said. "I'd work her. I'd get twenty-five."

Gertie ran the numbers through her head. It all came out somewhere around three grand. It may as well have been a million, for what she could put together. In the meantime, it was about what Republic would lose if she didn't get out of this chair, back down to Highland Park, dressed, and ready by the time the director swung by the bungalow in the morning. "I can get you two-seventy-five tomorrow," Gertie said. "And a hundred a month for a couple of years. We call that square."

Ma shook her head. "You'll get three hundred tonight and one-fifty a month for a couple of years. We'll call that square."

What could Gertie say? "It's a deal, Myrna."

Ma smiled. "Call me Myrna one more time and I'm gonna get you a drawer in the morgue." She looked up at John Sr. "Take this whore back home and get my money."

John Sr. stepped between the two lugs, reached his hand onto Gertie's lap, grabbed her by the chain between her handcuffs, and yanked her up onto her feet.

Neither spoke on the ride home. John Sr. rolled down both windows in his little Model A coupe. Cold night air rushed into the cab. John Sr. stuck a cigar into the right side of his mouth and lit it. The smoke filled the dead air between the windows, between him and Gertie. Gertie turned away from it and looked at the city lights along the Ventura Highway. Somewhere out there was a scheme to drum up three grand.

The first three hundred was the easiest. When they got back to Wilma's bungalow, John Sr. flung Gertie onto the loveseat and told her to stay there. He ripped Wilma's mattress off her bed. A nest of folding money lay scattered about below. He gathered it up. He charged into Wilma's closet, threw all her hats out into the bedroom, found the hat box in the deepest recess of the top shelf, opened it, and pulled out another clump of bills. Wilma's last stash was under a loose floorboard in the bathroom. John Sr. knew about that, too. He must've turned this bungalow upside down while Wilma typed at the Studio Club and Gertie worked on the sets.

He sat on the chair across from Gertie and laid the money out along the coffee table, divided according to denomination. Gertie counted while he counted. Wilma's life savings amounted to four hundred thirty-two dollars. John Sr. put a hundred thirty-two into one pocket and three hundred into the other. He told Gertie, "Stand up and turn around." Gertie did. John Sr. took the cuffs off.

"I'll be here next week for my hundred sixty-five dollars."

Gertie almost corrected him. Then she did the math and realized, as long as John Sr. knew about the deal, he'd get his ten percent.

Two nights later, Gertie swung by Musso and Frank's in hopes of raising the ransom. A platoon of Hollywood writers had assembled along the bar in the early evening. The studios kept them like factory workers, requiring them to clock in at nine and out at five. All the time in between, the writers were expected to have their ass in the chair and their fingers on the typewriter. Most didn't work that way. Some didn't work at all. Gertie was looking for those guys.

They hung out in the back room of Musso and Frank's: the writers who still dreamed of big literary prizes and thought everything about the studio system—save the paycheck—was beneath them. They gathered around small, round tables in their tan flannel suits and with their ink-stained middle fingers wrapped around some kind of double neat. Every other conversation was some has-been waxing melancholic about his talents going to waste.

Gertie knew from the Studio Club gossip that she'd find Meta and Bill here. Bill would be on his first public bourbon of the evening. Gertie would have to catch him before the bourbons replaced dinner for Bill, before he started singing slave songs and slapping anyone who tried to stop him.

Bill sat with Meta at the table closest to the cocktail waitress's station alongside the back bar. He wore a Harris Tweed coat and a wide tie tucked into a V-neck sweater. His brown hair was combed to a neat side part. His mustache was small and immaculate as always. He sat next to Meta with the straight-backed dignity of a Mississippi landowner. Meta wore a cream-colored work dress, one of the few items in her scant wardrobe. Gertie had seen her leave the Studio Club wearing it dozens of times. Only the accessories changed. On this evening, Meta had added a silk ribbon tied into a bow just above the top button. Gertie could imagine the pair in some antebellum ballroom for a niece's debutante party, downing one too many mint juleps and having to stagger home under a canopy of live oaks.

Gertie barged into their little twosome. She pulled out a chair and got straight to business. She said to Bill, "Rumor has it you're working on a new novel."

"Why, of course, Wilma. We talked about this."

"I'm Gertie," Gertie said. "Wilma told me about your new project."

Meta set her hand atop of Gertie's. "Wilma has been such a joy to have at the Studio Club."

Gertie looked at Meta's hand and didn't move her own. Meta's warmth radiated down onto Gertie's fingers. "We all love Wilma," she said. "Now, about this novel, Bill. How's it coming along?"

Bill lifted his bourbon to his lips and gulped it like water. He set the empty glass down. "Slowly."

"Hard to write a novel when you have Columbia breathing down your neck?"

Bill nodded.

Meta said, "They want him to write a swashbuckling
picture. Sailors and pirates and ports of call. It's ghastly."

"Way below a man of your talents, eh, Bill?"

Bill raised his hand to call for the cocktail waitress.

Gertie asked, "Have you thought of subcontracting the work?"

"Watch your tongue," Meta said. "Bill writes all his own scripts."

Gertie crossed her arms and leaned onto the table. Bill mirrored her actions. He tilted his head like an old hound trying to hear a far-off rabbit. "You don't have to, Bill." Gertie spoke in a low voice, the kind that doesn't drift to nearby patrons. "I've been working for Republic for seven years. I've written more scripts than half the drunks in this room combined. Ask around. I'm professional. I work quickly. I'm discreet."

In a whisper like a dagger, Meta said, "This is highly inappropriate."

Bill waved her off. "What do you charge?"

"What does the studio want from you? How many pages per week?"

"Twenty."

Gertie paused to run numbers through her head. She knew that, at one point, Columbia had paid Bill somewhere in the ballpark of twelve hundred a month. He'd had some shameful moments since signing that salary. A couple of flops, a bender that cost the studio a grand in wasted time. By now, his pay would be lower. But a man like Bill wouldn't accept less than a grand a month. Gertie figured she could chisel out twenty percent of that. She said, "Fifty a week. Two-fifty gets you the whole script. Meta can do rewrites as always."

Meta gasped. "Now, Gertie."

Bill raised a hand to quiet Meta. He leaned back in his chair. "Miss Greene, we have a deal."

The waitress dropped off Bill's bourbon. He ordered a third while she was there and made quick work of his second. He asked Meta to give Gertie the treatment.

"What treatment?" Meta wouldn't even look at Gertie while she spoke. "It's a swashbuckler. I already told you. Sailors, pirates, ports of call. Keep old Will Hays in mind and make all the sex a subtext."

Gertie stood and offered her hand to Bill. Bill shook it. Gertie rubbed Meta's shoulder. She said, "I know the score. I'll get you twenty pages by Friday."

JACK, 1946

WHEN JACK was a boy, six or seven at the oldest, still in knickers and barely able to read, his father enlisted him in a caper. At the time, the old man was making most of his living recovering stolen money and getting a percentage. A pair of yeggs from the Central Valley had been knocking over post offices. Jack still remembered their names. Joe Lanagan and Fast Eddie Carr. The old man was commissioned to find them and reclaim the loot. He'd put out feelers around Highland Park and was waiting for word.

Dave Hammond was a beat cop then. The old man had told him about Lanagan and Carr. Hammond knew who to look for and kept his eyes peeled. One afternoon, just after Jack had gotten back from school, Hammond swung by the house on Meridian with news. Lanagan and Carr had just ducked into a speakeasy on Figueroa between Avenues 56 and 57. The old man picked up a roscoe and said, "Come on, Jackie. Let's go to work."

Hammond and the old man charged down Avenue 52 toward Fig. Jack tried to walk with them for the six blocks across. He couldn't quite keep up. He'd trail behind and have to jog to catch them again. The two men didn't talk.

The old man stopped at a house on the corner of Marmion and Avenue 54. "You two stay out here," he said. Jack sat on a low wall and watched a cat stalking a bluebird perched in a green jacaranda. Hammond fiddled with his handcuffs. Two minutes later, the old man came out with a galvanized two-quart bucket full of draft beer. He handed the bucket to Jack. "You get a smack for every drop that spills. You got that?"

Jack nodded.

"Good. Now you walk in front where I can see you."

Jack started up Marmion. He kept a rigid grip on the bucket and walked as slowly as he could. Hammond kicked him in the butt. "Quit crawling, kid. We got to move."

Jack sped up. A little beer sloshed out of the pail. The old man cracked Jack across the back of the head. "Pay attention."

For two blocks up Marmion and one over on Avenue 56, Jack walked a tightrope between not being too slow and getting a kick in the ass and not being too fast, spilling beer, and getting a hard slap on the back of the head. The old man stopped him on the corner of Fig and 56. He squatted down in front of Jack, took the bucket of beer from his hand, set it on the ground, and took two photographs from inside his jacket. "See these two fellows, Jack?"

Jack took the photograph and studied their faces, the thick eyebrows and squashed nose of the one, the sleek mustache and chin dimple on the other.

"I need you to go into that doorway over there and find these two men. Walk up to them and offer to sell them this bucket of beer. If they don't buy it, sell it to someone else. But you notice where these two lugs are sitting. If they're sitting at a barstool, you count how many barstools are between them and the door. If they're sitting at a table, you draw a map inside your head and you come out here and draw that map for me with a stick in the dirt. You pay attention. Tell me what color suit they're wearing. Tell me if they have a hat on. Tell me who they're talking to. You notice everything and come back out here to paint that picture for me. Got it?"

Jack nodded. It seemed like the easiest part of the caper.

He walked the last half block to the speak with no one kicking or smacking him. He opened the large wooden door with a window slat at the top and stepped into the dark room. He waited for a half minute until his eyes adjusted. A long bar lined the wall to his left. There were no stools for him to count. Two women and six men stood along the bar. No bartender worked behind it. The men had a few bottles between them. An older kid sat on the end of the bar. Jack recognized him from grammar school. A working man in shirt sleeves and suspenders signaled the kid over. He gave the kid some coins and an order. The kid raced past Jack and out the door.

Six four-top tables sat to Jack's right. All of them were empty except the one farthest from the door. A man with bushy eyebrows and another with a sleek mustache sat with their back to the wall and eyes on the door. Joe Lanagan and Fast Eddie Carr. Lanagan wore a double-breasted pinstripe suit dark enough to match his wild black hair. Carr's purple jacket hung over the back of the chair behind him. He wore a white shirt and an empty shoulder holster. His gun sat on the table, barrel pointed toward the door.

Jack called out, "Bucket of beer. Twenty-five cents."

One of the workers at the bar dug into his pocket, grabbed a quarter and flipped it at Jack. The quarter splashed into the beer. Jack dug his dirty hand into the pail, fished out the coin, and passed the pail over to the man. The man shot Jack a mean look. Jack doffed his cap and said, "Thank you."

He raced out of the bar and around the corner to meet his father and Hammond. He'd picked up every detail and even drew a map in the dirt. Three times, he told his father that Fast Eddie had a gun pointed toward the door. The old man patted Jack on the cheek a couple of times. "You done good, kid," he said. "Now run on home."

Jack looked at Hammond and the old man, then took off at a sprint.

He turned left at Marmion and backtracked up to-ward Avenue 57. Halfway up the block, he heard gun-shots: four or five of them in quick succession. Jack picked up his pace. By the time he made the corner of Fig and 57, he could see the old man walking out of the speak. He held Joe Lanagan by the collar with one hand and Lanagan's money belt with the other. Hammond waited outside to slap the cuffs on the yegg. Fast Eddie Carr, Jack later learned, got himself shot that day, which made Jack the finger man.

Twenty years later, Hammond shoved Jack's cheek into a brick building side and fastened a pair of cuffs onto Jack's wrists. Jack thought about that long-ago bucket of beer and what he'd learned about Dave Hammond over two decades. First, Hammond never did the dirty work himself if he could help it. He let the old man walk into the gunshots at the speakeasy. He sent Jack into all the dangerous situations when they'd been partners. So if Hammond was the one waiting outside for Jack, tripping him up, pointing the gun at Jack with a shaky hand, and slapping the cuffs on, Jack could feel certain that Hammond didn't have anyone else to do this. So Hammond was working alone here. Jack summed it up. Dave Hammond—three months past his fifty-fifth birthday and never a tough guy when he was young—was out here trying to manhandle a twenty-six-year-old Jack Chesley, who'd survived on his own for months behind enemy lines in Germany.

Jack relaxed all tension in his shoulders. "You can peel my face off the brick, Dave," he said. "I ain't fighting you."

Hammond grabbed the chain of the cuffs between Jack's hands. He pressed the steel of the barrel against Jack's neck. "You're damn right, you're not going to fight."

Hammond stepped back and dragged Jack in the same direction. Jack asked, "Which way is your car?"

Hammond nodded in the direction of Alameda. Jack started walking that way. Hammond lowered the gun. He kept his hands on Jack's cuffs and walked a step behind. A train whistle echoed across the bare night. Occasional cars sputtered along the downtown streets in the distance. The rest of the street was vacant except for the concrete and bricks and metal shutters and shadows cast by distant lampposts. A '46 Ford sedan sat parked along the street a block away. Jack turned halfway back to Hammond to ask, "That your Ford?"

Hammond nodded.

"Sharp," Jack said. "I was looking at those when I first got back from Germany. They got a rhino under the hood, don't they?"

"It can get up and go," Hammond said.

"Don't want to ride in the backseat with those suicide doors."

"Hell, you know Gladys and I don't have kids. No one rides in the backseat."

Jack let a little laugh slip out. "Really? You going to let me ride shotgun, all cuffed up like this?"

Hammond smiled. "You're riding in the trunk."

And, in that split second when Hammond's guard dropped, Jack whipped around and head butted him in the nose. Hammond literally walked into the blow. Blood spurted out and across Jack's face. Hammond accidentally discharged his gun into the sidewalk. He dropped it and raised both hands to his face. Jack swung a kick into the side of Hammond's knee. The knee buckled from under Hammond, and he dropped. Jack kicked the roscoe down the sidewalk and buried his heel into Hammond's Adam's apple. "You got two choices, buddy," Jack said. "You can stay down because you're smart, or you can stay down because you're dead."

Hammond lay perfectly still. If he tried to speak, no air could get past Jack's heel.

Jack took another quick assessment of the situation. His hands were cuffed behind his back. Hammond had the keys. Jack couldn't unlock himself. He couldn't trust Hammond to unlock him. He couldn't stand there all night with his heel crushing a cop's throat. He couldn't run away or Hammond would pick up the gun and shoot him. He couldn't pick up the gun himself with his hands behind his back.

The way Jack had it figured, he could either try to knock Hammond out with a quick kick to the jaw, then rifle around for the keys, or he could go ahead and finish crushing the air out of his old partner, then free himself. Knocking people out was hard. Jack had been around enough to know that. And Hammond was wily. As soon as Jack lifted the foot off his throat, Hammond would start fighting dirty.

Jack whittled his options down to one choice. He leaned his weight onto the foot on Hammond's throat. Hammond squirmed and gurgled, grabbing for Jack's legs. Jack pushed down harder. A car swung around the corner and raced up Third. Jack could see Hammond's face growing purple in the lights from the car. The driver skidded to a halt with the lights on Jack and Hammond. Jack turned to look. He couldn't be sure at first, but that little coupe looked just like the one he'd inherited from the old man. The door swung open. Jack caught a glimpse of the driver's fluffy white cardigan.

The driver called out, "Jack, Christ, what are you doing?"

Jack shifted his weight somewhat. He figured it would be enough to keep Hammond down and keep him alive. He said, "Gertie?"

Gertie ran around to Jack. "What's going on here?"

"Hammond jumped me," Jack said. "I need you to grab his keys and his gun for me."

Gertie knelt and grabbed the heater. She tucked it into her purse.

Jack leaned a little harder onto Hammond. He said, "Dig out the keys to these cuffs and toss them a couple feet away from you."

Hammond moved one arm slowly toward his pocket, dug out the keys, and flung them against the wall. Gertie grabbed the keys. Her hands shook trying to work the key into the lock. It took her a couple of tries. When Jack's hands were finally free, he pulled his Springfield out of its holster. He took one step back. Gertie took several. Jack aimed the Springfield at Hammond's face. "You can thank Gertie here for saving your life," he said.

Hammond looked up at him with a pair of saucers for eyes.

"I mean it, Dave. This all would've been worse if she hadn't shown up. Be a square gee and thank her."

Hammond croaked out, "Thanks."

Just as Hammond said this, Jack got hit with a wave of something. His blood tingled and his temples tensed. He could feel his heart pounding and someone inside him screaming, "Kill him! Just fucking kill him!" The trigger of the Springfield felt warm under the middle knuckle of his forefinger. It would be so easy. Just a little squeeze, easier than opening the bomb hatches on his B-24.

Maybe something in these thoughts crept across his face. Maybe Gertie saw it. She said, "Jackie, take a deep breath and let's figure this out."

Jack sucked in the cool night air. It came in moist and tasted faintly of the ocean.

Gertie said, "Why did Hammond jump you?"

Jack waded through his clamoring thoughts and grabbed hold of one. "Bell sent him, I guess."

Hammond stayed on the ground. He rubbed his throat. Blood still trickled from his nose. A small puddle of it gathered underneath him. Gertie asked, "Did Bell send you?"

Hammond nodded.

"And where do you think he was planning to take you?" Gertie asked Jack.

"Probably somewhere in the north valley to kill me." Was that right? Jack spoke the thought as soon as it emerged. He didn't take time to swish it around and see if it tasted right.

Hammond shook his head wildly. "No, Jack. No." His voice came out raw and splintered. "I just wanted to have a talk with you."

"You could've called him on the telephone to talk," Gertie said.

Hammond chanced sitting up. Jack and Gertie both took a step back. Neither stopped him. Hammond said, "Well, sure. Maybe I wanted to do more than talk. Maybe I wanted to knock you around a bit, beat some sense into you. But I was always going to let you live."

"How generous," Gertie said. She propped a hand on her hip and turned to Jack.

Jack looked at her and looked at Hammond. A little kick couldn't hurt at this point. Just a little release. Jack whipped his foot into Hammond's jaw, maybe a little harder than he intended but not hard enough to break anything or knock anyone out. Hammond's hand slipped out from under him and he flopped back onto the sidewalk.

Jack pulled a handkerchief out of his pocket and wiped the blood off his face. He asked Gertie, "Did I get his blood all over my new suit?"

Gertie brushed her thumb across Jack's lapel. "Maybe a little."

"Is it ruined?"

A long red streak of blood sat where Gertie's thumb had just been. "It doesn't look good."

Hammond struggled to pull himself up again. Jack

looked at him and back at Gertie. "Should we go see Bell and find out what this is all about?"

Gertie shrugged. "Should we?"

Jack turned to Hammond. "What about you, Dave? You coming?"

Hammond tucked the foot of his good leg underneath and willed himself upright. He placed a little weight on the knee that Jack had kicked. "I don't think I can walk," he said.

Jack wasn't about to let Hammond touch him, much less use him as a crutch. He said, "I guess that's your tough shit, isn't it?"

Gertie climbed back into the driver's seat. Jack unfolded the rumble seat for Hammond, then slid into the passenger seat himself. They watched Hammond hop across the sidewalk and alongside the car. Hammond dragged himself into the rumble seat. Jack tickled the safety of his Springfield and kept an eye on Hammond, but really, with the back window separating him from Gertie and Jack, there wasn't much Hammond could do.

Gertie backed onto Third and started winding their way north and east to Pasadena.

WILMA, 1944

BROAD DAYLIGHT. The first Sunday of June, 1944. Wilma stood on the porch of her ex-father-in-law's house and wiggled the blade of a pocket knife against the window lock. Herbert Parker had shown her how to do this. She had practiced on the windows of her own bungalow until she could get the lock loose in fifteen seconds or less. John Sr. didn't live in the type of neighborhood where people called the cops whenever they saw suspicious activity. Still, Wilma didn't want to linger.

She sprung the lock, lifted the dining room window, and crawled inside.

On the first Sunday of every month for going on a year now, John Sr. had been collecting an ever-growing sum from Wilma and Gertie, then driving it up to Ma Breedlove in Oxnard. The trip took him no less than four hours. Wilma was sure of this. She'd timed it three months running.

She'd given John Sr. an hour head start, figuring he wouldn't turn around when he was halfway there. This left her two hours to ransack the place.

First, she checked the types of spots where Jack liked to hide things: closets, books in the bookshelf, under dressers, and behind the armoire. No luck. She lifted mattresses. She dug under every cushion in the joint. She checked sugar bowls and the folds of dusty tablecloths and between 78s beneath the Victrola. She tapped floor-boards searching for a loose one. There were a few in the bathroom. She lifted them. Sure enough, a suitcase of money was stashed there. A few grand, judging from the size and weight of the thing. She knew better than to take any of it. John Sr. would probably stash his ten percent here when he got back from Oxnard.

The search went on. She checked drawers and boxes for false bottoms. She lifted rugs and picked through the shed out back. Nothing.

As the morning drifted into the dangerous time when John Sr. might return, Wilma felt her options slipping away. Maybe it wasn't here. Maybe her information had been wrong. She walked back into the bathroom and looked at herself in the mirror. Half of her curly hair was matted to the sweat on her forehead and neck, the other half sprouted wild off the top of her head. The skin around her eyes was swollen and puffy. Had she been crying without even noticing it? Was she still? She moved in close to her reflection and said, "Think, Wilma. Where did the old man stash the goods?"

No thoughts came. She leaned back. A trick of the noontime light creeping in the bathroom window exposed a gap between the mirror and the wall. Wilma ran her finger along the gap. Sure enough, something was underneath this mirror. Wilma lifted it gently from its hooks, set the bottom edge onto the rug, and leaned it against the toilet paper roll. A manila envelope was pinned to the wall. Wilma pulled the pin.

The envelope contained about a dozen photographs, all eight-by-ten, all clear and well-lit. She flipped through them. A couple of the faces she recognized from films. A few other faces she knew from the society pages. The last two she knew from her nightmares: Myrna Laurie and

Leslie Bell, going at it like a couple of alley cats.

She snagged the photo, pinned the other eleven back to the wall, hung the mirror in its place again, and cleaned up the few flakes of paint and dust that had floated down when she pulled the mirror off. She raced out the back kitchen door, locking the doorknob behind her.

Wilma took the next day off from the hash house. Carlotta Bell and her mother, Lavinia, picked Wilma up at the bungalow. Lottie led them on a white-knuckle ride down Ventura Highway and through Topanga Canyon. Lavinia convinced her to take it easy once they hit the coast road. Lottie slowed her pace down to moderately insane. Lavinia turned back in her seat and asked Wilma a flurry of questions about the Camarillo State Hospital. Wilma did her best with the answers. Problem was, Lavinia had read Wilma's book so many times that she knew the book better than the author did. She gently corrected Wilma when Wilma's memory didn't match up to her prose. Wilma saved the morning by taking her little dobro ukulele from her valise and playing her ode to the bughouse. Lottie and Lavinia sang along to every "When I'm at Camarillo."

Wilma followed it up with a dozen more popular tunes. The Bell women sang along when they could remember the words. Lottie steered her mother's Cadillac through Malibu and Point Dume, past the Air Force base, and into the farmland of Camarillo. She parked near the administration building.

Wilma stepped out of the backseat and looked across hospital grounds. She said, "Wow. I thought I'd never come back here."

Lottie wrapped an arm around Wilma's shoulder and squeezed. "You and me both, sister."

Lavinia pointed across the parking lot to the steam rising from a long, narrow building. "That must be the laundry."

"It is," Wilma said. In her book, she'd written about her dream of working at the laundry and getting a few moments each day to walk freely between the laundry and the wards. It was the best she could hope for then.

Now, she was hoping for more. She and Lottie had planned this out. They'd been working on it since the day Wilma told Lottie about the money Ma Breedlove and John Sr. were extorting. Lottie knew more about Ma than Herbert Parker did. She told Wilma that Ma had never been the one jumping out of the closet, snapping photos of famous people having sex. It had always been John Sr.—Ma just hatched the scam. She seduced a rich or famous man occasionally. Mostly, she set up others and got John Sr. to photograph the scene. An old peeper like John Sr. was a specialist. He didn't even have to jump out of a closet, if he didn't want. He could get a shot of you in the act and leave you none the wiser.

When Wilma found this out, she knew there had to be photos of Breedlove and Bell. Bell wouldn't have funded the Hitching Post otherwise. And John Sr., if he took a picture like that, would keep a copy. Even if he sold the negative, he'd keep a clear, blown-up print and use it to reverse a new negative. All Wilma had to do was find that photo and throw a little blackmail at Bell to counter Ma Breedlove's extortion racket.

✦　✦　✦

A man in a slick double-breasted suit emerged from the green door of the administration building. He called out, "Mrs. Bell?" Lavinia waved to him. The man asked, "Are you ready for the tour?"

"Absolutely," Lavinia said. She introduced Lottie and Wilma.

The man shook Wilma's hand and said, "Welcome to our little brain emporium."

He led them through the new construction on the north side of hospital grounds, talking about progress and the groundbreaking techniques of the doctors. "We've improved even since you ladies were here," he said to Lottie and Wilma. The pair rolled their eyes.

He bought them all coffee at the café, walked them along the laundry building, and led them into the main entrance of the hospital. Instead of steering Wilma and Lottie to the baths as they'd done before, he walked straight into a small courtyard. He and Lavinia took a seat on a bench overlooking a modest tile fountain. Wilma and Lottie stood nearby, half-listening to his pitch about the hospital. Wilma took in the courtyard, the blooming lilacs climbing the stucco walls, the fresh red paint on the iron railings of the upstairs balconies, a pair of goldfinches fluttering around a lush sweetgum, the owl in the bell tower, so still he looked carved in place. Lottie leaned against her and whispered, "Just like you remember it, kid?"

Wilma pointed at the doctor's office overlooking the courtyard. "Give me that room and I'll finish my sentence for real. They can add all the time they want."

On the way out, Lavinia's tour guide said to Wilma, "I enjoyed your book."

Wilma smiled. "Why not? You got off easy."

The man laughed, deep and phony, special-made for Lavinia's ears.

Lottie drove the Cadillac off hospital grounds and north to Oxnard. She parked at a diner next to the Hitching Post. She patted her mother's knee. "I'm starving," she said. "Let's chow."

Lavinia didn't want to go inside. In fact, she flat-out refused. Lottie and Wilma went in without her. Lavinia stood in the parking lot, trying to decide which she feared more: being alone in this neighborhood or taking a chance on the food in the diner. She followed the girls inside.

She insisted on a table near the Cadillac in hopes of warding off potential car thieves. She asked the waitress to wipe the table down three separate times and still found the linoleum too sticky for her liking. She asked the waitress what the safest dish was and took her recommendation on the chicken salad. When the waitress left with their orders, Lavinia said to Lottie, "How did you ever find this lovely eatery?"

"Wilma found it," Lottie said. "Didn't you, kid?"

Wilma nodded. This was part of the plan. Lottie convinced Wilma that the truth, told to the right person, was stronger than blackmail. Wilma figured she'd give it a shot. She pointed at the cook sliding a tuna melt onto the expo line. "See that fellow there?" she asked Lavinia.

Lavinia turned. "The cook?"

Wilma nodded.

"Seems a charming bloke."

"He saved my life," Wilma said.

"How? Did he spare you from eating this poisonous cuisine?"

Lottie said, "No more jokes, Mother. You're going to want to hear this." She turned to Wilma. "Tell her how you got out of Camarillo."

"You finished your sentence," Lavinia said. "I know. I read *The Brain Emporium*."

Wilma sipped water from a dirty glass. She took a deep breath. "Actually, I bent the truth a little in the book."

"In the whole thing?" Lavinia asked.

Wilma shook her head. "Just in the end. Just about how I got out."

"What really happened?"

"My sentence got extended. I worried they'd never let me out. And living with a bunch of crazy people will make you crazy after a while. Lottie will back me up on that. So this guard, a fellow named Giroux, cut me a deal. He told me if I played my ukulele at a stag party, he'd get me my walking papers."

"Sounds like a good deal," Lavinia said.

"So I thought. I agreed to it. Giroux drove me up to that dive next door to here. It was a Hollywood shindig. A couple dozen men from pictures. Some of them you know. Roderick Hayles. You remember him?"

"Why, of course. What ever happened to the bloke?"

Lottie said, "Last I heard, he was assaulting Wilma."

Lavinia barked, "Carlotta Bell, you learn some manners."

Wilma said, "No. It's true. The men at the party insisted I perform a striptease. Giroux told me it was the only way to keep me out of the hospital. So I did."

"How humiliating," Lavinia said.

Wilma nodded.

Lottie said, "Not as bad as what happened afterward. They knocked Wilma out and raped her."

Lavina reached out her diamond-studded fingers and covered Wilma's hands. "My god, dear. That's awful."

Wilma looked down at the sticky linoleum. For a few seconds, she lived in two times: this lunch with the Bell women, and her morning after escaping the Hitching Post.

Lottie said, "It gets worse. The woman who runs that motor court insisted Wilma become a prostitute. Wilma has to pay her fifty bucks a week or else the madam sends some thugs over to drag Wilma back here and put her to work."

Lavinia squeezed Wilma's hand even harder. "That's positively frightful."

Wilma nodded.

Lottie said, "Tell her the worst part. Tell her who owns the whorehouse. Tell her who's pocketing all the dough you're paying out."

Wilma raised her bright blue eyes and caught Lavinia's gaze. She said, "A man named Leslie Bell."

Of course, Lavinia wouldn't take Wilma's word for it. After lunch, the three drove up to the Ventura City Hall and checked the public records. Sure enough, Leslie Bell's ghost corporation owned the Hitching Post. Lavinia stormed out of City Hall, down the polished stone steps, and into the Cadillac. Lottie stopped Wilma at the top of the steps. "Give her a second," she said. She pulled a couple of cigarettes out of her pewter case, handed one to

Wilma, and kept one for herself. Wilma struck a match on the stone wall alongside the stairs and lit both of their smokes. The two women gazed off, past the marble statue of Junípero Serra, down to the Pacific in the distance.

Lottie tried to engage her mother in conversation a few times on the ride home. Lavinia didn't take the bait. She lit one cigarette off the previous and blew smoke through a crack in the window and stared at the hills and farmland alongside Ventura Highway. Lottie chatted with Wilma a bit, filled her in on the latest with Chester Ellis, gossiped about some actresses she'd run into while doing film work. After a while, Lavinia's anger filled the cab of the Cadillac. It weighed down any hope of further conversation. The best Wilma could do was pull out her ukulele and strum chords that sounded good together but didn't add up to a song. Minor chords showed up more than was typical for Wilma, making the uke sound like a bluesy instrument, matching the mood.

Wilma waited for Lavinia to say something, to offer to intervene between her husband and the twins, but Lavinia kept her thoughts to herself. The photograph of Leslie Bell and Ma Breedlove called out from Wilma's purse. Wilma ignored it for as long as she could. When Lottie turned down Figueroa Street in Highland Park, Wilma knew it was time.

"Mrs. Bell?" she said. "I hate to do this, but that madam and your husband have been gobbling up every thin dime my sister and I could hustle for the last year. The more money we earn, the more they take. It has to stop." She dug the photo out of her purse and leaned onto the back of Lavinia's seat. "And as bad as they've been to me, they've been worse to you."

She handed the photo to Lavinia. Lavinia stretched it out as far as her arms could reach and squinted at it.

Wilma said, "That woman on top is Myrna Laurie. She's the madam who's been extorting me. The man on the bottom, well, you know him."

Lavinia handed the photo back to Wilma. She said nothing. Lottie tried to intervene. Lavinia raised a hand to stop her. Wilma stashed the photo back into her valise. She tucked away the ukulele, too. A breeze blew into the windows of the Cadillac. Lottie cruised slowly down a lane of craftsman houses. Women sat on porches, knitting. A loose chicken ran into the road. Lottie slowed to let it pass. Wilma set her goods on the backseat and waited for Lottie to drop her off.

Lottie pulled onto the gravel driveway leading up to Wilma's bungalow. Only then did Lavinia speak. She said, "Don't you or your sister pay another penny, Wilma. I'll take care of this."

JACK, 1946

HAMMOND TAPPED the shave-and-a-haircut rhythm on the doorbell. Jack stood behind him and resisted the urge to tap the bell two more times and finish the riff. Gertie walked across the expansive front porch and smelled the gardenias in the teak window box. "Get a load of this place. It's bigger than the Studio Club. How many people live here?"

"Two," Jack said.

"Three," Hammond said. He counted them on his fingers. "Bell, his wife, their butler."

"What about the maid?" Gertie asked. "Place like this, they'd need two or three of them."

"The staff live around back," Hammond said.

Gertie walked back to the front door. "Why does the butler get to live in the main house and everyone else has to live in the back?"

"What am I? Bell's fucking biographer?"

Jack set a hand next to Hammond's neck. His fingers dug into the soft spot between Hammond's collar bone and the muscles that stretched from neck to shoulder. He said, "Easy, Dave."

A shadow appeared behind the stained-glass oak tree on the giant mahogany front door. Hammond called out, "Renny. Hammond."

The burly butler opened the front door. He looked straight at Jack, who still had his hand near Hammond's neck. Jack lifted his hand off and let it hang by his side.

Renny nodded toward the inside of the house. He turned and walked across the foyer. Hammond limped after him. Jack followed. Gertie drifted away from the men, running a finger along the built-in bench seat under the stairs, cutting across the room, picking up a gilded water pitcher on the foyer table, setting it back down, checking her image in a giant antique mirror above the pitcher.

Renny turned right into a sitting room. Leslie Bell sat cross-legged in a chair near a lamp. He had a pipe in his hand and a sifter of brandy. He looked away from the approaching foursome in a forced way, as if this were a scene from a movie and he wanted to give his character a practiced nonchalance. Lavinia Bell sat in a matching club chair, hand-stitching the binding on a quilt.

Hammond was the first to speak. He said, "Mr. Bell, maybe Mrs. Bell and Renny have an errand they can run right now."

Lavinia set her quilt into a woven basket next to the chair. She brushed a few errant threads off the legs of her cotton slacks as she stood. Renny didn't move. He kept his eyes on Leslie Bell. Bell said, "You heard the man, Renny. Take the dame and dangle."

Gertie laughed. "Take the dame and dangle," she repeated. "Listen to the posh boy from the mean streets of Pasadena."

Bell stared at Gertie through slits for eyes. "You think I'm some kind of clown, lady?"

All eyes turned to Gertie. She fluffed the bottom of her loose, red curls with her right hand. She kept the smile on her mug and the light in her blue eyes. Either she didn't catch the threat behind Bell's words, or she didn't care. Jack looked at the purse hanging from her left hand. He remembered that she'd tucked Hammond's gun into it.

A heavy silence hung while Bell waited for Gertie to get the message. Gertie kept smiling. Hammond hobbled a couple of steps toward her. Jack filled the space between the two. Anything Hammond did, he'd have to go through Jack to do it. Lavinia cracked the tension. "Come on, Renny," she said. "I suppose you and I have to dangle."

Renny nodded and led Lavinia out of the room. Their hushed footsteps padded across the Turkish rugs, through the foyer, and out the stained-glass front door. When the door shut, Bell said, "What goes on? You got Carlotta, Chesley?"

Carlotta? Jack had forgotten about her, forgotten he'd been hired to drag her back, forgotten that they were still spilling lines from that script.

Gertie tossed the whole fiction out the window. "This ain't about Lottie, and you know it. We're here to find out what happened to my sister."

Bell looked at Hammond. "Who's the kitten trying to put the screws on?"

"It's Gertrude Greene. Wilma Greene's sister," Hammond said.

"Who's Wilma Greene?" Bell asked.

Hammond looked at Jack, then back at Bell. "The chippy what brings us all together."

Bell looked at Gertie and Jack. "And what?" he asked. "You two hinky chumps think I got something to do with your dead little dame?"

"You got smart real quick," Gertie said. "Two seconds ago, you don't know who Wilma is. Now you know she's dead without anyone saying that."

"Not true," Bell said. "Hammond just said it. He just said, 'The dead chippy what brings us all together.'"

"He didn't say dead," Jack said. He was about half-sure he was right.

Hammond hobbled back to a piano bench across the far wall. He sat down and kicked his wounded left leg in front of him. He rubbed the knee and rubbed his face. "Jackie, pour me a nip from that bar over there. I'll put an end to this mystery."

HAMMOND, 1944

HAMMOND HAD BEEN working the second shift on July 14, 1944. He ducked into the York station to grab a cup of coffee sometime around nine o'clock. While he chatted with the desk sergeant, a call came in about a hullabaloo on the two hundred block of Newland Street. Some drunk broad ran out into the street screaming. No one went out to help her. Her landlord didn't like the noise, though, so he called the York station to get her to shut up. "I'll run over and give it a look," Hammond told the sergeant.

A battered Packard was parked in the driveway of 243 Newland. Hammond recognized it. Herbert Parker, a peeper for the pictures, had been driving it around town for years. Hammond walked past the car and into the back bungalow. As soon as he rapped on the door, he remembered the joint. He'd been there a year earlier to visit his ex-partner's widow, Wilma. She'd claimed she'd been raped when really she'd been out whoring around. Someone filmed it. Wilma wanted the movie to be evidence.

Hammond checked the mailbox next to the door. Wilma's name was still on it. Only she'd dropped the Chesley and was going by Greene again.

Hammond knew this. Wilma's book had come out a few months earlier. She used the name Greene on that, too.

Hammond knocked on the door and called out Wilma's name. He could hear scuttling inside the bungalow.

No one opened the door. Hammond yelled, "Wilma, I'm coming in." He tried the knob. It was unlocked. He opened the door and flipped on the light. Wilma lay on the floor, just inside the door. Her throat was black and blue; her face drained and pale. She had vacated her bowels. Hammond had seen plenty of corpses in his day. This was one more. He didn't have to feel for a pulse to know she was dead.

Hammond drew his heater and called out, "There's no back door to this bungalow. Time to come out and face the music."

Footsteps plodded in the bedroom. Hammond held his piece fixed on the bedroom doorway. A silhouette emerged into the light. He had his hands up. Hammond figured this to be one of the easiest murder cases in Highland Park history. Only the shadow was too big to be Parker. Even in creepers, Parker stood under five and a half feet. Something was familiar about the walk, too. The way the murderer shuffled into the light. Hammond knew he'd seen it a thousand times. He couldn't place it. The other man stepped into the halo of living room light and things got more complex.

The murderer was Hammond's old pal and Wilma's ex-father-in-law. John Chesley, Sr.

Chesley held his hands high and said, "Hello, Dave."

Hammond kept the gun fixed on Chesley. "What's going on here?"

"Looks like I'm being framed," Chesley said.

He told Hammond that Wilma called him. She had an incriminating photo that she'd stolen from Chesley. Chesley wanted it back. She told him to come over and bring a hundred and thirty-two dollars. The number was that specific. One hundred thirty-two. So he gathered the cash and came by to find Wilma lying dead on the floor. "You showed up not two minutes later."

"So you brought the hundred thirty-two?" Hammond asked.

Chesley nodded.

"In your wallet?"

Chesley nodded again.

"Toss that wallet over to me."

Chesley did. Hammond opened it, pulled out six twenties, a ten, and two singles. He stuffed them in his own pocket and tossed the wallet back to Chesley. "Where's the photo?" he asked.

Chesley shrugged. "Not here, as far as I can tell. I thought I knew all of Wilma's hiding places. She must've gotten a new one."

Hammond nodded. "We won't look too hard," he said. "We'll play this simple. I'll keep your hush money. You drive out of here with Parker's car. I call in a couple of favors. We say she fell in the tub. Everything's jakeloo."

"One problem with that," Chesley said. He reached back and flipped on the bedroom light. "Come back here and take a look."

Hammond holstered his heater and walked to the back of the bungalow. Chesley stood over Wilma's bed. Parker lay there tangled like a discarded rag doll.

"Is he dead?" Hammond asked.

Chesley shook his head. "Passed out."

"You drag him here?"

"Nope."

Hammond lifted his peaked cap and rubbed the bare skin underneath. "We'll play it the same way," he said.

"You drift out of here. Leave the car. I'll wake up shamus and put the squeeze on. He'll pay. We'll call it an accident. All will be forgotten soon."

Chesley chewed his bottom lip for a piece. He nodded. "Yeah," he said. "Yeah. I think that could work."

"Close the door behind you," Hammond said.

Chesley cleared out.

Hammond went into the kitchen. He grabbed a quart pot off the stove. It looked clean enough. He filled it with water, headed back to the bedroom, and dumped the water on Parker. Parker sprung to his feet like an alley cat. "What gives?"

Hammond shifted the pot to his left hand and held his gun with the right. "I got you dead to rights, peeper," he said.

Parker looked around the room. "Where am I?"

"Where'd you go tonight?"

Parker took a deep breath. He nodded to himself. "Okay," he said. "I know."

"Good," Hammond said. "And now maybe you can tell me why you murdered Wilma."

"Murdered? Wilma's dead?"

"Don't play coy with me. You killed her and I caught you."

Parker reached into his back pocket. Hammond wiggled the gun. Parker didn't react to the threat. He pulled out a handkerchief and comb. He wiped the water off his face and slicked back his hair. "We both know I didn't kill her," he said. "It doesn't make any sense. No one kills a girl and then goes into her room to take a nap. I was set up. I suppose you showing up with that gun is the last scene of the setup. So what do you want?"

"What do you have?"

Parker stashed the comb and handkerchief in his back pocket. He took his wallet out of the front pocket. It was fat with cash. Wilma must've been blackmailing him, too. Parker grabbed a stack of bills. "Five large," he said. "More or less."

Hammond tossed the pot on the bed. He took the money with his left hand and kept the heater trained with his right. He stuffed the money into his bulging front pocket. "Five large gets you clear," he said.

Parker shuffled past Hammond and toward the front door.

"Keep your eyes off the floor," Hammond said. "And don't vomit on the premises. I still have to clean this mess up."

In Leslie Bell's sitting room two years later, Hammond summed up his story. He said, "And from there, everything worked to plan. I stripped Wilma, got rid of her soiled robe, stuffed her face-first into the tub, called Frenchy, and told him my story. Eggs in the coffee."

Jack took a seat on the bench next to Hammond. He shook his head violently enough to loosen a few strands of hair from their pomaded place. "I'm confused," he said. "Who framed my dad and Parker?"

Hammond rubbed his knee. "It was no frame," he said. "Your dad killed Wilma. Simple as that."

GERTIE, 1944

JULY 14, 1944. Gertie noticed the cop as soon as he stepped inside the joint. Tall and lean, ropy muscles under policeman blues, he reminded her of her brother-in-law Jack. Former brother-in-law. The cop couldn't have been more than a few months past his twentieth birthday, but something about him looked older. It was in the eyes scanning the room. There was something serious about them, like he'd already been to Germany and back, or maybe had just seen too much death here in Los Angeles.

Gertie's dinner companion prattled on, something about a pair of shoes he'd seen Veronica Lake wearing on the lot the other day. If he'd been half as charming as he thought he was, she'd have listened. Instead, she watched the young cop. He caught her looking at him and headed straight for her.

She took a quick mental inventory. What had she done that could lead to arrest?

Well, this dinner date wasn't exactly on the up-and-up. It was all about her selling a screenplay to this dandy. He was a novelist who'd lucked into a big-money studio contract. Only problem was, he had no idea how to write for pictures. He'd been assigned a crime movie. Nothing special. Just the usual corpse at the beginning and a pretty boy talking tough until he finds who made the stiff stiff. The dandy was a pretty boy, all right, but he couldn't fit into the rest of it. He had no idea how to kill someone, in fiction or otherwise. And even if he did, he'd be more interested in solving the mystery of where the actress got her lovely pearls than of who committed this made-up murder. So the dandy did what so many of the other scribblers on the studio dole did: he hired Gertie to write his screenplay for him. It was her little cottage industry. All hush-hush. Maybe a little fraudulent, but doubtfully illegal.

Not the type of thing that inspires the law to crash Gertie's gimlet and cake.

The scribbler's love life wasn't exactly legal in the State of California, either. But he was here with Gertie—a woman—and there was nothing too obvious to suggest that they couldn't be a couple. Gertie nodded to the cop as approached her table and tried to figure the angle.

The cop asked, "Gertrude Greene?"

Gertie saw no harm in admitting that.

"We need you to come down to the coroner with us."

"Us?" Gertie asked, because there was only one of him.

"You're the only next of kin we can find." The cop held out his hand. Gertie tossed back the rest of her gimlet. Next of kin? It must be her mother.

The scribbler stood. "I'll come along."

Gertie shook her head. He already had his screenplay. She already had her money. She doubted she'd cry over her mother's body. She didn't want to. But this dandy was so safe, such a doll, that his sympathetic eyes could turn on her waterworks. She ran her fork across the icing on top of her cake, licked the fork clean, said goodnight, and followed the cop out.

✦ ✦ ✦

The kid didn't say much on the drive down Sunset other than to answer how her next of kin had died: "Slipped in the tub. Hit the edge face first. We suspect she was drinking."

"I haven't seen my mother in so long," Gertie said. She counted the time in her head. She'd moved out when she was sixteen, which would make it—could it be already?—ten years. "I'm not even sure I'll recognize her."

The cop turned on the siren and gunned it. He weaved around cars, occasionally whipped into the opposite lane to pass, and took turns sharp enough to tax his wartime retreads. Gertie couldn't see the angle in this, either. Her mother wouldn't get any more dead. What was the point in racing? She wasn't sure if the cop wanted to impress her or scare her. He did neither. If he just wanted her to shut up, well, his driving accomplished that, at least. They charged through Silver Lake, Echo Park, Chinatown, and eventually over the bridge into Boyle Heights.

When they climbed out of the cruiser at the city morgue, Gertie forgot to breathe for a few seconds. It was strangely beautiful. A marine layer had settled in, making the moon less of a ball in the sky than a general glow. Fog glistened around the globes of electric light along the sidewalk. The building itself looked like a turn-of-the-century dance hall: long granite steps, high windows with keystones over them, austere bricks, delicate stonework. A light was on in the attic. Gertie could see the wooden rafters through the window. Just above it, like the morgue's own crown, was a marble sculpture. It resembled a looking glass in a bed of flowers, like something from the Brothers Grimm, maybe.

The boy in blue tapped the small of Gertie's back and

led her inside. He still had nothing to say. His silence was
fine in the car, with city lights racing by and the bells of
the interurban cars ringing and drivers laying on horns to
let the kid know that, police cruiser or not, this driving
wasn't right. But here at the quiet morgue, with the ocean
air seeping under her skin, Gertie needed a little dialogue
to fill in the empty spaces. As they crossed the marble foyer of the morgue and took the automatic elevator down
to the basement, Gertie started chatting again. "I'm surprised you grabbed me to do this instead of Wilma. She
should be home." Because Gertie had invited Wilma to
join her and her friend at Musso and Frank's. He was
springing for dinner. He'd just as happily feed the both of
them. But Wilma had worked a long shift that day. She
said she was staying in, taking a bath, going to sleep early.

"Wilma?" the cop said. He opened the elevator door.
Gertie stepped out.

"Wilma's my twin sister," Gertie said. "She lives in
Highland Park. It's closer to here than Hollywood. You
should've called her first. She has a phone and everything."

The cop grunted. Gertie wound the film back a few
frames and looked at it again. Maybe he hadn't added a
question mark to Wilma's name. Gertie stared down the
dim hallway to the bright room a dozen steps away. She
was here to ID her mother, right? Her mother was the
drunk. Her mother was the one likely to slip in a tub and
die. And her mother's death was the death that Gertie
could handle. Her mother had never given much of a shit
about Gertie or Wilma, hadn't been to Wilma's wedding
or the funeral for Wilma's husband, hadn't gone with
Gertie to visit Wilma in the mental hospital or helped
out at all. Nothing. No word for a decade.

It was her mother under that sheet Gertie was rapidly approaching, wasn't it?

Gertie wanted to ask the cop, but here they were already, turning into the bright room. Another flatfoot in uniform stood next to a corpse on a metal table. He was a short guy, maybe a hard heel over five-foot-two. His eyes had a way of looking in Gertie's direction and somehow not seeing her. The coroner—or at least a man in a white coat—sat behind a metal desk on the other side of the room. He was bent over, writing something on the paper in front of him. His bald spot sparkled under the overhead lights. Drawers lined the adjacent wall, a card catalog of corpses. Everything smelled like iron and antiseptic and blood. The cop led Gertie to the metal table.

"Please tell us who you see under the sheet," he said. He nodded to his partner. The little flatfoot lifted the sheet.

Gertie took a glance and gasped. She could've been looking at herself lying on that metal morgue table. That could've been her face with the broken nose and cold lips. It looked so much like her. Those same blue eyes and clusters of freckles and wild red hair. Gertie said, "Wilma?"

The flatfoot whipped the sheet down again. The cop turned to the coroner and said, "Gertrude Greene has positively identified the deceased as her sister, one Wilma Greene Chesley of 243½ Newland Street, Los Angeles, California." The coroner checked a box on his form. Gertie reached for the sheet again. The flatfoot held it down.

"What happened to her neck?" Gertie asked. "Why was there blood pooled along her throat?"

"She had a broken nose," the flatfoot said.

"I know she had a broken nose. I saw that. Why was her neck bruised?"

The cop who'd led Gertie in grabbed her by the elbow and pulled her away from Wilma's body. "Come with me, Miss Greene."

Gertie yanked her arm out of the cop's hand. She grabbed the sheet over Wilma. The flatfoot pushed her. The cop wrapped his arms around her midsection and pulled. Gertie got just enough of the sheet to see under it again. Deep bruises, like a sunset spreading from purple to red to yellow, lay across Wilma's throat. The cop lifted Gertie and turned her away from the table. Gertie held on to the white sheet. The flatfoot pulled it from his end. The cop started to carry Gertie away. She let go of the sheet. "All right! All right!" she screamed. Her legs grew wobbly. She would've hit that polished vinyl floor if the cop hadn't held her in his arms. "All right." Sobs started flooding out now. "Give me a break."

The coroner hopped to his feet. He rolled his desk chair over to Gertie. The cop set her down on it. Gertie let the tears flow as they would. The coroner and the cop rolled her into the dim hallway. "It's okay," the coroner said. He reached behind his white coat, pulled out a handkerchief, and handed it to Gertie. Gertie blotted her eyes. A thick streak of mascara blackened the cloth. The coroner knelt in front of her. "You just lost your sister. It's okay to cry. Take your time."

Gertie nodded. She closed her eyes to squeeze the tears out, and when she did, she saw the bruises on Wilma's neck. As much as everything seemed to be falling apart around her, she was smart enough to keep from saying what she wanted to say more than anything: that

Wilma didn't die by falling in a goddamn tub. Wilma had been murdered, choked to death, and Gertie knew exactly who did it.

JACK, 1946

JACK STARTED to cry. Not heavy sobs. His old man had beat that habit out of him before Jack started grammar school. Not even a whimpering cry. Just the tight-lipped, tears-sneaking-out-of-the-corner-of-the-eyes kind of cry, the kind of cry he'd learned to fight through on the school-yards and street corners of his childhood. He watched Bell across the room. Surely Bell had a gun somewhere. Gertie had Hammond's Browning. Jack had his Spring-field. Hammond had nothing or he would've shot it already. Three guns in the room. Two on his side. He let another tear slip.

Christ. His father had killed his wife.

Gertie was the first to react. She walked over to Jack and put her hand under his chin. "Stand up, Jackie." Her hand guided him to his feet. She held his face so he was looking straight at her. She said, "Take your hanky out and wipe your face." Jack closed his eyes, squeezed out the last of the water, and wiped his face. He took a deep breath. He told himself to pull it together at least until he left Bell's house. Crying would be for times when no one had a weapon or a motive.

Gertie took her hand off Jack's chin. She snapped her purse open and took out Hammond's Browning. She put it in Jack's hand. "Point this at Bell," she said. "Don't let him shoot me in the back."

Jack aimed the Browning at Bell. Bell rocked in his chair. He stared at Hammond. Hammond didn't move.

Gertie said, "About half of that story you just heard is true. Think about it. Your father didn't kill Wilma. It doesn't make any sense. Hammond said the old man was looking for a picture and hadn't found it. You know your father. Do you think he would kill Wilma before he got her to give him the photo?"

Of course not. She was right. Jack lowered his aim to Bell's chest. It made for a bigger target.

Hammond spoke up. "It was probably an accident, Jack. He probably just meant to scare her and went a little too far."

Gertie put her thumb on the button of Jack's chin and her forefinger just underneath. She held his face so he had to look at her. She asked, "When you were a kid, how many times did your father beat you within an inch of your life? How many times did you see him beat your mother? How many times did you see him strong-arm a thug? Did he ever fuck up? Did he ever accidentally kill anyone?"

Jack shook his head. The old man knew what he could and couldn't do. He knew his own strength. And, by 1944, he would've been too damn old to accidentally kill someone.

Hammond started to protest. Gertie reached into Jack's blood-stained coat, pulled the Springfield from its holster, and pointed it at Hammond. Hammond piped down.

Gertie said, "I know the photo he was looking for. I have a copy of it in my purse." She took a couple of steps back, tucked the Springfield under her arm, and dug the photo out. It was a small one, three-and-a-half-by-five inches. She held it up for Jack to see.

It looked like the postcards they sold in the back room of that antiquarian bookstore over on Cahuenga. "I don't get it," Jack said. "Why would my father be looking for a dirty picture? Why would Wilma have it? Why would you have copies?"

Gertie said, "Look at the man on the bottom and look at the man you're pointing a gun at."

Jack did both. It was a picture of Bell. The more he looked, the more he recognized the woman on top. It was the broad in charge of the Hitching Post. "I don't understand any of this."

"Jackie, you're a sweetheart, but you're a terrible detective." Gertie slid the photo back into her purse. She pointed the Springfield at Hammond. She laid it out for Jack as simply as possible. "Bell was extorting money from Wilma and me. Wilma got sick of it. She found that picture your dad took, and she gave it to Bell's wife. Bell's wife got hot under the collar and told Bell to kill the caper. So Bell killed it for a couple of months. He stopped sending your old man over to collect money. He stopped giving Ma Breedlove a cut. He left me and Wilma alone. But you don't stay in a business that gets you a house like this if you let some little chippy working in a hash house get the better of you. As soon as Bell's wife stopped looking, he took action. He either killed Wilma or he had Hammond do it."

"Wait a second, now," Hammond said.

Jack looked down the barrel at Leslie Bell and said, "Let her talk."

Gertie said, "A lot of what Hammond told you was probably true. He just left out the first part of the story. The way I figure it, before your father or Parker got to

Wilma's, Hammond or Bell came by and killed her. Then they called a couple of dicks in hopes of pinning it on one of them. Parker got there first. He got knocked out and dragged into the bedroom. Either Bell called Hammond at the York Station or Hammond slid out and waited for your father. Either way, Hammond walked in right after your father did. This way, he could cover it up. If anyone looked deeper into things, they'd find that both your father and Herbert Parker were at the scene of the murder. One of the two of them would swing. Bell and Hammond would be in the clear."

Jack looked at Bell and said, "Is that right, Dave?"

Hammond didn't answer. Bell placed his hands on the arms of the club chair and shifted his weight.

"Stay in that chair," Jack said.

Bell sat back.

Gertie said, "Only thing I'm not sure about is which one of these two bastards did it. My guess is Bell. He's vicious. Dave, here, is kind of a nance."

Jack looked over his shoulder at Hammond. Hammond still sat on the piano bench with a hand warming his wounded knee. He stared at the Turkish rug under his feet. Bell did something. Jack could see movement out of the corner of his eye. He started shooting before he could fully turn back and aim. The first shot missed wide and lodged into the oak paneling. Jack was more careful with his next two. He aimed for the middle of Bell's chest and shot twice. The force of the bullets threw Bell back into the chair. Jack sent a fourth and fifth shot into Bell's head. The luger in Bell's right hand dropped to the floor.

Jack turned back to see Hammond rushing after Gertie. Gertie dropped the Springfield and screamed. Jack fired at Hammond. The Browning clicked. Empty. Jack swung it, butt first, into Hammond's chin. Hammond tumbled down. Jack kicked him as he fell, catching the chin again. Hammond lay on the hardwood floor. Out cold.

Jack threw down the Browning and looked for his Springfield. Gertie had it in her hands. "Come on, Gertie," he said. "We gotta cheese it."

Jack hopped over Hammond and ran out of the room. He reached the stained-glass front door before he heard Gertie yelling, "Jack! No!"

Jack swung around and raised his fists. There was no one in the foyer to fight. No one seemed to be in that giant house but Jack and Gertie. Gertie yelled, "Get back in here."

Jack paused at the doorway. He took several deep breaths. He couldn't make heads or tails of things. He wanted to run but a thought from Gertie popped in his head. Bell's wife had seen him there. Renny had seen him. Bell was a heavyweight. Either the cops or Bell's boys would come after him. There was nowhere to run.

Gertie called out again, "Jack, I have an idea. Come back."

Jack took a deep breath. He walked across the foyer and back into the sitting room. Gertie stood over Hammond. Hammond slowly pulled his arms underneath himself. "First thing you do," Gertie said, "is knock that fucker out again."

With all the adrenalin pumping through his veins, Jack felt like he could knock out Joe Louis. He grabbed Hammond's lapel, spun him around, and launched another right into Hammond's jaw. Lights out. It's always easier to knock a man unconscious the second time.

"Give me my gun," Jack said.

Gertie took a step back. "What for?"

"I'm gonna kill this fucker. He killed Wilma."

Gertie kept backing away. "No, Jackie. Bell killed Wilma."

Jack shook his head as if he were trying to rattle his brain loose. "How? How? How?" His arm was still outstretched, waiting for Gertie to hand him his gun. "How do you know?"

Quietly, in her most soothing voice, Gertie said, "Sit down, Jackie. Breathe deep."

Jack let himself flop onto the piano bench. The seat was still warm from Hammond's ass. Jack pulled out his tobacco pouch and forced his shaking fingers to roll a cigarette.

Gertie kept her distance. "Think about it, Jackie. If Hammond did it, Bell wouldn't protect him. He'd let him dangle. He'd have him killed, if he had to. But Hammond would cover for Bell. There'd be an angle in it. Money. A little power over a powerful man."

Jack nodded. He lit his smoke. Fingers still shaking, but his head clearing a little. "Bell reached for a gun. He was going to shoot me." He nodded to himself. "A murderer would try to kill you, not tackle you." Jack set a steadying hand on the edge of the bench and squeezed. He took a long drag, pulled the cigarette from his lips, leaned his head back, and exhaled a cloud of smoke. "Hammond tried to tackle me. He tripped me and cuffed me downtown when he could've just shot me and been done with it. It couldn't have been him who killed Wilma. He was never a killer. He never had it in him, did he?"

Gertie stepped closer. "That's it, Jackie. You're coming back to me."

She leaned over him, placed a tender hand on his cheek, and gazed at him with those dazzling blue eyes so much like Wilma's. Thoughts flashed across Jack's brain like lighting in a summer storm. *Did Gertie know all along who killed her sister? Is that why she always steered me in the right direction and figured everything out so quickly? Did she enlist me not to investigate, but to kill Bell?* Gertie smiled at him. He didn't want to believe it. But evidence was evidence, even for a lousy detective like Jack.

Gertie lifted her hand off Jack's cheek. She patted his shoulder twice and walked over to the phone sitting near Bell's fresh corpse. She said, "Now follow my lead and we'll be just fine."

JACK, 1946

JACK DIDN'T KNOW the homicide cop from Pasadena. By the time the guy made the scene, Jack and Gertie had told their story enough times to have it down pat. The pair sat on the bench near the front door. The sleuth introduced himself as Jimmy Carmody. He sat on the short end of the L-shaped bench and said, "So, tell me what happened here."

Gertie looked at Jack. Jack nodded. He ran through the lines of the script Gertie'd put together on the spot. "Bell hired me to coax Hammond into dropping by for a visit. He didn't say why. I didn't want to take the job. Hammond's my old partner. But Gertie and I were out at Al's Continental tonight when we ran into him. I laid it all out on the table. Hammond said, 'Hell, I'll swing by.' So the three of us rode over here in my little coupe. Hammond's Ford is still downtown. We should've taken that. We could've talked on the way. As it stood, we had no idea what was going down between Hammond and Bell. We get here. Hammond pulls out a picture of Bell and some hooker in the act. Turns out Hammond's shaking him down."

"Blackmail?" Carmody asked.

Jack nodded. Gertie handed Carmody the picture from her purse. "I picked it up from the floor," she said.

Carmody slid on a pair of reading glasses and studied the picture. "I guess I can figure out which one's Bell. Go on."

Jack said, "Well, Bell wanted me to shoot Hammond. He told me to do it. But I'm no killer. I'm not even a detective, really. I don't have a license or anything. I think Bell meant to hire my father."

"Your father a detective?"

"Was."

"Retired?"

"Dead."

"Murdered?"

Jack shook his head. "Not unless you know something I don't."

Carmody said, "Go on with the story. Bell tells you to kill Hammond and you won't do it."

"Right," Jack said. "So Bell says, 'Hell, I'll kill the dirty son of bitch.' He digs out a luger and points it at Hammond. Only Hammond got the drop. Unloaded his clip into Bell. Five or six shots. It wasn't fully loaded. But he shot that heater until it went click."

Carmody rubbed the stubble on his face. A red mark still ran across his cheek from where the pillow had been pressed against it when the call came in. Jack reckoned Carmody couldn't have been awake for more than fifteen minutes. "And Hammond's a cop, huh?"

Jack nodded.

"The two of you saw all of it."

"We did," Gertie said.

"Christ on a cross," Carmody said. "It's a good, old-fashioned shitstorm." He called one of the crime scene guys into the room. "What's Hammond's hand look like?" he asked.

Jack felt a flush of panic. Of course they'd check for powder nitrates to see if Hammond had been the one to shoot the gun. And Hammond hadn't shot, had he? Jack couldn't remember.

The crime scene cop said, "Covered in residue."

This took Jack a second. He vaguely remembered Hammond accidentally firing the gun on Third Street. Was that tonight? It seemed like months ago. But, no. It was barely hours ago. Jack stifled a relieved sigh. Lucky.

Carmody asked, "Is he singing, yet?"

"Nah," the cop said. "He's out of it. Don't know his own name. We asked him about Roosevelt, he thought we were talking Teddy."

Carmody turned to Jack. "Why'd you knock him out?"

"I didn't want him to pin this mess on me."

Carmody nodded, more to the thoughts in his head than to Jack's response. "Aren't you a cop, too?"

Jack shook his head. "I'm barely back from Germany."

"Yep," Carmody said. "Good you brought a witness. Good you knocked him out." He rubbed the pillow dent on his cheek. "Bell didn't happen to give you a receipt when he hired you, did he?"

Jack checked his wallet. As luck had it, the receipt Renny'd given him was tucked behind the twenties. Jack pulled it out and passed it over. Carmody studied it.

"I'm going to keep this receipt and this photo," he said. "And you're going to keep your mouths shut." He looked over his reading glasses with the face of a stern father in a Hollywood picture. "Go home and forget any of this ever happened. You didn't see shit. You don't know shit. Got it?"

Jack stood first. He put out a hand to help up Gertie. Gertie took the hand and pulled herself to her feet. Jack

said to Carmody, "We're like a couple of ghosts. Say poof
and we're gone."

Carmody leaned forward on the bench seat. He rested his elbows on his knees and cradled his head in his hands. He let out a long, heavy breath.

Jack and Gertie vanished before he had time to look up again.

EPILOGUE: JACK, 1947

JACK SAT ALONE in the darkened Highland Park movie theater. The newsreel and cartoon and short had run their course. The Republic logo shimmered across the screen, followed by the title—*Darkness and Sweet*—and top billing. Tom Fillmore as Hank Chelsea.

In the opening scene, a vixen with wild, curly hair runs screaming out of a bungalow and into a street. A man whose face is hidden in shadows walks after her. She runs right, runs left, dodges his grasp a couple of times. She makes a play for the bungalow again. The man forces his way in. Screams followed by silence.

In the next scenes, Tom Fillmore as Hank Chelsea returns from Germany to find out his wife has been murdered. He travels around Los Angeles in search of the killer. He knows who to visit and what questions to ask. He leaves a trail of corpses in his wake, but finally catches up to the big money man running a gambling casino in the North Valley. There'd been some blackmail, some extortion. Chelsea couldn't be fooled. All it took was for him to point a heater at the big man, and the big man sang like nightingale. Chelsea's buddy in the Pasadena PD swung by to make the appropriate arrests. Justice was restored.

The movie had been Jack's idea. A few months earlier, he'd dropped in at the Studio Club in hopes of getting Gertie to speak to him again. She'd shut down once she'd found out he killed her pal, Herbert Parker. Jack couldn't forgive himself for that. He felt like Gertie's forgiveness was the best he could hope for. So he pitched a movie to Gertie. He said, "We write what happened to us, but we fix everything. We make the world simple again."

Gertie was an easy sell. She started swinging by Jack's place early mornings, before that first studio call. They'd talk over ideas. Gertie would type. She'd turn the jumbled thoughts into snappy dialogue and fast-paced scenes. It didn't take her long at all. Ten working days plus a couple of weekends. Jack was more than a little impressed by the way she'd work. He was amazed, really. Whenever he told her this, she'd shrug and say, "I've written dozens of these."

Selling the script was an education for Jack, too. Even though Gertie worked for the studios and did the thinking for a couple of directors, she wouldn't take credit for the screenplay. "They don't really pay women," she told him. So she'd gone to the back room at Musso and Frank's and sold the script to some sweetheart scribbler there. Jack had gone with her. She'd pointed to Jack and said to the writer, "See this palooka? You change a word and he rearranges your face."

The old dandy just nodded. He passed the project off as his own, got paid a couple of grand for it, and the three of them divvied up the dough. Jack insisted Gertie should get half, he and the dandy should split the other half evenly. The dandy was probably more intimidated than convinced. He agreed, anyway.

Jack even got a small role in the production. He played the big man's butler. He and Gertie had written the butler as a Filipino, but come shooting time, all the Filipinos on contract at Republic were out in Lone Pine, playing Comanches in a John Ford picture. So they changed the name of the butler to Ronnie and Jack said his line.

Gertie was nervous when *Darkness and Sweet* hit theaters. She told Jack that they were poking a sleeping bear. Jack wasn't worried. He'd seen his share of cover-ups in the LAPD. Buried shit tended to stay buried. And he'd followed up on this one, found out that Lavinia Bell and her butler Reynaldo both made out like bandits. Between a huge life insurance policy, a modest inheritance, and pockets of cash they kept excavating among the crevices of that old house on South Orange Grove, they had it made. They weren't about to start digging up any corpses.

As for Dave Hammond, he wasn't in a position to dig up anything. He retired from the force within days of the Bell shooting. His knee wasn't healing, so he'd taken to using a cane to get around. And his head didn't really come back from those two concussions. He couldn't remember what happened that night. He called Jack once, about a week afterward, to meet him down at Cole's and fill him in. Jack went down, Springfield loaded, ready for trouble. But Hammond was hazy and hobbled. Jack had never seen him look so old. Hammond had asked, "What happened after I jumped you outside of Al's?"

"You don't remember?"

Hammond shook his head.

Jack piled another lie upon all the rest. He said, "You dragged me up to Bell's. Bell tried to shoot me. You got the drop on him."

Hammond had a fork in his hand at the time. His hand started shaking. The fork rattled on the plate so much that a waitress stopped what she was doing and took the fork from Dave. Hammond whispered to Jack, "I never killed anyone. Thirty-seven years on the force. Never killed anyone."

Jack looked him in the eye. "You killed Bell," he said. "You saved my life."

Hammond pulled a handkerchief from his back pocket. He buried his face in it.

After *Darkness and Sweet* ended, Jack walked out to the concession counter. He'd gotten to know the girl who worked there over the two weeks the movie'd been running. He leaned against the counter and said, "How's life, Edie?"

Edie grazed her fingertips across the paper hat her boss made her wear to work. "Glamorous as always."

Jack pulled out his tobacco pouch. He rolled a cigarette, handed it to Edie, rolled a second for himself, and lit them both. Edie took a long drag and blew smoke into the low ceiling of the lobby.

"You staying for another showing, Mr. Chesley?"

"I was thinking about it."

This was the last day of the run. One more showing, then it would be replaced by a musical with that kid from *The Wizard of Oz*. Jack couldn't see himself leaving the theater now.

"Is your lady friend joining you?" Edie asked.

"I don't think so. The studio keeps her pretty busy."

"Tell me about it." Edie spread her hands wide, as if

she were presenting the concession stand for sale. "Life in show business."

Jack ordered his dinner from Edie: a hot dog, a bag of popcorn, a bag of peanuts, and a bottle of pop. He finished his smoke and went back into the theater after the newsreel. He ate his hot dog during a cartoon about a party girl; he ate his peanuts during a Three Stooges short. Then the Republic logo came across the screen again.

The theater was mostly empty. He could hear footsteps clicking down the aisle. The sound was sharp and hollow, like a woman's high heels. She paused at Jack's row, then came down and sat next to him. He knew without looking it was Gertie.

Jack kept his eyes on the opening scene. Gertie reached over and grabbed his bag of popcorn. Jack offered what remained of his bottle of pop. Gertie said, "I have my own."

Tom Fillmore came onto the screen again. He was everything Jack wanted to be: beautiful, smart, one step ahead of everyone else. A good detective. A man who could figure things out based on the evidence in front of him. A man who didn't need his ex-sister-in-law to solve the mystery and explain the solution to him. A man who could walk through the filth and depravity of the modern world and come out clean. A man who saw death and inflicted death and wasn't haunted by it. A man who lived in two dimensions.

Jack gave himself over to the flickering images at the front of a shadowy room. All the while, he knew in the back of his mind that this movie's run would end in an hour. The world would return to three dimensions. Justice would never be restored. He'd still have massive holes inside dug out by the war and Wilma's murder. But he was scarring up just fine. And he was ready to follow Gertie toward whatever madness she flung him into.